A ROOM W

She went over to the wall, and pressed a switch. I gasped. The entire floor of the room had become transparent. We were sitting immediately over a huge double bed upon which lay a naked Chinaman of around forty. He was lying on his back, being pleasured by an equally naked, very beautiful Chinese girl of maybe eighteen or nineteen. She was kneeling between his spread thighs, her long black hair falling over her face as she went about her task. The man was resting his head on a pillow, his eyes were wide open, and he appeared to be staring straight up at us. 'Don't worry,' said Cherry. 'He can neither see nor hear us. He doesn't know that we exist. He is simply watching himself and his activities in the mirrored ceiling. All he knows is that the young lady who is attending to his needs is his for however long he wants her for. She will do anything that he wants. Absolutely anything. This particular girl is famous for her special skill. Her house name is Heavenly Mouth . . .'

Also in paperback from New English Library

The Pearl: volume 1
The Pearl: volume 2
The Pearl: volume 3
The Pearl Omnibus
The Oyster: volume 1
The Oyster: volume 2
The Oyster: volume 3
The Oyster: volume 4
The Oyster: volume 5
The Oyster Omnibus
Rosie – Her Intimate Diaries: volume 1
Rosie – Her Intimate Diaries: volume 2
Rosie – Her Intimate Diaries: volume 3
Rosie – Her Intimate Diaries: volume 4
Rosie – Her Intimate Diaries: Omnibus
The Black Pearl: volume 1
The Black Pearl: volume 2
The Black Pearl: volume 3
The Ruby: volume 1
The Ruby: volume 2
The Ruby: volume 3
Arousal
House of Lust
The Uninhibited
Submission
Summer School 1: Warm Days, Hot Nights
Summer School 2: All-Night Girls
Summer School 3: Hot to Trot
Summer School 4: Up and Under
In the Pink 1: Stripped for Action
In the Pink 2: Sin City

In The Pink: Getting It

Tony Andrews

NEW ENGLISH LIBRARY
Hodder and Stoughton

Copyright © 1996 by Tony Andrews

First published in Great Britain in 1996
by Hodder and Stoughton
A division of Hodder Headline PLC

A New English Library paperback

The right of Tony Andrews to be identified as the Author of
the Work has been asserted by him in accordance with the
Copyright, Designs and Patents Act 1988.

10 9 8 7 6 5 4 3 2 1

All rights reserved. No part of this publication may be
reproduced, stored in a retrieval system, or transmitted,
in any form or by any means without the prior written
permission of the publisher, nor be otherwise circulated
in any form of binding or cover other than that in which
it is published and without a similar condition being
imposed on the subsequent purchaser.

All characters in this publication are fictitious and any
resemblance to real persons, living or dead,
is purely coincidental.

British Library Cataloguing in Publication Data

Andrews, Tony
 In the pink
 1. English fiction – 20th century
 I. Title II. Getting it
 823.9'14 [F]

 ISBN 0-340-63489-8

Typeset by
Letterpart Limited, Reigate, Surrey
Printed and bound in Great Britain by
Cox & Wyman Ltd, Reading, Berkshire

Hodder and Stoughton
A division of Hodder Headline PLC
338 Euston Road
London NW1 3BH

CONTENTS

PROLOGUE — 1

CHAPTER ONE
Cold Feet — 3

CHAPTER TWO
La Vie En Rose — 37

CHAPTER THREE
Moscow Mischief — 67

CHAPTER FOUR
The House of a Thousand Dreams — 119

CHAPTER FIVE
Food for Thought — 149

CHAPTER SIX
Keeping Abreast — 181

CHAPTER SEVEN
A Surprise Goodbye — 217

PROLOGUE

In July, 1976, my little world seemed complete. My cup, as they say, was filled to overflowing. I'd been working in New York as deputy editor of *Tiptop* magazine, standing in for Fred, the real editor – and my friend and mentor – while he visited our mutual boss Wally back in London. Whilst he'd been over there, Fred had asked me if I would like to stay on in New York as his permanent deputy editor, an offer which I accepted with alacrity. Right now, I was heading back to New York myself, following a week-long trip down to Puerto Rico, where I'd been staying with my fiancée, Annabel, the nightclub manager whom I'd met in London prior to my trip to the States. We had become engaged during her two-week visit, and I had bought her a pretty diamond ring from Tiffany's.

Fred would be back in New York when we arrived, and had told me that he'd worked out a deal for me with Wally, our publisher, who was the owner of the company. Also awaiting my return to work was Eileen, Fred's sexually predatory secretary, who had demanded that I provide her with my sexual services (again!) immediately after Annabel's return to London. And then there was Pauline, the uninhibited air hostess whom I'd met in Daly's Dandelion, the singles bar on Third Avenue. And Dee Dee, from the topless and bottomless pussy bar, who had modelled for the magazine and – privately – for me. As had Lucy, the six-foot tall, bald and beautiful black model with the shaven snatch. Not to mention my friend June, and the six obliging hookers in the brothel which she owned, who seemed keen to lay their sexual favours out for me. Three of these girls reckoned I still owed them. And not forgetting the entrancing Jenny, from the S&M club. And now I was engaged to Annabel, and was supposed to be getting married when I returned to England in a few weeks' time to sort out my affairs, before moving permanently to America.

CHAPTER ONE: COLD FEET

I think I first started getting cold feet when I was buying the engagement ring with Annabel in Tiffany's the previous week. Much as I loved her – and I still believe that I really did – I was beginning to wonder just how long my marriage to her (or to anyone, for that matter) could possibly last, bearing in mind the fact that I earn my daily bread largely surrounded by beautiful women. Mostly highly sexed beautiful women. The *lingua franca* of the world in which I work is sex. The magazine which I edit deals in copulation. It approves of sexual relationships between men and women. It actively supports them. *Encourages* them. The essence of a really good girl set published in *Tiptop* is that the girl looks fuckable. In my experience, girls who look fuckable generally look that way because they fuck a lot.

The purchase of the ring somehow brought these worries to the surface. How many times had I been unfaithful to Annabel since I'd been in New York? I'd no idea. Daily, almost. Dozens of times. With at least eight different girls. How was that going to change, simply because I was getting married? Could I really do my job properly as a married man? I didn't think so. Not when I really got down to it. If, when we got back to New York, later on that day, I kept my promise to Eileen the next day, after I'd seen Annabel off on her 'plane to London, what was the first thing that I was going to do? Fuck

Eileen, that's what. If I kept my promise. And anyway, thinking about it, I *wanted* to keep my promise. Thinking about it, I *wanted* to be able to fuck as many different, beautiful, sexy women as my working life offered me. Without feeling guilty about it. Without getting nagged. Marriage, I suddenly realized, as the 'plane banked and began its final descent into Kennedy, simply wasn't on.

But how, for God's sake, to tell Annabel? I obviously had to tell her before she left. Of course I did. Didn't I? I couldn't tell her on the telephone, after she'd gone, could I? Or write to her? Could I? No, of course I couldn't. Which meant telling her today. Now? I looked at her. She was looking out of the window, watching the ground coming up to meet us, seeing the sun reflecting from the myriad swimming pools that are a feature of the houses in outlying, suburban New York. No, not now. It needed to be in private. Definitely not in a public place. Nor on this aircraft.

I stumbled through Customs and Immigration, my head in a whirl. In one way I was relieved that I had taken the decision but, in another way, I dreaded having to tell Annabel. In the end *she* told *me*. We were sitting down in Fred's apartment, sipping a glass of champagne before going out to supper. Fred, unusually for him, was in the office. I'd spoken to him earlier, and he said he'd probably not be back until late. He suggested that he and I should hold off any serious conversation until the following evening, after Annabel had gone. Annabel twirled her glass, watching the bubbles rising. Then she looked up at me. 'I guess I'd better put you out of your misery,' she said. I looked at her. 'What do you mean, darling?' I said. She put her glass down. 'You've been so miserable, ever since you gave me this lovely ring,' she said, taking it off her finger, 'that I can't possibly let you go through with it. I'd rather keep you as a friend than marry you, and eventually lose you. Here, take it back. Please.' I looked at her, totally amazed. 'Don't be ridiculous,' I said. 'I don't know what you're talking about.' 'Oh, yes, you do,' she said. 'You haven't had a moment's happiness since I put this ring on last week.'

I won't bore you with the whole scene, but suffice to say that I persuaded her to keep the ring, and she persuaded me to call off the marriage. What a truly remarkable woman. There were no tears. Not that I saw, anyway. We went off, after our conversation, to the same little Italian trattoria where we had eaten such a romantic meal just before we left for Puerto Rico, and she actually managed to make me laugh. Mostly at myself. We fucked all night, with what seemed like mutual enjoyment, and considerable passion, and the following morning I took her out to Kennedy in the same stretch limo that I had met her with. My last sight of her was as she went through the departure lounge doors, waving and smiling, her blonde hair shining, her eyes bright, her face the relaxed, beautiful face that I had thought I knew so well. It was at that moment that I realized that I probably didn't know her at all. From a long, long way away, I heard Pamela's voice saying 'Please don't turn into a frog. Please.' Pamela was an earlier, lost love. But lost for different reasons.

I took a deep breath, and went back to my limo. I got very drunk that night. Eileen was torn between pleasure at the reason for my drunkenness and anger that I was too drunk to fuck her. In the end, she put me in a cab and sent me home. When I got there, there was still no sign of Fred. I rang Annabel, but there wasn't any reply. I checked my watch. With the five-hour time difference between London and New York, I reckoned that she would still be at the club. If, of course, she'd gone to the club. On reflection, it seemed unlikely that she'd go to work the evening of the day that she had arrived back in London. I dialled the number again, wondering if I'd misdialled the first time around, and I fell asleep listening to her telephone ringing, unanswered, three and a half thousand miles away.

Eileen telephoned at ten the following morning, and woke me. 'Hey, lover boy,' she said 'Are you coming into the office, or what?' 'Probably what,' I said. 'What's the time?' She told me. 'Shit,' I said, full of early-morning eloquence. 'I'll be there in about an hour. OK?' 'You're the boss,' she said. 'Well sort of.' She rang off before I could think of anything witty to counter with. When I eventually got to the office, she brought me coffee, aspirin and a pile of mail. She poured the coffee for both of us.

'I've been through all of this,' she said, indicating the pile of letters. 'Most of it's rubbish, but it's the kind of rubbish that you need to reply to yourself. Unless, of course, you trust me to take the right decisions.' I pushed the pile back towards her. 'I trust you,' I said. 'Thank you.' 'Terrific,' she said. 'Now then, what's happening with you and Fred?' 'As far as I'm concerned, nothing,' I said. 'I spoke to him while he was in here yesterday, but I've not seen hide nor hair if him in the apartment. I don't think he was there when I left this morning.'

'Hmmm,' she said. 'No, actually. He wasn't. He rang from somewhere over on the West Side, just before you got here. He didn't say who he was with. He says will you met him at Maxwell's Plum at twelve-thirty? I've booked a table in his name.' She looked at her watch. 'If you leave in half an hour, you'll be about right. OK?' 'Sure,' I said. 'No problem. How was he when he got back from London? Was he in good nick?' 'Yes, I think so,' she said. 'He seemed pretty up about everything. Apparently Wally has forgiven him for not being in the office all day. He says he's sorted out a pretty good package for you. And he tells me you're going to become a permanent fixture here. Is that right?'

'Assuming that the package is as good as he says it is,

yes,' I said. 'Wow,' she said. 'How about that? Then that'll mean that you'll be looking for your own apartment quite soon, won't you?' she asked. 'I guess so,' I said. 'When I get back from London. But one thing at a time. Let me have lunch with Fred, and we'll see how it goes from there. There are all kinds of minor problems.' 'I'll bet,' said Eileen. 'But like what, for example?' 'Well,' I said, 'off the top of my head, I understand that I'm being offered the post of deputy editor, underneath Fred, with Fred retaining the title of editor.' 'Yes,' she said. 'That's as I understand it.' 'Well, think about it, Eileen,' I said. 'You've already got a deputy editor. She's called Angie. Right?' 'Damn,' she said. 'You're right. I hadn't thought about that. Is that a big problem?' 'Not with me,' I said. 'Not so long as whatever they call me, it's obvious that I'm number two to Fred. I wouldn't accept anything that made me look like number three.' 'No,' Eileen said. 'I understand that. But what about Angie?' 'What indeed,' I said. 'But I'm sure that is something that we can cope with. It's not a big problem, it's just an example of the kind of detail that I'll need to think about, if I accept Wally's and Fred's offer.' Eileen stood up. 'You should probably go off to your lunch with Fred now,' she said. 'But do me a favour, will you? A personal favour. Please?' 'What's that?' I asked. 'Say yes,' she said. 'Whatever they offer you, say yes. I promise you, you'll never regret it.' I got up myself, and put my arm around her, and gave her a big squeeze. 'Thank you, sweetheart,' I said. 'I appreciate that. I'm not making any promises, but I'll certainly remember that when I'm making my mind up.'

I kissed her, gently, on her mouth. She put both her arms around me, and pulled me to her, violently, and then she kissed me back. Hard. Hungrily. I pulled away after a moment. 'Let's continue this tonight, darling,' I said. 'If you're free, I'll try and make up for my misbehaviour last night. OK?' 'Oh, yes, darling,' she said. 'Please. I'm free.

I'm always free for you. I always will be. What will you do? Ring me here? Ring me at my apartment? What?' I laughed, gently. 'It depends what time I get away from Fred, sweetheart,' I said. 'But I'll ring you here, if I get away before the office closes. After that, I'll ring you at your apartment. All right?'

She gave me another passionate kiss. I felt my cock beginning to stir from it's alcoholically-induced lethargy. 'Yes, darling,' she said. 'I'll be waiting by the telephone.' I left before I could become more physically involved than I presently had the time for. I caught a cab up to First Avenue at 64th Street, where Maxwell's Plum was situated.

To my surprise, Fred was already there. As was his wont, he was talking to a pair of extremely attractive young women. 'Hey, Tony,' he said. 'Great to see you. How was Puerto Rico? How's the almost blushing bride? How are you?' He didn't pause, or wait for a reply. 'Girls,' he said. 'I'd like you to meet another Britisher. This is my colleague, Tony Andrews. He, like me, lives out here.' He winked at me. 'Tony,' he said, 'Meet these delightful young ladies. This is Wanda, and this is Margot.' I shook hands with them both, and muttered something that seemed appropriate. Wanda was a big, busty redhead. She had the most enormous tits, and a lovely, friendly smile. Her friend Margot was black-haired, small, slim, and distinctly pretty. 'I've asked the girls if they would like to join us for lunch, Tony,' Fred said. 'They said it would depend upon what you looked like when you arrived.' He turned to the girls. 'So, ladies,' he said. 'I told you he wasn't a dog. Perhaps now you'll believe me. What's it to be? Lunch? Or not? Speak.'

'Lunch,' they both chorused, to my relief. 'Yes, please,' said Margot. She came and stood beside me, and slipped an arm through mine. 'This one's mine,' she said to Wanda. She looked up at me and smiled. 'I just love Limeys,' she said. 'Especially when they live in New

York. Are you into sex?' I smiled down at her. 'With you, baby,' I said, 'yes. Shall we skip lunch?' Margot giggled. 'I should say not,' she said. 'I've never been bought lunch at Maxwell's Plum. But I'm a much better fuck after food than I am before. It kinda gives me stamina. Know what I mean? Aren't I Wanda?' she asked her friend. 'So they tell me,' said Wanda. She looked at me. 'I think she probably is,' she said. 'I don't think she's kidding you.' Oh, fuck, I thought. There goes my conversation with Fred. But what the hell. Who wanted to talk work anyway? And I mustn't forget that I'm seeing Eileen later, I thought. I tied a knot in my mental handkerchief.

'What's this about a blushing bride?' asked Margot, looking at me. 'Oh, it's nothing,' I told her. 'Just a private joke. No one's actually getting married. Speaking of which,' I said to Fred, 'where were you last night?' 'Me?' said Fred. 'I was at home. Where were you?' He looked directly at me. If I hadn't *known* that he wasn't at home, I would have believed him. 'I was at home, too,' I said. 'It was obviously an evening for stay-at-homers.' Fred grinned at me. We ordered lunch, and the time passed pleasantly and amusingly. Fred is genuinely charismatic.

By the end of the meal, both Margot and Wanda were relaxed, happy, and raring to go. Margot was sitting on my right, and her left hand was stroking my half-erect prick beneath the table cloth. I wasn't complaining, but neither did I make any suggestion, either to Margot or to Fred, about what should happen next, or where we should go next. I was there at Fred's invitation, and it was his party. If he wanted to remember that we had originally agreed to meet to talk about my future with him out here in New York, that was his privilege. If he preferred that we took the girls back to his apartment, that was his privilege too. Fred was a friend of long standing, but one ignored his status at one's own risk. He had always been like that, and he wasn't ever going to change. Mind you, when he was your guest, or with you at your invitation, he never, ever pulled rank. That was something different. Quite frankly, I would have preferred to talk business. But it was obviously not to be. I could tell by the way Fred was leering at Wanda's huge breasts.

If you are fortunate enough to work with Fred, and are also a friend (the one does not guarantee the other) it is important to remember two things. The first I have just described: his occasional self-regard, in certain circumstances. But I should also say that, as long as you don't put it to the test – intentionally or otherwise – then you will probably never suffer from it. The other thing to remember is that, if you are with him in circumstances where you and he (and other men too, should that be the case) meet a group of women (as now, if you accept two women as a group: the principle remains the same) then Fred regards *all* of the girls as his property. If he wants to, and is able to, and the girls will permit it, he likes to fuck as many of them as possible. However much you might take a particular shine to one of them for yourself, he will almost certainly regard her as fair game at some stage of the occasion.

If she tells him to fuck off, that is fair enough, too. But as editor, and managing director, of *Tiptop* magazine in both Britain and America, he has strongly developed feelings of *droit de seigneur*. I should also say that if you are with a girl that you have brought with you, then she is sacrosanct. He wouldn't dream of making advances. Well, not serious ones, anyway. Thinking these thoughts, I was glad that I had no strong feelings about Margot. She was pretty, and seemed to fancy me. Her raven hair and her slim, shapely body turned me on. As did her hand on my prick. But I wasn't going to get uptight if Fred wanted to fuck her after he'd fucked Wanda.

In the event, Fred didn't seem to be in any kind of a hurry. When we'd finished our coffees and liqueurs – the latter the most important part of any meal for Fred – he suggested that we go back down to ground-floor bar level at Maxwell's. The time was only three-thirty, but it was heaving. New York bars, unlike London bars in those days, are open all day. There were a number of obvious tourists amongst the natives, and I was reminded about Fred's remark to Wanda and Margot, earlier that day, emphasizing that we lived in the Big Apple. Most New York girls who frequent singles bars aren't just looking for a quick fuck. The majority of them are looking for ongoing relationships. Consequently, if you announce that you are only there for a week, or whatever, you are unlikely to get your end away, if that is what you had gone there for. It is what most of the men who go there go for. It was certainly what Fred went there for.

The girls weren't too pleased to be put back into the arena, as it were. I think they had probably believed that they had hooked a couple of likely lads in Fred and me. We patently had enough money, always something that gladdens the hearts of New York girls. Well, to be fair, no girl wants a boyfriend who can't afford to take her out and about, does she? And we were although I say it myself, reasonably attractive. Plus the fact that we had the added attraction, to most New York girls, of being British. They just love the accent. And we were also, perhaps more importantly, intrinsically more polite, and more courteous, than many American men. Less aggressive. I guess it's all a matter of national characteristics.

Down in the bar, I concentrated on talking to Margot, while Wanda concentrated on keeping the other women whom the irrepressible Fred kept talking to at bay, something she did with considerable panache, and complete success. Margot told me that both of the girls were native New Yorkers, from Brooklyn Heights, where they had both been born, and where they went to school, and where they now shared a small apartment. They were the same age – twenty-three – and were both working as secretaries in the Wall Street area. Although Margot freely admitted that they both enjoyed a good time, and that good sex was an essential part of a good time, she admitted that they both hankered, long term, for the kind of relationship that would lead, eventually, to marriage and children.

Their shared disadvantage, she told me, was that, working in the Wall Street area amongst well-educated, highly-paid executives, in one of the city's largest financial institutions, their Brooklyn accents put them completely out of court as women, other than simply as sex objects. It was rather a sad story, and I felt a genuine sympathy for them both. I told her that I couldn't tell a Brooklyn accent from a Bronx accent, or indeed from any other kind of American accent, and she laughed, and said it was nice to be appreciated for what she was, and not for how her voice sounded. I realized, thinking about it, that, sadly, we do exactly the same kind of thing back home in England. I asked her what the answer to her problem was, and she thought for a moment, and then put her arm through mine, and kissed me gently on the lips. 'I guess one answer could be to marry you,' she said, smiling. I kissed her back, feeling rather touched by her remark.

I'd been talking to Margot, but I'd been keeping an eye – and an ear – in Fred's direction, and I was beginning to get the impression that only one of two things could happen now. Either he'd dump Wanda (and, inevitably, Margot with her) and look for something newer, and perhaps more challenging, or he'd accept that he wasn't going to attract anyone else whilst he had these two girls in tow, and bow to circumstance. In other words, take them home and fuck them. From his shortening conversation, I didn't think it would be long before he decided which of the two options to pursue. When the decision came, it was to invite Wanda and Margot home. They accepted immediately. (What took him so long? Margot asked). We went out onto Third Avenue, and caught a cab coming downtown.

It took us along 64th Street, almost to our door on Park Avenue. I'd stopped looking at the faces of the doormen as I went into the block these days, but I must admit that this time I looked, since it was the first time that I had come back there with Fred since I first arrived from London, all those weeks ago. What was it now? Three months, almost. Something like that. They looked just the same as they always did. The only difference was that Fred spoke to them. 'Hi, guys,' he said, full of *bonhomie*. 'What do you think of these two, then?' It was a purely rhetorical question. He didn't expect an answer. Nor did he get one. The two doormen gave him a sort of sickly grin, and one of them actually dragged himself out from behind their desk, and pressed the button for the elevator. Wonders would never cease. Not to be put down, Fred made the classic, international, working class, hand-under-the-elbow-with-clenched-fist gesture, indication of sexual things to come. The doorman ignored him. Well. Fred was a sublet, wasn't he? New York apartment doormen have a finely developed sense of the appropriate. Except in the month before Christmas. But this was July.

The two girls loved the apartment, and ran around in it, oohing and aahing as they went. Fred suggested, as we went through the door, that it was probably time for a bottle of champagne, and we all agreed. I looked at my watch. It was just after five. I'd just catch Eileen at the office, with any luck. I excused myself, and went into my bedroom to telephone her. 'Hello, sweetie,' I said, when the switchboard put me through. 'I'm still with Fred. We've just got back to the apartment. I'm not sure what's happening from here. So that you don't spend the evening hanging around waiting for someone who may not turn up – I mean, it's not exactly within my control – why don't I take a raincheck, and say that I'll call you early tomorrow?'

'Thanks a lot,' she said. 'That's really made my evening.' 'Hey, come on, Eileen,' I said. 'This is my whole future we're supposed to be talking about here. Fred and me. We haven't actually got very far. You know what Fred's like, for God's sake. What do you expect me to do? Say "Hey, Fred forgive me, I don't really want to know what you've got in mind for me for the next few years. I've actually got to go off and fuck someone. I'll maybe see you tomorrow." Are you kidding?' I heard her take a deep breath. 'Fred is probably one of the few people who would actually understand that,' she said. 'But I hear what you're saying.

'Tell me,' she said, changing the emphasis with which she had been speaking up until now. 'Tell me, how many girls have you and Fred got with in the apartment right now, and what does yours – or should that be and what *do* yours? – look like?' I could understand her attitude, and if I'd been her, I would probably have asked the same question. But it wasn't my doing. All I wanted was to discuss my forthcoming relationship with Fred. In strictly business terms. Had I really dumped the lovely Annabel for nothing more than to spend my days picking up girls in singles bars, and taking them back to Fred's apartment to fuck?

'Look, Eileen,' I said, trying to be patient. 'Whatever is going on here isn't my doing. You know Fred as well as I do. The answer to your question is that there are two girls here with Fred and me. Neither of them is "mine", as you so unfairly put it. I didn't ask them here, I didn't want them to come here, and I wish they weren't here now. The sooner they go, the happier I shall be. And perhaps *then* I'll be able to talk to Fred about the things that he originally invited me to lunch to discuss with him. But don't give me a hard time. Please. All right?' 'I'm sorry, darling,' she said. 'Please forgive me. But you haven't fucked me for three weeks now. You were either tied up with, or were away with your fiancée, for two weeks. You've been back now for two days. Yes, you spent your first night back here with me. But you were so drunk, all you did in bed was snore. You may or may not remember that I sent you back to Fred's apartment in a cab. You may or may not know that I love you. You may or may not care that I need to be fucked. By you. Now.'

Right at that moment, there was a rather cursory knock at my bedroom door, and it opened to reveal Fred, carrying a glass of champagne. 'Who's that?' he asked, handing the glass to me. I put my hand over the mouthpiece. 'Eileen,' I said. 'Oh, great,' he said. 'Put her on.' He stretched out his hand. I handed over the phone. 'Eileen, darling,' he said. 'Fred. We're having an orgy. Would you like to join us? We're a bit short of women.' He looked at the telephone in a slightly surprised fashion, and put it back on its rest.

'So what did I say?' he asked. 'She put the phone down on me. She'll have to go.' He looked at me. 'So,' he said. 'Wanda obviously wants my body, and Margot patently wants yours. It can't be a bad start, can it?' 'I guess not,' I said. 'But let's not be boring, shall we?' he asked. 'What do you mean, boring?' I said. 'Well, you know,' he said. 'I mean, let's keep the bedroom doors open. That sort of thing. You know. Let's not be selfish.' 'Whatever you say, Fred,' I said. 'It's your party.' 'That's the spirit, Tone,' he said. 'That's more like the Tony I used to know.' He put his arm around my shoulders, and escorted me back into the living room. Wanda and Margot had entered into the spirit of things by removing their outer wear, leaving them both in just bras and knickers. Wanda's bra was a miracle of contemporary brassiere construction. That such delicate material could restrain such enormous breasts was almost unbelievable. 'You can take that off for a start, darling,' said Fred, walking over to her and putting down his champagne glass, whilst he busied himself with her bra fastening. Wanda stood still while he unhooked her, and then she shrugged the straps off over her shoulders and arms. Fred dropped the brassiere on the floor. Wanda's breasts, when released, were much prettier than I, for one, could have imagined. They were large, yes. Full and ripe. But they didn't droop in the least. They stood out firmly, their conical ends tapering to large nipples, which were now standing erectly in the centre of her areolae. These were dark brown in colour, and sensually puckered in their thrusting rigidity.

Fred took a breast in each hand – or at least, as much breast as each hand could hold – and began to squeeze and feel and knead them, pulling on the nipples until they were engorged and swollen with, presumably, excitement. Then he stopped what he was doing, unzipped his fly with fumbling fingers, and sat down on the edge of the sofa. 'There's only one thing to do with a pair of tits like those,' he announced. 'Come here, darling.'

Wanda went over to him as he pulled his almost fully erect penis out of his trousers. 'Now kneel down in front of me,' he said. From his behaviour, he and Wanda might have been on their own. In fact, I knew Fred well enough to know that he actually loved an audience for his sexual adventures. He preferred it. His idea of sex seemed to be far more about humiliating the girl or girls who he was with than in any kind of real sexual enjoyment. Certainly giving pleasure didn't come into it. Perhaps he'd had too many complaisant women around him for far too long. I sometimes expected that he needed the audience to make sure that his staff knew that he was still able to get it up. He had by now got Wanda masturbating him with her breasts, one in each hand, jacking off his prick as he pushed it up between their luscious curves. As I watched,

COLD FEET 17

he took her head between his hands and pulled it down towards his cock. 'Now suck it as well,' he instructed her. He looked up at me. 'Nothing like the old French necklace, Tone, is there?' he asked. He didn't seem to expect a reply, so I didn't make one.

Looking at them, the sexiest part, for me, was to see Wanda's glorious ass, as full and as ripe as her breasts, showing tautly through her transparent knickers as she knelt in front of Fred. I could see curly, ginger anal hair surrounding her rectum, which was winking tightly at me through the hair as she bobbed her head up and down over Fred's prick. Her sphincter was the same puckered dark brown as her nipples. I felt my cock standing to attention. Had there been just the three of us, I think I would have stripped off, pulled down those tantalizing white see-through knickers, and fucked Wanda whilst she was entertaining Fred with her mouth and tits. I don't know what Wanda would have thought, but Fred would have loved it.

Just then I felt a hand on my arm, interrupting my fantasy. It was, of course, Margot. 'Hey, baby,' she said. 'Don't you want to play games too?' She was looking at me and smiling. Why not, I thought to myself? It didn't look as if I was going to have my conversation with Fred. Not this particular evening, anyway. And I could hardly abandon Margot, who seemed keen to get down to basics. In any case, Eileen could hardly be expecting me now, after her telephone conversation with Fred and me earlier. 'Of course I do, sweetheart,' I said, finally. 'Let's go and find ourselves a little privacy.' I took her by the hand and led her along to my bedroom, closing and locking the door behind me. Margot looked somewhat askance at me as I turned the key. 'Don't worry, sweetheart,' I said. There's no problem. I'm just not really into threesomes. Or foursomes, come to that. That's just to keep Fred out.' She relaxed, visibly. 'Oh, that's OK, then,' she said. 'I thought perhaps you were going to do something nasty to me.' 'Nasty, darling?' I said. 'What do you mean, nasty?'

'Oh, I don't know,' she replied. 'Some men like doing nasty things to girls. You know, beating them. Hurting them. Tying them up. Whipping them. All that sort of stuff. I'm just into fucking. I don't mind giving head, but I'm not into doing what Wanda's doing right now, not in public, anyway. And in any case, my tits aren't big enough.' I took Margot by the hand, and pulled her towards me. She was wearing a brassiere that was intended to tantalize rather than support, and tantalize it did, thrusting her firm young breasts together and forward, creating deep cleavage where there wasn't really any cleavage at all, making the most of her small but, I was certain, very pretty breasts.

The bra was in the palest green chiffon, and she was wearing matching French knickers, with full, open legs, the crotch unbuttoning via four tiny buttons. The chiffon was completely transparent, and the legs of the knickers, at the bottom, were lacy. There was only one way to describe them, to my mind, and that was as 'fuck me' knickers. And that was what I intended to do. I put my arms around Margot and began to kiss her. Her tongue instantly met mine, and we explored each other's mouths, wetly and erotically, and at the same time she ground her crotch against my rampant prick, taking a deep breath as she felt my hardness against her. I reached around behind her and unfastened her bra. She shrugged out of it, rather as Wanda had shrugged out of hers earlier, and freed her pretty little breasts.

They *were* perfect, as I had imagined. Absolutely perfect. Small, firm, pointed, with tiny pert nipples, which were burgeoning as I looked at them. Like little bullets. I leaned down and began to suck one. Margot reached down with her right hand and began to caress my cock through my trousers. She grasped its girth, and began what I can only describe as a masturbatory movement, pulling my foreskin backwards and forwards. She pulled her mouth away from mine for a moment. 'Maybe we should get into a better position for this kind of activity?' she suggested. 'I mean, like, how about on the bed? I love to feel and play with your cock through your trousers, but think how much more fun for both of us it will be if you take them off.' 'I can't argue with that, sweetheart,' I said.' But do me a favour. Keep your knickers on for me, will you, please? I'm a knicker freak. I just love to peel them off myself. Amongst other things.'

'What a funny word to use, knickers,' said Margot. 'To Americans, knickers mean those sort of plus-four type trousers that golfers sometimes wear. As in knickerbockers. What I'm wearing are panties. But, sure, I'll keep them on for you. Whatever turns you on, baby.' 'Thank you, sweetheart,' I said. I let go of her, and she went over and lay on the bed, still wearing her pale green French knickers. (French panties? That's ridiculous!) I undressed quickly and went, naked and preceded by my tumescent cock, over to the bed. Margot smiled up at me expectantly. 'I kept them on,' she said, smiling up at me. 'Thank you, darling,' I said, as I spread her legs widely, and buried my mouth and nose in her delicately scented, lacy chiffon crotch. The material – lined with cotton – was wet with her juices, and the fresh, intense smell of hot cunt was like the strong scent of a carpet of orchids in a rain forest; heavy, sensual, erotic. Added to that delightful aroma was the taste and feel of the damp fabric, which I found libidinously, electrically stimulating. I sucked and licked at the wet fabric, inhaling as I did so, luxuriating in the combined attack on all of my senses – sight, taste, feel and smell. The chiffon got wetter and wetter, and Margot began to move her hips beneath my mouth.

'Oh, fuck me, darling,' she breathed, softly. 'Fuck me. Please. Now.' I abandoned my oral attentions to her somewhat reluctantly, and, using my fingers, I undid the four small buttons which closed the crotch of her French knickers. Once opened, I pulled them widely apart, revealing her black, tightly curled pubic hair surrounding her large, fleshy, pink cunt lips, open, like the petals of an exotic flower, and surprisingly wet, as if just rained upon by a tropical shower.

'Oh, yes,' she whispered. 'Yes. Now. Please. Fuck me.' As I watched, she released a small quantity of love-juice from her open vulva, which trickled, rather than spurted, out on to the bed sheets. It was, I think, sheer sexual excitement which caused her so to behave. I do not believe that she was entirely in control of herself at that moment. I don't think she even knew what she had done. I raised myself up, and, kneeling over her, I lowered my engorged cock over her cunt, and, using my fingers, I spread her wet cunt-lips, and thrust myself deeply inside her. The sharp, slightly acrid smell of her aroused quim reached my nostrils. It acted – I know not why – as an intensely effective aphrodisiac, and I began to fuck her seriously hard. She responded to me, and gathered herself together and matched my rhythm with her own.

After a while, she grasped my buttocks, and began to knead them, which I found intensely erotic, moving faster as a result. She then kept one hand kneading, and with the other felt for, and found, my anus. She massaged it gently, and after my initial reaction, which was to hold it as tightly clenched as I knew how, I began to relax, and ultimately, to enjoy the sensation. She continued to massage it, and then she took her hand away, put it up to her mouth, spat on her fingers, and, putting them back where they were before, she slid a forefinger inside me. My instant reaction was as previously. I closed my sphincter as tightly as I knew how. 'Relax, baby,' she whispered in my ear. 'I'm not raping you. Just touching you up a little. Let go, and enjoy it. It doesn't make you gay, for God's sake. It's real sexy. I promise. Trust me. OK?'

Realizing that what she said was true, I did as she suggested, and after a few moments, I began to really enjoy the feeling of her finger massaging my anus from inside. Once I became accustomed to it, and began to relax into what was happening to me, it certainly added to my enjoyment of what I was doing, and I began to start my journey up towards the inevitable ejaculation, which I could sense – rather than physically feel – was now commencing, somewhere down around my ankles. It rose, slowly, with increasing speed, up my legs, up my thighs, to my balls, where it immediately exploded, causing me to ejaculate wads of hot come up inside Margot's receptive pussy. 'Oh, baby,' she said. 'I can feel your spunk spurting up inside me. That feels real good. You'll never know just how good that feels. Oh, my God. I love it. Thank you.' 'My pleasure, sweetheart,' I said, completely truthfully. 'My pleasure.'

We lay there for a while, sweating quietly, arms around each other, not feeling the need to talk. Simply enjoying the total relaxation of mutual sexual release. After maybe ten minutes, I turned over towards her, and kissed her. 'Thank you, darling,' I said. 'That was good. Really good. I enjoyed myself.' 'Me too,' she said, grinning up at me. 'I loved it when I shoved my finger up your ass, and you closed up like a virgin. Haven't you ever had a girl finger-fuck your asshole before?' I thought for a moment. 'Well, since you mention it, yes, I have,' I said. 'But not for a long time. And never on the first occasion that we've been to bed together.' 'Does that mean that you've never fucked a girl in the ass?' she asked me. I felt my cock stiffen at the very mention of heterosexual buggery.

'Er, no, not exactly,' I said. 'As a matter of fact, it's something I'm rather fond of. Provided everyone's happy about it.' 'Oh, great,' she said. 'I love it. Do it to me now. Fuck my asshole. Will you? Please? I love it. I love it.' 'I'd love to,' I said. 'Thank you. Just hang on in there, baby. I'll just go find some KY jelly.' 'Are you sure you're not gay?' she asked, laughing at me as I went through to the bathroom. I found the KY, and went back into the bedroom with it. 'To answer your question, sweetie,' I said, turning her over onto her tummy, unscrewing the cap of the KY jelly, and squeezing out a goodly thread of it onto my forefinger, 'I'm not gay. At least, not unless fucking girls up the ass makes me gay. If that's the case, then yes, I am. You tell me.'

I began to rub the KY jelly into her asshole, and she wriggled her bottom at me provocatively as I did so. She had a beautiful, tiny, tight little asshole. I thrust my finger deeply into it, and I felt her relax and open, accepting my finger up to the hilt, then closing tightly around it, and squeezing it for all she was worth. Despite my recent ejaculation, I nearly came over the bedclothes in my anticipatory excitement. I pulled my finger out, squirted more KY over it, and put it back up her ass again, again thrusting my finger in as deeply as it would go. She took it right up to the hilt again, and began to move her bottom about beneath my finger. 'Oh, baby,' she said. 'I love it. Take your finger out, and put your cock up there. Up my ass. Fuck me, anally. Bugger me. Do dirty things to me. I love it. I want your prick up my ass. Do it to me. Do it now. I want your cock up my ass.'

She looked back at me over her shoulder. 'I've said please,' she said. 'What the fuck else do I have to do?' She raised herself up on her knees in front of me, and, putting both her hands behind her and grasping her buttocks firmly, she pulled her asshole open as wide as she could. I could see deep down inside it. It was dark pink inside, the same as her cunt. It was both wet and greasy. My cock was standing up like a flag-pole. 'It's all yours, baby,' she said. 'Do it now. Fuck my ass. *Please.*' I grabbed her by the buttocks and spread my knees each side of her knees. I pulled her body with the proffered asshole towards me and, using my right hand, I guided my throbbing cock towards her anus. I pressed against it, gently, and felt her pushing backwards, at which point my cock slid into her. She was very tight, and I kept pushing, and it slid more deeply into her. I felt her clenching and unclenching her sphincter muscles as I began to fuck her, and I knew I wouldn't be able to hold my ejaculation back for more than a few moments, despite my recent performance. She felt hot, and the KY jelly had made her pliantly greasy, to my intense pleasure.

Margot bucked and pressed against me, obviously revelling in the feeling of my prick thrusting up her asshole, and she began to make animal noises deep in her throat. She clenched her muscles more and more tightly, and suddenly, almost without warning, I was ejaculating great jets of come inside her, my cock pulsating as it discharged, spurting rhythmically, and then Margot was coming too. I could feel her spasms in her rectum, throbbing all around my cock, milking it of its juices.

She turned her head, and looked at me. 'Wow, baby,' she said. 'Some piece of ass, yes? Was that anything like as good for you, huh?' 'It was sensational, sweetheart,' I said. 'I'm sorry I didn't last so long. It was all too much. I just couldn't hold it.' 'Don't worry about a thing,' she said. 'We'll do it again in a little while. You're bound to last longer the second time around.' 'Third,' I said. 'Who's counting?' she asked. She lay down on her stomach, with my cock still inside her, and I turned with her as she lay on her side. Her asshole was so tight that my cock stayed half erect inside her, the pressure of her muscles stimulating it.

After a few minutes, sheer lust overcame me, and I began to move, slowly at first, and then I felt her pressing back against me. My cock was fully erect again, and I began to fuck her anally once more. 'Oh, yeah,' she said. 'That feels so good. You just don't know how good that feels.' 'I do, baby,' I said. 'I really do.' Don't ask me why, but at that moment I suddenly noticed that she was still wearing her French knickers. They'd been there all the time, of course, but I simply hadn't taken them in. I'd obviously been totally distracted by what I had been doing. Well, it isn't every day that I get to fuck a pretty, new young girl in the ass. I'd undone the buttons at her crotch, but I hadn't actually taken them off. They looked rather appealing, hanging from her waist, the loose ends moving in rhythm with my copulatory strokes.

Her rectum felt just as tight and hot this time as it had the first time around, and she was using her sphincter muscles as enthusiastically as she had before, but I was confident I was going to last much longer. Time to enjoy the gorgeous, libidinous, sheer *naughtiness* of what I was doing to her. I watched my cock thrusting in and out of her tightly clenched anus, surrounded as it was by her tightly curled, shiny black anal hair. I was spreading her pinky-brown, puckered flesh as I delved and withdrew, seeing it distend as I thrust in, contract as I pulled back, my cock greasy from the jelly that was now covering its length, making its repeated journeys so smooth. I felt that I was discovering, experiencing, what carnal knowledge really meant, even accepting that it isn't a description normally used for buggery. I knew that I was sodomizing her, but I found that I was enjoying debauching this delightfully willing girl, invading her most private of private parts. I felt like a satyr, or a whoremaster, deflowering his newest whore, raping her anally, forcing her to accept his swollen, invading tool up her ass. I felt deviant as I had never felt before. I was a sexual pervert, a sodomite, a true degenerate. And I was loving every minute of it. I bent down to Margot's ear. 'Talk dirty to me, baby,' I said. 'Tell me what I'm doing to you. Say naughty things. Where's my cock? Tell me.'

'You're fucking my asshole,' she said, obligingly. 'Your

huge, stiff cock is fucking my ass, spreading my tiny little bottom-hole, forcing its way into my anus. You're buggering me, making me take you up my ass. My little hole's spread wide open by your huge prick. You're raping my asshole, fucking my bottom. And, oh yes, now you're spurting spunk inside me. You're coming in my asshole. I can feel great jets of spunk inside my bottom. Oh, I love it. I really, really love it. You can fuck me in the ass any time you want, baby. Any time at all.'

This time I did pull out of her, and we both lay there for a while, breathing deeply, recovering from our exertions. After a while, I got up off the bed, went into the bathroom and began to shower. A few minutes later Margot joined me and, taking the soap from my hand, she began to lather my cock with it, pulling my foreskin back, ensuring that it was properly cleansed. To my surprise, it began to swell in her hand. 'What a naughty boy you are,' said Margot. 'Don't tell me you want me to jack you off, not after you've fucked me three times. I don't believe it.' She began to masturbate me. I put a hand on her arm, and gently stopped her. 'Thank you, sweetheart,' I said,' but no, thank you. Take no notice of it. It's just boasting. It doesn't know what it's saying.' I took the soap back from her, and spent an enjoyable while soaping and rinsing her pussy, then her asshole. Then I washed her tits, very, very carefully, simply for good measure.

We got out of the shower, and towelled ourselves dry. Margot put back on her pale green bra and French knickers, at which point she realized that she had left the rest of her clothes in the other room, where she had taken them off. Having dressed myself, I volunteered to go and get them, and, unlocking the bedroom door, I went through to where we'd left Wanda giving Fred an enthusiastic French necklace, combined with a blow job. There was no sign of them, but Margot's skirt, blouse jacket, and shoes were there where she'd dropped them. I collected them, and took them back into the bedroom.

'There's no sign of the others,' I said. 'And Wanda's clothes aren't in the room. I wonder what they're up to? If I know Fred, he's gone off somewhere. Otherwise we'd have had him knocking on our door, if he's still about. I'll go and have a look in his room.' I went through to his bedroom. The door was open, but there was no sign of either of them. There was a mirror glass lying on the bedside table, plus a razor blade, and faint traces of Fred's favourite nose candy on both of these items. Hmmm, I thought. I looked around, and then went through to the living room, and looked carefully there, but there was no sign of a note anywhere. I was surprised that Wanda hadn't left a note for Margot, if nothing else, but there is no explaining what people do or don't do when they're high on cocaine. I checked the time. It was just after six. I went back into the bedroom.

'No sign of anybody anywhere,' I told Margot. 'They obviously found something better to do. How about a drink?' 'That's strange,' she said. 'I wouldn't have thought that Wanda would go off without saying anything, or leaving me a note. Something. Anything. And yes, I'd love a drink. Thank you. Do you think there's any champagne left? It's not often I get the chance to drink decent champagne.' She paused. Then: 'Actually, it's not often that I get to drink *any* kind of champagne.

'Sure, honey,' I said. I doubted there was any left in the bottle that we'd opened earlier, but there was plenty more where that came from. I went into the kitchen and took a bottle out of the fridge. Margot found me in the kitchen as I was opening it. 'Hey, you guys live well, don't you?' she said. It came out as 'Don chew.' I guess that was part of what she'd meant earlier, talking with a Brooklyn accent. I found it rather touching. 'Grab a couple of glasses out of that cupboard over there, will you please, sweetheart?' I asked, pointing at the corner cupboard. 'Yes, I guess we do pretty well,' I went on. 'But we earn it. What we do for a living results in more and more people buying the magazine that we produce, which means more and more profit for our publisher. It seems only fair that we too should get some benefit from that. Don't you agree?' 'Sure I agree,' she said. 'But you're dead lucky to actually share in the magazine's profitability. You must have a generous boss.' As she was speaking, I could hear voices in the corridor outside, and then came the sound of a key in the door that opened to let in Fred and Wanda. I went out of the kitchen to greet them.

'There you are,' I said, somewhat obviously. 'We wondered where you were.' 'We got bored,' said Fred. 'So we did some coke, and then we decided that we wanted to see a dirty movie. So we went to that nice dirty movie house up on, what is it? Fifty-fifth Street?' 'Something like that,' I said. 'What did you see?' 'We saw your friend Lucy,' said Fred. 'Lucy?' I asked. 'You mean bald black Lucy, who's recently modelled for us?' 'The very same,' said Fred. 'We've seen her sucking cock, sucking pussy, having her pussy sucked – by both girls and men – and being fucked every which way. She was terrific. Wasn't she?' he asked Wanda. 'She was quite something,' said Wanda, who obviously had her own opinion of Lucy's abilities. 'They certainly kept her busy.' 'But that's good,' said Fred. 'When we run her girl set with . . . who was it?' he asked. 'Dee Dee,' I told him. 'Dee Dee from the topless bottomless bar. You know?' 'Oh, yes,' said Fred. 'That's right. Anyway, when we run her pictures, we can write some cover lines tying them in with the movie. It'll be great publicity. We should probably run a few extra thousand copies. What do you think?' 'Why not?' I said. 'Great idea.'

'What are cover lines?' asked Margot. 'They're the sales pitches that all magazines run on their front covers,' said Fred. 'You know, things like "Eat as much as you like and lose weight" on women's magazines. We'll say something like "America's top porno actress reveals her all" or "America's top porno star's live-in lover." Something like that. Cover lines are designed to make you want to buy the magazine, so that you can read about whatever it is that the cover lines are about. They're sort of teasers. Tony writes good ones.' 'Oh, right,' said Margot.

One of the things that has always fascinated me about New York is that blue movies are shown there legally. And I do mean *blue* movies. High quality, first-rate, hard-core pornographic films, made to the production standards of the mainstream films you see at home in London. With attractive men, beautiful girls, and every possible kind of sexual perversion that you can imagine. And probably one or two that you haven't thought of yet. Nor are all such movie house in sleazy areas. Some of them are, of course, but some of them – the one that Fred and Wanda had just been to, for example – are in up-market residential areas, and are newly built, well-decorated, comfortable movie theatres. They just happen to specialize in showing fully explicit pornography. The scripts are usually modestly believable and the actors and actresses are every bit as famous in their field as their more 'respectable' Hollywood counterparts are in theirs. And, as Fred had just indicated, they perform every conceivable kind of sexual act, in close-up, with girls sucking girls as probably the most popular of the many variations on offer. When it's simply old-fashioned fucking, the man always withdraws as he ejaculates, and spurts his semen over the girl's face and/or breasts. I used to wonder why this was done, until somebody told that it is to show that the people involved are *really* fucking. There's no make-believe.

'That Lucy is too much,' said Fred. 'I wouldn't mind giving her one myself. That shaven black cunt is a right turn-on.' He looked at me. 'Don't you think, Tone?' 'Please, gentlemen,' said Wanda. 'Manners, please. Do you mind? I don't mind pussy, but cunt is an ugly word.' 'Would you prefer wee-wee?' Fred asked her, doubling up with laughter at what he perceived as his wit. 'Come and sit on my face, so that I can kiss your wee-wee, baby.' He almost fell on the floor with mirth. One thing I have to say about Fred, he really enjoys a joke. Especially if it's one of his. But I thought I'd answer Fred's question, in order to change the subject. I could see that Wanda didn't share Fred's particular sense of humour.

'I refuse to answer that question, on the grounds that it might incriminate me,' I said. 'No, joking apart, yes, I think that bald wee-wee *is* a right turn-on, and yes, I have fucked her.' In more ways than one, I thought, thinking of my recent session with Margot. My prick stiffened at the memory. Down, boy, I said to myself. 'Wow,' said Wanda. 'Superman.' She turned to Margot. 'You should see this black hooker Lucy,' she said. 'She's at least six feet tall, and she fucks like a rattlesnake. Your friend here must have been doing you quite a favour while Fred and me were at the cinema. Tell Auntie Wanda all about it. Has he got a ten-foot shlong?'

I laughed. 'No, he hasn't,' I said, quickly, not wanting Margot to say anything at all. Fred was very self-conscious about the size of his rather small cock, and I didn't want the conversation moving in that direction. It was yet another subject to get away from as quickly as possible. 'But shaved pussies have always turned me on,' I said. 'Why?' asked Margot, curiously. I grinned at her. 'I'm not going to tell you,' I said. 'I don't know you well enough.' 'I'll tell you,' said Fred. 'It reminds him of young nuns. He can look at a girl's shaved pussy, and fantasize to himself that he's fucking a novice nun who has just shaved her pubic hair for Jesus for the first time. Dirty sod.' 'Well, that's as maybe,' said Wanda. 'But there's nothing nunlike about this Lucy, I can tell you. She'd scare me shitless if I were in the same room with her.' She looked at Margot.

'She's a dab hand with a dildo,' she said. 'Terrifying. And you should see her suck pussy. I don't suppose she needs to eat anything else.'

We all laughed. 'Hey,' said Fred to me. 'Was she a great fuck? Did she suck you in, and blow you out in little bubbles, as we used to say at school, long before any of us had ever fucked anything, other than our hands? I can imagine that she would be.' 'Come on, Fred, old love,' I said. 'That's not the kind of question a gentleman asks about a lady. Least of all when there are other ladies present.' 'I don't see why not,' he said. 'Mostly because, first of all, I'm not a bloody gentleman. Do you really mean that I've got to wait until these ladies have gone to ask you if the lovely Margot was a good fuck? Or if she gave you a blow job? Or if she takes it up her arse?' He looked at Margot, and grinned at her evilly. Margot blushed. 'Really, Fred,' I said. 'Let's change the subject, shall we?'

'Oh, fuck the lot of you,' said Fred. 'You're all dead boring. Tone, open another bottle of champagne, will you, there's a good chap? I can't be doing with all this pompous morality. First I mustn't say cunt, and now I can't ask if anyone enjoyed a good fuck. Cunt, cunt, cunt, cunt, cunt,' he said, childishly. He relapsed into sulky silence as I went off to the kitchen to do as I was bid. The two girls were talking quietly in the corner as I left. Margot followed me into the kitchen a few moments later. 'Tony,' she said, 'Wanda's a bit pissed off with Fred, and she wants to go. I'd stay if I were on my own, but I'm not. That's if you wanted me to stay, of course,' she added, hastily. 'Of course I do,' I said. 'But I do understand. I'm sorry about Fred. He's a bit over the top at the moment. It's the cocaine. It makes him paranoid. He'll be better in the morning. Do me a favour, please, Margot, will you? Call me at the office? Please? The number's in the book. I'd love to get together with you again, real soon. OK?'

She stood on tiptoe and kissed my cheek. 'Of course I will, darling,' she said. I grabbed her and kissed her hard. Her tongue met mine and we explored each other's mouths for a moment or two, and then she pulled back. 'I must go now, sweetie,' she said. 'Ciao, baby.' 'Ciao, darling,' I said. 'See you soon.' She left, and I heard them both making their farewells to Fred. Wanda put her head around the kitchen door. 'See you, Tony,' Sorry about this.' 'No problem, Wanda,' I said. 'I understand. See you soon, I hope.' Wanda blew a kiss, and disappeared. Fred came shuffling morosely into the kitchen. 'Boring cows,' he said. I looked at him. 'Well, all right, then,' he said. 'Boring cow. *Was* yours a good fuck? *Did* she take it up her arse?' I looked at him again, but I didn't say anything. 'Oh, come on, Tony,' he said. 'Don't *you* give me a hard time, for God's sake.'

'Oh, very well,' I said. 'Yes, she was a terrific fuck. One of the better ones. And as to does she take it up the arse, I don't know,' I lied. 'I didn't ask her.' I handed him a fresh glass of champagne. 'Now just drink that, and shut up about women,' I said. 'How about a game of backgammon?' 'Oh, great idea,' he said. 'Yeah, I'd like that. For money, of course?' 'Of course,' I said. 'A dollar a point?' 'Done,' he said. 'I'll go and set the board up.'

Fred thought he was the world's best backgammon player, just as, in the same way, he thought that he was the world's best poker player. He wasn't actually that bad at either, but he certainly wasn't the quality player he thought he was. But he was very rich, and if you're very rich, you can usually win, because you simply raise everyone else out of the game. But that doesn't work quite as well in backgammon. There is no real element of surprise in the game. The pieces are all there, on the board, for both players to see. The only chance is in what your throw of the dice will produce. And if you don't know the odds for and against any given combination of numbers coming up when you throw, you shouldn't be playing backgammon. Not for money, anyway. Yes, the doubling dice gives you the opportunity to increase the stakes, but it doesn't affect the odds in any way.

But Fred's money always came in handy in backgammon too, in that, if he was down financially at the end of a backgammon session, he'd offer his opponent the opportunity to play a final game for double or quits. If you think about it, it's a very unfair offer. Imagine that I'm playing him, over a period of, let's say, two hours, I win a hundred dollars from him, at a dollar a point, that means that I've played – and won – quite a few games over quite a long period of time. Yet Fred is expecting me to gamble that whole amount, at the end of the session, on one game, lasting perhaps ten minutes. Yes, of course I can win, and end up with two hundred dollars. But if he's lucky enough to throw exceptional dice, I can lose, and end up with nothing. And of course the thing that we never discuss is the fact that, because Fred is my boss, I can't actually refuse. Or, at best, I would be very ill-advised to refuse. But that's life.

I went through to the living room. Fred was setting up the pieces on his beautiful antique backgammon table. It was a great pleasure to play on that table, and it was the one thing in the apartment that I really envied him. I'm not, basically, a very envious person, but this table made me make an exception to my usual philosophy. It was something else. The mahogany top was inlaid with ivory and teak for the black and white points, and the pieces were in carved white and dyed red ivory. It was a good size. So many backgammon boards are far too small. The table was what is today regarded as international tournament size; something like two feet by three feet. (I've never caught up with the metric measurements.) Fred took one red piece and one white piece and, putting his hands behind his back for a moment, he brought them out in front of himself again, the hands closed. I touched his right hand, and he opened it to reveal the white piece. A good omen.

I don't mind playing from left to right, or right to left. It's immaterial to me. (It should be to all backgammon players, but some people have strong preferences.) But I'm very superstitious about preferring to play with white, rather than red, or black, pieces. Don't ask me why. There's no real reason. 'Fancy a snort before we start?' asked Fred. 'Why not?' I said. 'Thank you.' If you can't beat them, join them. In any case, I really enjoyed the occasional snort. I just didn't want to make a habit of it. Ho ho. 'Is it good stuff?' I asked. 'Pretty good,' said Fred. 'Not too bad at all.'

He got out his silver two-gram phial, and tipped out a quantity of small rocks onto the mirror glass that he used to cut his cocaine on. He then cut and chopped them into powder with a silver-mounted razor blade, and arranged the resultant powder neatly into four equal lines. Next he took out his wallet, and selected a clean, new, one hundred dollar bill. He rolled it carefully, put one end up his nostril, and inhaled the cocaine sharply up the other end, moving the rolled note along the line of powder as he did so. He repeated the actions with a second line, and handed the note to me.

It hit me quickly, It *was* good stuff. I almost immediately felt on top of the world. Light-headed, in the nicest of ways. Every word that passed my lips was a word of genuine wisdom. Everything that I said was amusing. Fred sat down at the table, and grinned at me. 'Not bad, eh?' he asked. 'Terrific.' I said. 'Good stuff. Thank you.' 'Plenty more where that came from,' he said. 'Where *did* it come from?' I asked. 'Some contact of Eileen's,' he said. 'I think she gets a small percentage for introducing me. But I don't mind that. It's always good stuff. They'll deliver at any time of the day or night. And they always let me try it before I buy. I reckon it's a good deal.' 'How much?' I asked. 'Two hundred dollars a gram,' he said.

'Not bad for good stuff.' Shit, I thought. That's about three thousand dollars' worth of coke a week, at the rate Fred snorts it. Shit.

'House rules?' asked Fred. 'Sure,' I said. 'No automatic doubles. No beavers. Or anything else like that. No throwing again if you don't like your throw, with an added double. 'In fact,' I said, 'international rules. OK?' 'OK,' said Fred. 'If that's the way you want it.' 'That's the way I want it,' I said. We both threw our dice.

Beavers are when someone offers you the doubling cube and, after consideration, you not only take it, but you can – if you so wish – hand it straight back again, before you throw the dice. It is, to my mind, an unnecessary way to play, since, if you accept a double, you can offer it back at your next throw anyway. What's so clever about giving it back and forth? It gets back to who's the richest player. I don't believe that's what the game is about. I threw a six and a one. A lover's leap. Fred threw a two and a three. 'Fuck,' he said. 'My move,' I said. I offered him the doubling cube before I made my move. He took it. His next move, he gave it back to me. I kept it. That meant we were playing for four dollars a point. I won the game. We played, gently until about midnight, at which point the cocaine, and the whisky that I had been drinking since we started playing backgammon, began to catch up with me. I yawned, long and loud. 'If you'll forgive me, Fred,' I said, 'I think I'll make for bed.' 'Of course I won't forgive you,' he said. 'I owe you money.' 'How much?' I asked. He took up the score sheet that he had been keeping, and totted up our scores. 'It looks like just over twelve hundred dollars,' he said, 'I'll play you the best of three for double or quits.' 'Oh no, you won't,' I said. 'I've worked long and hard for that money. Now I've had enough. I'm tired. Just shut up and pay up.' He looked at me long and hard, but he didn't say anything. Then, 'I'll have to give you a cheque.' 'That's OK,' I said. 'I'll take a cheque.'

Fred kicked back his chair and, with considerable lack of grace, went into his bedroom, returning with a chequebook. 'Have you got a pen?' he asked. I gave him my pen. 'Just Tony Andrews?' he said. 'Fine,' I said. He wrote out the cheque, signed it and handed it to me. 'Thank you,' I said. The cheque was made out for twelve hundred and forty-six dollars. Not a bad evening's backgammon. I put it in my wallet. 'Drink?' said Fred. 'Last line of coke?' 'Why not?' I said. 'I'll get the scotch. You do the coke.' I found some clean glasses, poured four fingers of neat scotch into both, and put ice in Fred's, water in mine. I took his glass over to him. He was busy with the razor blade. 'Cheers,' I said. He looked up. 'Oh, cheers, Tone,' he said. We clinked glasses, and drank. There was silence for a while.

'What's the matter, Tony?' said Fred. 'You look fidgety.' 'That's probably because I feel fidgety,' I said. 'Why's that?' he asked. 'Because I told you a fib, earlier,' I said. 'Oh,' he said. 'That's no big deal.' 'No,' I said. 'Perhaps not. But I'd like to put the record straight. You know when you asked if Margot was a good fuck, earlier on?' I asked him. 'Yes,' he said. 'Go on.' 'Well,' I said, 'you asked me if she took it up her arse. I said I didn't know, because I hadn't asked her.' He looked at me. 'Yes,' he said. 'Well.' I said. 'That was a lie. I did fuck her up the arse. Twice, as a matter of fact.' 'I know,' he said. 'I came to see what you were up to at one stage, and I could hear her through the locked door, saying, I don't know, "Stuff it up my arse." Something like that.' He grinned at me. 'It doesn't matter, Tone,' he said. 'It's not important. We all have our little secrets. Don't we?' I looked at him, long and hard. 'You bastard,' I said. 'You absolute bastard. And, yes. I guess we do.' He laughed, and raised his glass towards me. 'Cheers, Tony,' he said. 'Cheers, Fred.' I said. We went our separate ways off to bed a little later, both of us relaxed and happy. Friends again. A good feeling.

CHAPTER TWO:
LA VIE EN ROSE

To my surprise, Fred was up and about the following morning when I made it to the kitchen. Unlike me, he was shaved and dressed. 'Morning, Tony,' he said. 'And how are we this beautiful summer morning?' 'Morning, Fred,' I replied. 'All right, I think. All the better for seeing you.' I looked at my watch, just to check that it hadn't stopped, or something. But no. The second sweep hand was moving slowly around. The hands said nine a.m.

'I thought I'd get into the office a bit early this morning,' he said. 'Shake the staff up a bit. Nothing like a surprise to keep them on their feet. I'll see you there later,' he said. 'Come and see me when you get in. No hurry. We'll talk over this draft contract. OK?' 'Great,' I said. 'Terrific. Thank you.' He got up, brushing toast crumbs off his expensively tailored Californian jeans. Where else would you find tailored jeans, except in California? Except that – I remembered now – my mate David Jones, who worked these days for Paul Raymond's magazine company in New York, once told me that Paul Raymond had *his* jeans tailored. Apparently by the same theatrical tailor who fashioned the clothes for some of Paul's theatrical ventures. It being 1976, Fred's jeans were, of course, flared. Very. I had gone so far as to purchase sixty dollars' worth of Fiorucci jeans in New York's Fiorucci shop on East 59th Street. Very daring for me. But flared jeans were something else altogether.

'Cheers,' said Fred, on the way out. 'See you,' I said. I finished my coffee, shaved and showered, and got myself together.

It was a beautiful morning down on the sidewalk, bright and sunny, but with a breeze that kept the temperature down to bearable levels. I decided to walk to the office via my bank, on First Avenue and East 49th, and pay in Fred's cheque from the night before. You never knew with Fred. If he remembered losing the money (which was doubtful) he might well stop the cheque, under the pretext of some imagined, manufactured foul.

On arrival at *Tiptop*'s offices, I looked in on Eileen on the way through to my office. 'Hi,' she said. 'Are we well this fine, sunny morning?' 'I think so, sweetheart,' I said, thanking God inwardly that she seemed to have forgotten her irritation of yesterday. 'How was the meeting with Fred?' she asked. 'Don't ask,' I told her. 'We didn't have it. We played backgammon instead. But at least I won some money off him. But don't mention that either, please. At least not to him. He wasn't greatly pleased.' 'Don't worry,' she said. 'I won't say a word. I'll bring some coffee along to your office in a minute, and we can go through your mail. OK?' 'Thanks,' I said. 'I'll just pop my head around Fred's door.' 'You do that,' she said. 'Hey,' he said, when I did just that. 'Come in. I'll get Eileen to bring us some coffee.' I didn't say anything about Eileen taking coffee to my office. I thought I'd let her work things out for herself.

'So,' said Fred. 'You ran things pretty well while I was in London. Wally was delighted. And he's more than happy for you to join me out here. So I guess that all you have to do is go back to London and tidy up before you come out here permanently. I'll get Eileen looking at apartments while you're in London. Do you have any preference about which part of town you'd like to be in?' 'Well, yes, I do,' I told him. 'But where and how I live depends to a large extent on how much Wally's going to pay me.' Fred smiled at me. 'Don't worry about a thing,' he said. He told me the annual salary that Wally proposed. It was almost three times my London salary. 'Plus the company will pay your apartment rent, and basic expenses, like ConEd, gas, cleaning, and so on,' he said. I whistled. 'That all adds up to serious money,' I said. 'It does, doesn't it?' agreed Fred.

'But don't forget that what you do on a day-to-day basis here will make Wally about twelve million dollars a year, net after tax, the way things are going at the moment. If sales drop, of course, you're dead.' He grinned at me. 'But that's life. What do you say?' 'I say yes, please. And thank you,' I said. 'It's a hell of a good deal. My thanks to you, Fred. I'm sure it's more to do with you than Wally.' 'Not really.' said Fred. 'Wally's not stupid, you know. Don't think that he doesn't realize that in you he's got a first class long-stop, if I should happen to blot my copybook. Oh, and by the way, I forgot one small point.' I looked at him, expectantly. 'Your expenses,' he said. 'You can spend up to five hundred dollars a week without having to justify anything to anyone. Just don't spend more than that without checking with me. That's meant to cover real expenses, but you're also expected to make personal profit. And don't forget to put receipts in. You'll need those, for the IRS. Restaurant bills are fine. OK?' 'Fantastic,' I said. 'Absobloodylutely fantastic.'

'So,' he said. 'What's this I hear about you getting engaged, all set for a trip down the aisle, prior to moving out here with your virgin bride, and then – so I'm told – it's all over? This is Annabel, isn't it? What happened? Tell Uncle Fred all about it.' He leaned across the desk, and gripped my arm. 'Seriously, Tony. Is there anything I can do to help?'

I told him what had happened. I didn't leave anything out, and I didn't try and make myself look like the poor abandoned, would-be bridegroom. I told him that I thought that I really was in love. Perhaps for only the second time in my life. And I told him that, although it was Annabel who had brought the subject of my doubts and fears up, she was, in fact, quite right. Sad as it made me, I told Tony that I thought that she had made the right decision for both of us. I would, I said, have gone through with it. But I wouldn't have given too much for its chances of lasting. 'My dear old chap,' said Fred. 'How absolutely dreadful for you. And now you're full of remorse. You feel that you've ruined this lovely girl's life. Am I right?' 'Absolutely right,' I told him. 'I can give you some advice that will help, if you take it seriously,' he said. 'What's that?' I said. 'Anything that would help would be very much appreciated.' 'Fuck everything that moves,' he said. 'Take it from me. I've been there, once or twice. Drown yourself in cunt. It works very well, and very quickly.' I had to laugh. I'd have cried, otherwise. 'I'm serious,' he said. 'I know you are,' I told him. 'And I know you're right. I'll do my best. I promise.' 'Good,' he said.

'Now,' he continued. 'There are just a couple of other things to sort out, and then I suggest that we go and have some lunch. When do you want to go back to London, and how long will it take you to get things together there? I'll tell Wally on the phone that you've accepted his offer, and he'll get a contract to you for you to sign, either here or there. And I'll tell accounts to start your new salary package from today. It includes all the usual things. You know. Medical insurance. That sort of thing. And we've got a consultant out here to help with applications for work permits. Green cards, they call them. They're not green at all, of course. But apparently they were originally, many years ago. You'd better go and see him while you're still here. He can start right away. Eileen will give you his address and so on. *Tiptop* will pay his not inconsiderable bill. And tell

LA VIE EN ROSE

Eileen to call real estate agents, about an apartment for you.'

I was somewhat dazed by all this excitement. Get yourself together, Andrews, I said to myself. What was it now? Almost the end of July. I guess a month back in London – bearing in mind that I'd still have to go into the London office – would be enough to tidy up my arrangements. I looked at Fred. 'How about my starting here formally on September One?' I said. 'A month,' said Fred. 'Yes. Great. Now let's go and get some lunch. And let me know if there's anything you think of that we haven't touched on. Or sort it out with Eileen. God, I need a drink.' He stood up. 'Let's go, shall we? Where do you fancy?' 'I don't mind,' I said. 'You choose. But there is one thing I've just remembered.' 'What's that?' he asked. 'My title,' I said. 'What about it?' asked Tony. 'Well,' I said. 'When you asked me if I'd like to come and work for you out here, you said as deputy editor.' 'So?' he said. 'Well, that's fine,' I said. 'Except that we've already got a deputy editor. That's Angle's title.' 'Shit,' he said. 'So it is.'

We were down on Third Avenue by now, the taxi horns blaring, the pedestrians crowding, the street sellers shouting their wares, the traffic cops blowing their whistles. Fred managed, by dint of sheer bad manners, to get us a cab. 'Sorry, buster,' he said, as he pushed a furious American out of the way. 'This one's mine.' I didn't hear what the man said to Fred, but I heard Fred's reply. 'And fuck you, too,' he said, slamming the cab door shut behind him. 'The Russian Tea Room,' he said to the cab driver. 'One fifty, West Fifty-seventh.' 'I know where the fuckin' Russian Tea Room is, Mac,' said the cabbie, irritably. 'That makes a bloody change, then,' said Fred, sitting back comfortably in his seat. The cabbie looked at Fred in his rear view mirror, and apparently thought better of it. Fred *is* very large. I hadn't been to the Russian Tea Room myself, although I had heard about it. It wasn't a tea room at all. It was a very popular restaurant.

We had an uneventful journey across town, thank goodness. I've been with Fred having fights with London cabbies. I didn't want the same experience in New York. It inevitably ended in tears, usually with the taxi driver demanding that Fred – and everyone travelling with him – leave the cab instantly. When the driver pulled up outside the restaurant, Fred looked at the meter and, over-tipping horrendously, handed a twenty to the cab driver, saying 'Thanks, Mac. Keep the change.' He began walking away before the man could even say thank you.

'Have you been here before?' he asked me, as we went in. 'No,' I said. 'Hello, darling,' he said to the woman in charge of the reservations desk. 'How's my lovely Olga?' I don't know if her name was really Olga or not, but she must have been well over fifty, and going about fifteen stone, which was far too much for the under five feet that she stood behind her desk. The lovely Olga simpered, and blew Fred a kiss. 'Oh, you naughty man, Friedrich, darlink,' she simpered. 'I always tell you, *pleeze* telephone and make ze reservation. You 'aven't got a reservation, 'ave you?' 'Yes, of course I have,' said Tony. 'I told my secretary to telephone you and ask for a table for two. Do you mean she forgot to do it? Shit.'

Olga looked at her watch, and then at her reservation book. 'I do my best for you, Friedrich, darlink,' she said. 'I give you a table, but eet is not a very good table. You do not mind?' 'Of course not, darling Olga,' said Fred, reaching out and pinching Olga's voluptuous, tightly corseted bottom. Olga jumped about a foot in the air, and came down blushing and simpering even more. 'Follow me, pleeze, you *naughty* man,' she said, swaying her armoured hips with *élan* as she led the way out to our table. She gave us a menu each, and left us to it. 'Vodka?' asked Fred. 'If you like,' I said, not wanting to spoil Fred's wish to be Russian. He looked up at me from the menu. 'I tell you what,' he said. 'We ought to be celebrating today, oughtn't we? Well, *you* should be celebrating, anyway. And I'm more than happy to join you. So let's order a large vodka first, as a snort, and then I'll order some decent vintage champagne. How about that?' 'Sounds good,' I said. 'Thank you.' Fred waved at a dazzlingly pretty young waitress who was passing by. She stopped and said 'Yes, sir?' 'I'd like to order some drink,' he said. 'Certainly,' she said. 'I'll send the wine waiter right over.'

She was as good as her word, and the wine waiter arrived a few moments later. Fred looked at the wine list, and then ordered two large Russian vodkas, on the rocks, with a slice, and a bottle of Mumm. The '71. 'Very good, sir,' said the waiter who, from his accent, had to be American. Just as the pretty waitress, from hers, had to be Russian. Or Ukrainian. Or whatever. 'A good year,' said Fred, when the waiter had gone. 'A bit young, but they don't half whack on the price for the champagne here. But I'm sure you'll like it.' 'I'm sure I shall,' I said. 'I wouldn't mind taking your advice about fucking everything that moves with that waitress. She's gorgeous, isn't she?'

'She certainly is,' said Fred. 'You get dancers from the Russian ballet chorus working in here sometimes on their day off. It's always worth a try. They don't get paid very much, and because of what they do, they're usually starving.' He put his menu down. 'Do you see anything you fancy?' he asked, adding quickly, 'On the menu?' 'I haven't really looked,' I said. 'What do you recommend?' 'The blinis with caviar are excellent to start with,' he said. 'So is the borscht. They do amazing things with goose here. And of course their Chicken Kiev is the best in town.' Just then a waiter whom we hadn't seen before brought our vodkas. Fred ground a little pepper from the pepper mill onto the top of his. He laughed at my expression. 'If it was all right for James Bond,' he said, 'it's all right for me. Actually, Olga tells me that the Russians in Russia really do do it. It's supposed to draw the diesel to the top, where you can avoid it, or throw it off, leaving rather purer vodka behind.' He poured a little of the top of his vodka, on which the pepper floated, onto the floor beside the table. 'Basically, it just amuses me,' he said. 'Cheers.' 'Cheers,' I replied.

And then the beautiful young waitress was beside us again. 'Have you decided what you want to eat?' she asked, smiling prettily. I crossed mental fingers. Please, dear God, I said to myself, don't let Fred make some dreadful remark about how my friend Tony here would like to eat your pussy. I'd heard him do worse, in my day. We told her that we had decided, and Fred ordered the borscht, while I went for the blinis, and then we both ordered the Chicken Kiev. I chatted up the girl as much as I possibly could in the circumstances, without doing or saying anything brash, and she chattered back seemingly happily, asking me about which part of England I came from. She had been to London, she said, with the ballet. She *was* one of the off-duty ballet dancers Fred had described earlier.

We has a delightful meal. Fred was at his best, which meant interesting, amusing and full of fun. He seemed genuinely to welcome me to American *Tiptop,* and I began to remember how much I had enjoyed working with him as a freelance before he had left London. 'Why don't you give that little waitress your office telephone number, Tony?' he said, towards the end of the meal. 'Tell her you'd like to set up a test photographic shoot? She'll probably wet her knickers. Not to mention drop them. You obviously fancy her.' I pondered for a moment whether to tell him what I really thought, or not, and then decided I would. 'Maybe, Fred,' I said. 'But I think I'll do it my way, which is ask her which day – or days – of the week she works here. Then I can come in another day, and talk to her again, and perhaps make a pitch then. I think today's too soon.'

'Whatever you want to do, Tony lad,' he said. 'If it was me, I'd probably get my cock out and wave it at her, and say, what do you think of that, baby? You know me. Like the old joke about the chap who walks down the King's Road in Chelsea every day, handing out cards that say "Do you fancy a fuck?" Like him, I get a lot of slapped faces, but I get a lot of fucks too.' I laughed. 'You've got better nerves than I have, Fred,' I said. 'And you almost always win, because basically, you don't care. One pussy's much like another to you. You don't get emotionally involved. Am I right?' He gave me a slightly strange look, and then took a swig at his champagne glass before he answered me.

'You're a perceptive old bugger, aren't you, Andrews?' he said, eventually. 'I wouldn't admit it to too many people, but yes, sure, you're absolutely right. I don't actually give a fuck about any of them. So long as they've got a hole I can dip my wick in, that's all I'm after. If they're pretty as well, so much the better. If they're amusing too, well, wow, they might last as long as three days. Who knows?' He winked at me. 'But I didn't think it was that obvious. But changing the subject, while I think of it, there's something I'd like you to do for me, if you will. It's a possible story for the magazine. I'm told that there's a cabaret club or night-club somewhere downtown that's putting on a show called Pouff! Yeah, I know,' he said. 'Not that kind of poof. Americans don't know that word. It's the kind of "pouff" you'd use to describe the way a magician makes something disappear. You know what I mean?' I nodded.

'Anyway,' he continued, 'apparently it's a terrific show. They tell me it's got a tremendous new star, called Crysis – spelt C-R-Y-S-I-S – who's going to be really big, and fantastic chorus girls and boys. I'm told it's a real, fast-moving, well-dressed – or undressed, if you prefer – late night spectacular. Will you go and have a look for me? Don't tell them you're coming. We don't want to commit ourselves to anything until you've seen the show. Just book and go. Take someone with you if you wish. And come back and tell me what you think. If it's as good as I'm told, maybe we could do a photographic feature. See what you think. Will you do that for me? Please?' 'Of course I will,' I said. 'It sounds fun.'

The waitress who had been serving us (yes, the pretty one) came to see if we wanted anything else, and Fred ordered coffee and large brandies. When she brought the coffee, I tentatively asked her name, and she told me immediately, with a delightful smile, that it was Katrina, and she asked me mine, which I told her. She went away again before I could ask her which days she worked at the Russian Tea Room. But I was delighted when she came back with the brandies, because there was a folded piece of paper tucked under my coffee cup, which read, in a rather childish scrawl, 'If you would like to take me out, I would enjoy that very much, Tony. You can call me any morning (after ten a.m. please!) and before four p.m. except Wednesdays, when I'm working here at the Russian Tea Room. My number is 265 79401. I'm not free in the evenings, except on Sundays (when I'm free all day too). I hope you will call me, Tony. Katrina.'

I showed it to Fred. 'Fuck me, Tone,' he said. 'I don't know how you do it.' When Katrina brought the bill, I held up the piece of paper, and smiled at her. 'I'll call you,' I said. 'Tomorrow.' She smiled back sweetly, and actually blushed. 'I'd like that,' she said, looking at me with the bluest eyes I think I've ever seen. 'I'd like that very much.' She took Fred's credit card and the bill, and went away. When she returned, she spent the time that Fred was signing the chit, and adding his tip, looking at him. When he was finished, and she had given him his

LA VIE EN ROSE

receipt, she gave me a quick smile as she turned to go, and then she was gone.

'I think you're on to a great fuck there, Tone,' said Fred, as we left the restaurant. 'These young Russian ballet dancers are supposed to be great little goers. Just think how supple they must be.' He looked at me, an evil grin on his face. 'She can probably do that thing acrobatic dancers do. You know, where they do the splits, and then lean right over backwards, and put their head up between their legs.' I didn't say anything, so he continued. 'Just think about it, Tone,' he said. 'If she can do that, you can fuck her mouth while you suck her pussy. That should earn you a place in the Guinness Book of Records, at least in that position, shouldn't it?' I punched his arm. Hard. 'The trouble with you Fred,' I said, 'is that there's no romance in your soul. Shame on you.' 'Ouch,' said Fred. 'That hurt. But you miss the point. I'm not talking about romance. I'm talking about fucking. Why do you always have to be in love? It only causes problems when the relationship comes to an end. My way, there's lots of fun, and no tears. That aside, I bet that Katrina goes like the nine ten from Paddington.' He looked at me with that evil grin again. 'Or should I say Vladivostock? How old would you say she was? Eighteen? Nineteen? Something like that? I bet it's like a mouse's earhole. I bet she shaves her cunt, too. I mean, if you spend your time on a stage with your legs up in the air, showing everyone your tiny, high-cut knickers, you're bound to shave your cunt, aren't you?'

'Please, God,' I replied. 'You know it's always been a big turn-on with me.' I hailed a cab, and gave the driver our office address. I spent the journey across town fantasizing about Katrina. She had long, blonde hair, the colour of ripe corn – to go with those amazingly blue eyes – pulled back into a braided chignon. She wasn't tall. About five six, I'd guess, with a slim – but not anorexic – figure, and beautiful, long, slim legs. Her tits were small, but exquisitely formed. Pointed, and firm over her chest muscles. She was patently very fit. I tried to envisage her naked body, and I wondered if Fred was right about her shaving her pubic hair.

I shut my eyes, and imagined her small, nunlike little pubis, completely hairless, with her pink little pussy lips showing wetly down the centre, oozing clear, scented, teenage love juices, as she lay on her back, pulling her sex lips apart for me, saying in that beautiful Russian accent, 'Fuck me, please, Tony. Fuck me now. I want you in my cunt.' And then I suddenly realized that the cab had stopped. I opened my eyes to see that we had arrived at the office. Fred had paid the cabbie, and was standing on the sidewalk, holding the door open, laughing at me. 'Come on, lover boy,' he said. 'Dream time is over. It's back to the real world.'

I didn't say anything, but I tried – probably unsuccessfully – to look nonchalant as I got out of the cab. 'Great lunch, Fred,' I said. 'Thank you. I really enjoyed it.' 'And so you bloody should,' he said. 'So would I, if I'd fixed myself up with a little dolly ballerina to fuck. All I'm likely to get to fuck out of the Russian Tea Room is vulgar Olga.' ' I noticed you had your hands all over her on the way in,' I said, trying deliberately to wind him up. 'I assumed she was a regular.' 'Regular what?' he asked. 'Fuck,' I said. 'You must be bloody joking,' he said. 'I wouldn't fuck her with yours.' I let it go at that. It had been a good day. There was no point in antagonizing him.

And he was quite right. I probably *had* set myself up with something delicious. We'd see. I got back to my office, and looked through the mail and messages on my desk. The only one of interest was one from Eileen, which said 'Busy tonight?' I rang her through on the intercom. 'Hi, sweetie,' I said. 'Thank you for your note. How would you like to go and see Pouff! later on tonight?' I wondered if she had heard of it. 'Oh, way out,' she said. 'I'd love to. Everyone says it's good news.' 'Oh, good,' I said. 'Would you like to book us in?' 'Sure,' she said. 'It's one of those places where they expect you to have dinner first. Let me check the timings. But if I'm right, it'll be eat at about eight, eight thirty, show starting at ten, ten thirty. If that's what it is, is that OK with you?' 'Sure,' I said. 'We can welcome the end of the day with a few drinks somewhere on the way.' 'Great,' said Eileen. 'I'll get back to you.' 'Don't mention *Tiptop*,' I said. 'I'll explain why later.' 'No problem,' she said. 'Hang in there, good buddy.'

Spare me the truck driver colloquialisms, I thought. It transpired that she was quite right about the timing, and she booked us a table for eight thirty. The fact that she knew about the show, and wanted to see it, encouraged me, since she was very on the ball, and would have known if it was basically crap. At five thirty she knocked on my door, and put her head round. 'Ready, Tone?' she asked. 'Or would you rather meet me somewhere later?' 'No,' I said. 'Now's fine. I'm pleased to be able to stop. So where do you fancy? P.J. Clarke's? Michael's Pub? Somewhere else?' 'Oh, let's go to P.J. Clarke's,' she said. 'It's the nearest, and I like it. It brings out the Irish in me.'

'What Irish is that?' I asked. 'Oh, come on, Tony,' she said. 'Don't do all that poxy British bit with me. I know I'm not Irish. But that doesn't stop me enjoying the St Patrick's Day Parade, or drinking in Irish bars. And bars don't come much more Irish than P.J. Clarke's. Not in New York, anyway. If I want to feel Irish when I'm in there, that's what I'm going to feel.' 'All right, all right, all right,' I said. 'Don't come the old prawn with me. If you want to feel Irish, feel Irish. I don't give a damn. At least in P.J. Clarke's they don't play those appalling songs full of propaganda for the IRA, and take up collections for them.' 'Come the old prawn?' she said. 'What on earth are you talking about?' I got up from my desk, walked towards her and, putting my arms around her, I pulled her to me and gave her a very wet kiss. 'Don't worry about it, sweetheart,' I said, eventually. 'It's not important. And I love you. Let's go and be Irish at P.J. Clarke's.' She giggled, and we disengaged and took ourselves off down the corridor towards the elevators.

'How was lunch with Fred?' she asked. 'It was good,' I said. 'Lunch was good. We went to the Russian Tea Room.' 'Oh, nice,' she said. 'And the meeting before the lunch was good,' I continued. 'The contract – yet to be signed – is good. Everything was good.' I looked at her, and put my arm around her waist. We were outside the office now, waiting for the bank of elevators to take us down to the ground floor. 'And this evening is going to be good.' She looked at me, smiling. 'And tonight?' she asked. 'And tonight, my darling, is going to be fabulous,' I said. Always assuming I'm going to spend it with you.' 'Who else?' she asked.

As we walked the block and a half to P.J's, I told her about my upcoming trip to London, my starting officially in New York on September one, and my new title. 'But you won't be managing editor,' she said, looking puzzled. 'No, I know I won't,' I said. 'I won't be doing the job of managing editor. That would bore me rigid. But we don't want to upset Angie. And personally I don't give a damn about titles. As long as the money's OK.' She looked at me, questioningly. I grinned at her. 'The money's OK,' I said. 'Well done,' she said. 'Congratulations.' For the record, in magazine publishing, a managing editor isn't an editor at all. At least, not in my book he or she isn't. It's a responsible position, in that he or she is accountable for the successful management of the editorial function, but it is purely an administrative responsibility. It has no creative content whatsoever.

At *Tiptop,* we didn't have a managing editor, as such. It was assumed to be part of Fred's job. In status terms, managing editor ranks higher than deputy editor, which was really what my function was going to be. But Fred was never a one for titles or responsibilities. Not for other people, anyway. He took a simple view. He was the boss. Everyone else worked for him, and took orders from him. I had no quarrel with that. For the rest, he usually left his staff to jockey for position with each other. I had no quarrel with that either. I was more than confident of my ability to discharge my editorial responsibilities with *Tiptop*. I certainly lacked Fred's charisma, that was for sure. And I lacked some of his natural flair. But I didn't half know my bloody job.

We got to P.J. Clarke's and I ordered a Bloody Mary for Eileen, and my usual scotch and water, no ice. 'Cheers, darling,' I said. 'Here's to a jolly evening.' We clinked glasses. 'And night,' she said. We clinked glasses again. 'And night,' I repeated. Please God, I thought. I told Eileen about the fact that Fred had suggested that she might make some preliminary enquiries about an apartment for me, whilst I was away in London. 'Of course, darling,' she said. 'Where do you want to be?' 'Oh, Upper East Side, I think,' I said. She just looked at me. 'And how much do you want to pay?' 'Well,' I said, 'within reason – sort of – I don't really care, since the company's going to pick up the tab.' 'Fuck,' she said. 'I wish I'd been born in England. You guys just don't know you're living, do you?'

'Oh, come on, sweetheart,' I said to her. 'Don't come all that how-spoiled-we-Brits-are bit. I've worked my butt off, writing what I write, for bloody years, to get to do what I'm doing now. Fred's good at his job. I'm good at mine. Successful magazines don't just happen, you know. Successful magazines happen because of successful editors. Hugh Heffner started all this off with *Playboy*, all those years ago. Bob Guccione brought it up to date with *Penthouse*. First with pubic hair, then – after the Presidential Enquiry into pornography decided that the printed reproduction of male and female genitalia were not pornographic (always provided that the one wasn't pictured being inserted into the other) – then he followed pubic hair with all the rest. Tastefully, of course. Tony Power started *Club,* and I think I'm right in remembering that *Club* reproduced the first female arsehole legally published in the States. And Fred brought everything up to date with *Tiptop*. I keep going what Fred started off when he's not here, and now I'm going to come out here permanently and help him to do it all the time.

'I don't know whether you know how much money this magazine of ours makes, but it makes a hell of a lot. Don't you think that the top people who are largely responsible for its success should share – at least to a certain extent – in it's profitability?' 'Oh, I'm sorry, darling,' she said. 'Please don't misunderstand me. It's just plain, ordinary, understandable jealousy. At least, I hope it's understandable. I've been working *my* butt off ever since I came to New York and, yes, *Tiptop* pay me well over the odds for what I do for them. I like the people I work with – I *love* some of them,' she said, smiling at me. 'And I enjoy what I do more than anything I have ever worked at before. I'm also living better than I've ever lived before, and that's entirely due to *Tiptop*. Well, to Fred I guess.

'It's just that this is the first time I've been involved with the senior people in a company. With the management, if you like. Americans with top jobs aren't anything like as forthcoming as you and Fred are. They never ever discuss their salaries, or how much their rents are, or what kind of perks they get, with their secretaries. Secretaries are just wage slaves, to them. So I find it difficult to handle, sometimes, when I hear details of how much money you and Fred are making, or how well you are doing, and I can't help bur compare these things with my salary, and my own cost of living. I'm sorry, darling. It's just plain jealousy, like I said. But it's not a problem. I guess I just

LA VIE EN ROSE

need to watch my mouth occasionally.'

I leaned over and kissed her. 'It's not a problem with me either, sweetheart,' I said. 'I'm sorry if I snapped. Now then, how about another Bloody Mary?' She leaned over and kissed me, in return. 'Yes, please,' she said. 'That would be good.' I got the round of drinks, and we chattered on for a while, talking about the differences between working in New York and working in London. And then, eventually, it was time to get a cab down to go and see the show at La Vie En Rose. It turned out to be a small, but real theatre, with stalls and a circle, which had been converted into a supper club by the simple process of taking out all the seats, and replacing them with chairs and tables, at which patrons were seated for their meal, prior to the show itself. Eileen had reserved us a good table, nicely near to where the action would be later in the evening. I didn't realize at the time, but it became obvious later that the waiters and waitresses were actually the boys and girls from the show. The food was of excellent quality, if erring perhaps a tiny bit on the unexciting side. Eileen and I both chose soup to start with, followed by steak. But the steak was of really prime quality, and cooked exactly as requested: rare for me, medium-rare for Eileen. The salad and vegetables were fresh, and beautifully undercooked, and the Californian house red wine perfectly and pleasantly drinkable.

When the table was finally cleared, we ordered another bottle of the wine to drink whilst we watched the show, which started promptly at ten. It was fun. Energetic, fast-moving, well choreographed, with an excellent band, and good music. The dancing was first-class, as was the singing. Both chorus boys and chorus girls were pretty, as is so often the way.

The star of the show, the quaintly-spelled Crysis, was gorgeous. A tall blonde, with terrific legs, and a fantastic pair of tits – most of which were visible over the top of her low-cut dress – she had an amusing line in patter, told some extremely *risqué* jokes with great panache, and sang like Marilyn Monroe. I wasn't absolutely certain, but I thought that she was possibly miming to tapes of Marilyn's voice. However she was doing it, she was tremendous, and the audience loved her. I totally agreed with whoever it was had suggested to Fred that she would make a good subject for the magazine, and I asked Eileen if she would mind asking the management if we could go backstage and talk to Crysis, my thought being that an American, and a woman at that, would probably be given more co-operation than an Englishman, who might easily be thought to be just another sozzled fan who wanted to try and persuade Crysis to drop her panties.

In the event, Eileen came back to say that Crysis would come and join us at our table in a little while, which seemed a very civilized way of getting to talk to her. Eileen had, of course, explained that we were representing *Tiptop,* and wanted to talk about putting together some kind of a feature about both Crysis and her show.

Crysis looked even more gorgeous close to than she had up on stage doing her act. She'd changed into another extremely *décolletée* dress, revealing deep cleavage and split almost to her thigh. She was beautifully made up, and her voice was deep and sexy. She sat between Eileen and me, and I felt my cock stiffening at the combination of her proximity, her sensuality, and her scent. She waved a languid hand at the waiter, and ordered a bottle of champagne. When I told the waiter to put it on my bill, she insisted that no, this was on the house. She knew *Tiptop,* which saved a lot of explaining, and immediately agreed to pose nude for us. 'If you're sure that's what you want, honey,' she said. I said that I was sure that it was, and she said something that I didn't really understand, about perhaps being topless, rather than completely nude, but I said, that was up to her, of course, and suggested that perhaps she leave the decision until the photography was arranged, to which she agreed.

I said that the way in which the shoot was done would be up to the magazine's art director, and she said fine, and if anyone – no matter how many – from the magazine wanted to come and see the show, then all we had to do was to call her, and she'd make the necessary arrangements. I thanked her, and said that we would probably like to send the art director, and a photographer, and that, if I might, I'd like to come and see the show again myself. She leaned over, put a hand on my knee, squeezed it, and said, in that lovely husky voice, 'Any time, Tony, absolutely any time.' I nearly came in my trousers. Does she fancy me, I wondered? There wasn't a lot I could do about finding out, not with Eileen sitting a few feet away. Eileen and I did, after all, have to work together, and I was promised to her, as it were, for this particular evening. Not forgetting that I'd let her down once this week already, the evening I had spent with Margot. But next time I came to La Vie En Rose, I'd make sure that Eileen was left behind. This fantastic, sexy woman *had* to be a fabulous fuck. I looked at her full, passionate lips, and imagined them around my cock, her pink tongue wrapped around mine, doing lovely, naughty things to me. She saw me looking at her lips, and she licked them, wetly, lasciviously, and smiled a sexy smile at me. I wriggled in my seat in an endeavour to make more room for my swollen prick.

All around us the other customers were dancing to the band, now that the show was over. I wondered if Crysis would think it gross were I to ask her to dance. Then I remembered that, once more, I'd do my relationship with Eileen more damage than it was worth, even if Crysis did actually want to dance. She was very probably dog tired from her efforts on stage.

I deliberately kept the conversation fairly general,

wanting to keep the more intimate questions for the interview that I was mentally planning to do to accompany the photographs that would eventually be taken. I'd set the meeting up somewhere extremely private – perhaps Fred's apartment, having first made certain that he wouldn't be there. Yes, I thought. That would be ideal. It would be a natural place to suggest doing it, because of the privacy, and the unlikelihood of being interrupted. It also had my bedroom, with its king-size bed. Absolutely perfect.

Finally, it seemed that we had taken the conversation (and everything else, for that matter) as far as we could go right now, and I thanked Crysis for her time, and her forthcoming co-operation. I told her that I looked forward very much to our next meeting, and she thanked me for the magazine's interest, and, leaning across the table – so that those fabulous tits almost fell out of her low-cut dress – she kissed my cheek, setting my blood on fire with the closeness of her body, the bewitching aura of her scent, and the touch of her lips on my skin.

In the cab on the way back to her apartment, Eileen gave me a very old-fashioned look indeed. 'If I didn't know you better, Tony,' she said, 'I could have persuaded myself that you fancied Crysis,' she said, looking at me with that slightly strange look. I thought for a moment. I didn't see any harm in saying that yes, she was quite right, I did fancy Crysis, since I hadn't made any kind of a move towards following through on my desire. I had been perfectly well behaved, and had come away with Eileen, as promised.

'Since you mention it, sweetheart,' I said, smiling to keep the whole thing conversational, and not confrontational, 'I *do* fancy her. Very strongly indeed. But why do you say "If I didn't know you better?" ' She gave me that look again, just for a moment, and then she burst into laughter. She damn near fell off her seat, actually. 'What's

LA VIE EN ROSE

so funny?' I asked. 'I do believe that you actually don't know,' she said, still spluttering. 'You're damn right,' I said, crossly. 'I don't know. Tell me.' I waited for her to get her act together. She put out a hand, and grabbed my arm. 'I'm sorry, Tony,' she said. 'If you really don't know, I can see that's it's not that funny. But Crysis is a fella. She's a TV. A transvestite. A man. She's taking the tablets. I mean, just look at those fantastic tits. But she hasn't had the operation, although I understand that it's possibly on the cards. Her playing all coy about just wanting to be photographed topless, and not exposing her all, is because she was trying to tell you, in case you didn't know, that her "all" is a cock. She doesn't mind airing it. I've seen photographs. But she wasn't sure that *you* knew that. Do you see what I mean now?' I was totally shocked. Completely devastated.

'Yes, of course I do, sweetheart,' I said. 'Thank you for telling me.' What a cunt I felt. What an arsehole. What a berk. 'Did I make a terrible fool of myself?' I asked. She took my arm, and tucked hers through it. 'No, of course not,' she said, kindly. 'But Crysis wasn't sure whether you fancied what she *actually* is, or what you *thought* she was, which are, as you now know, two quite different things. She certainly fancied *you,* that's for sure.' 'Thank you very much,' I said, bitterly.

It was the first time that I had stayed with Eileen at her apartment. It was a small but pleasant studio apartment on the Upper West Side, not far from Columbus Circle. The apartment was small, but the bed was large, thank God. Previously, we'd always been at Fred's place, but whilst he was away.

I fucked for England that night. Well, Wales actually, as the original joke has it, and in line with the fact that my father was Welsh, and I was born in Towyn, in Merionethshire. I was trying to prove something, I'm not entirely sure what. That I was straight, probably. I sucked Eileen's succulent, hairy snatch until she came and came and came again. 'Oh, lover,' she said at one point. 'If I could find girls who suck pussy like you do, I'd go back to being a lesbian. I would, I promise you. But you're much better than any of the girls I've had suck my pussy.' I sucked her breasts too. And devoured her mouth. 'I can taste my cunt-juice,' she said, at one stage, as I kissed her. 'How lovely,' I said. Eventually, after I'd been sucking her off for some considerable time – as much for my enjoyment, I have to say, as hers – she said, 'Please fuck me now, darling Tony. My cunt needs your prick. It needs fucking. Now. Please?' I raised myself up from between her legs, her juices running down my chin and down her thighs, and knelt over her, my rampant cock throbbing with blood-swollen desire, and Eileen reached down and pulled her pussy-lips apart for me. 'Oh, yes, 'she said, taking hold of my cock. 'Oh yes, please. Now.'

She took it and fed it into her hot, wet vulva. She was throbbing inside, as I was outside, and our potent sexual parts met in a delightful agony of sexual desire, her open love-hole gripping my cock in her own, feminine version of the Venus Fly-trap. I thrust and delved, and Eileen spanned and gripped, and we both started to work our bodies together, our rhythm increasing as our lust expanded, our need to achieve orgasm exceeding even our need to copulate. We came together. Not delicately. Not gently, but in a rush of mutual, explosive, joyful release. I pumped my ejaculate into her receptive pussy, and she orgasmed again and again, until we both of us were finished. Exhausted. Replete. Done. 'Oh, baby,' she said. 'I needed that. I really needed that. Thank you.'

After a while, Eileen got out of bed, and came back with an ice-cold bottle of champagne and a couple of glasses. It was vintage Mumm's, actually. She handed me the bottle. 'I put this in the fridge last night,' she said. 'You open it, darling.' She held the glasses as I poured. 'I hoped we'd need it,' she said. 'I certainly do. How about you?' 'Magic,' I said. 'Absolute magic. And yes, it's exactly what I need right now.' Champagne after sex is one of the most civilized habits I know. Apart from being civilized, it's also very good for the libido. We finished the bubbly, and then we fucked again. Slowly, this time. Gently. Elegantly. Almost lovingly. In the old straight up and down, just-like-mum-and-dad position. When we'd finished, I leaned down and kissed Eileen's cheek, to find tears. 'What's the matter, sweetheart?' I asked. 'Nothing, baby,' she said. 'I'm just so happy.' Women are the strangest creatures, aren't they? I had been thinking of going back to Fred's apartment, but there was no way that I could get up and leave Eileen after that statement. We slept together, comfortably entwined, like long-time lovers. I rose at seven, and crept out, leaving a note for Eileen, who was still asleep. I took a cab back to the apartment, where I showered and shaved, breakfasted, and took myself off to the office. I didn't see Fred at either place.

I spoke to Dave, the art director, and asked him to get Eileen to arrange some tickets for him to see Pouff! He had already seen it, he said, but he'd be more than happy to see it again. I told him that Fred had thought it would make an interesting feature for *Tiptop,* and that I'd got Crysis's agreement to be photographed. 'Hey,' he said. 'Wow. You've been talking to Crysis, then? What did you think?' 'I thought it was a great show,' I told him. 'And Crysis is very decorative. I'm not certain whether we should photograph him totally naked, or simply topless, and not refer to his gender in the article. He seems happy either way.'

'Oh, man,' said David. 'Let's do him starkers. Let's shock the pants off everyone.' 'Well,' I said, 'you talk it over with him, and then perhaps you and Fred and I should sit down for ten minutes and talk it through, then make a decision. My own feeling is to run maybe four pages, two spreads, the first showing shots from the show, with the chorus boys and girls, and with shots of Crysis doing her act, and then to show her topless, with those terrific tits, and then finally nude, with everything in view. What do you say?' 'Sounds good,' he said. 'Leave it with me. I'll get back to you.' As he was leaving, I said, 'I must say, Dave, that Crysis is bloody attractive. As a woman, I mean. I really quite fancied her.' He chortled. 'Hey, great, man. We'll have you down in one of the leather bars' back rooms yet.' We both laughed, and he left. I deliberately hadn't told him of my not initially recognizing Crysis as a man.

I realized that I felt sort of strange. I wasn't sure what the problem was. Only that there was a problem. I guess it began with Annabel. And then continued with . . . What? I thought about it, but I didn't come up with any solution. I'd enjoyed my night with Eileen. But I felt sort of constrained. Thinking back, my sex life had been pretty mundane for a while. Much as I found Annabel and Eileen both sexually exciting, there hadn't been anything sexually very inflammatory in my life for a while. And then it hit me. Suddenly, I knew what the answer was. Or rather, *who* the answer was. I picked up the phone and dialled June's number at the brothel. The well-remembered charms of Charlene, Rita and Victoria, and the – as yet – unexplored delights of Gloria, Louise, and Andrea. *That's* where the answer to my need for a little sexual excitement is going to come from. Yes, sir! I heard June's voice, and I said 'Hello, sweetie,' before I realized that I was talking to a taped message, I looked at my watch. It was only ten thirty. I guess that's early when your work ends after midnight. I didn't leave a message. I'd call back later.

I spent some time typing out a few pages of notes about my visit to Pouff! while my impressions, and particularly my reactions to Crysis, were still sharp. I recorded my feelings, both before I had realized my mistake, and then my thoughts upon those reactions after I had learned what you might call the full facts. I decided that I might write the words that would eventually accompany the photographs that were to be taken from the point of view of a man who did not, at first, realize that Crysis was a man. And then his reaction, once he discovered that 'she' was a he. Carefully done, it could be both amusing and effective. I looked at my watch. It was noon.

I took my wallet out of my hip pocket and found the piece of paper I was looking for. I dialled the number written down there: 265 79401. Katrina's pretty voice answered the phone. 'Yes?' she said. 'Katrina,' I said. 'It's Tony Andrews. From *Tiptop*. We met at the Russian Tea Room yesterday. Do you remember?' 'Of course I remember, darlink,' she said. 'And now you are telephoning me. That is nice. I am very pleased. Thank you.' She paused. 'I wonder if you would like to come out with me?' I said. 'Lunch next Sunday? What do you say?'

'I say yes, please,' she said. 'I would like that very much.' I thought for a moment. 'Do you like Chinese food?' I asked her. 'I love it,' She said. 'Do you know the Oh Ho So?' I asked her. 'No,' she said. 'But I can find it. Wait, please, while I get a pencil and paper.' I heard her put the telephone down. Moments later she was back. 'Yes, darlink,' she said. 'I am ready now. Where is it, this Oh Ho So?' 'It's at 395 West Broadway,' I said. 'Down in SoHo. I'll make the reservation in my name. What's a good time for you?' 'Anytime,' she said. 'OK, then,' I said. 'I'll meet you there at twelve noon next Sunday. I'll make sure I'm there before you.' 'Thank you, darlink,' she said. 'I will be there. But there is one thing I must tell you. I am due for my period this coming weekend. So we will not be able to make much love. But we will do something. Do not worry. I do not want you to feel, after lunch on Sunday that I do not want you. I do want you. So now I tell you the problem. Yes? Soon after that – two or three days – we will make love. I promise. Is OK?' 'Is OK,' I said. 'Until Sunday, darlink,' she said, and put the phone down.

Phew, I thought. Different cultures, different habits. Different strokes for different folks. She was actually telling me that she wanted to fuck with me, before we'd even been out together, and she was warning me that she would be menstruating by the weekend, so that it wouldn't be possible. 'But we will do something' she had said. What did that mean? Would she fellate me? Give me one off the wrist? Let me fuck her anally? Get one of her other ballet chorus girlfriends to fuck me? I had a hard-on just thinking about it.

And then the straightforward way in which she had referred to her period. I don't believe that any Western European or American girl that I have ever known would dream of telling a new man that she hadn't yet been out with that she would be menstruating by the weekend, and therefore unable to – what was the phrase Katrina used? 'Not be able to make much love.' That was it. *Much* love. Not that we wouldn't be able to make love at all, but that we wouldn't be able to make *much* love. Or, put differently, we *would* be able to make *some* kind of love. I remembered what her lovely little tush looked like as she walked away from our table at the Russian Tea room. I remembered the pointed shape of her tiny breasts through the thin material of her dress, and the apron that she wore over it, as part of the Russian Tea Room's uniform. I remembered her smile, and her note, and her suggestion that I telephone her. Jesus, I thought. Suddenly life is looking up again. I began to feel better.

It was lunch time. I decided to go to lunch by myself, so I simply walked out of the offices without looking to right or left. I'd go, I thought, in my life-is-for-enjoyment mode, to Dee Dee's topless/bottomless bar, enjoy a couple of drinks and a sandwich, and look at some prime pussy, including Dee Dee's. When I got there, the bar was fairly full, and I had to wait at one of the side tables for a while, before I could get a seat at the pussy bar itself, the circular bar along the top of which the naked girls walked, jived, danced and otherwise perambulated, displaying there wares as they went. I couldn't see Dee Dee anywhere, or any of the other girls that I had got to know, either by sight or by name, on earlier visits, but there was plenty of wide-open pussy displaying itself around the bar.

I particularly liked the look of one little girl. I say little deliberately. She was. She couldn't have stood much more than about five six in her five-inch heels, which was all that she was wearing at the time, apart from the obligatory garter in which customers could tuck dollar bills of various denominations, in exchange for rather closer glimpses of her open pussy. She was either Puerto Rican, or Latin American of some kind. She had a pretty, young, coffee-coloured skin, devoid of a blemish, a wrinkle, or a stretch mark of any kind. She could only have been about eighteen at the very most. Her face was beautiful, with a smile to match, and the garter that she wore around her upper thigh was bulging with dollar bills. I waited for her to come around to where I was sitting, and then I waved a ten at her. She knelt down, smiling as she did so, and her pussy lips parted in front of me, naturally, as she squatted before me. 'Do you like what you see, honey?' she asked me. I looked at it.

It was a really pretty cunt, with delicately shaped, pale pink inner labia, shining wetly now, both from the exercise, and – presumably – the fact that she got turned on by displaying it to all and sundry. I could see quite a long way up it, despite its smallness. It looked as if it was capable of closing tightly around any cock that thrust itself inside. I could smell its strong, fresh odour. Her pubic hair was clean, shiny black, and tightly curled. Her outer labia were rather a darker pink than her inner lips. It was, in my estimation, grade one pussy. I could feel the blood engorging my prick. 'Yes, sweetheart,' I said, handing her the ten bill. 'I like what I see. What's your name?' 'Conchita,' she said. Oh, yeah, I thought, and my name's Billy Bunter. But what the hell. She smiled at me. 'How much do you like it?' she asked. 'It's all yours, if you want it.' I looked up at her face, tearing my eyes away – just for a moment, you understand – from her pussy.

'How much?' I asked, seeing no point in beating around the bush, so to speak. She tucked my ten under her well-stretched garter, and, using the fingers of both hands, she pulled her pussy widely open. 'It's all yours, baby,' she said. 'You can suck it, fuck it, jerk off into it, do anything you like to it. I'll even piss on you through it, if that's what you like. It's young, fresh, clean, and it loves to ride cock. How long depends on how much. You can rent it by the hour, the day, the week, the month, or for ever. You tell me how long, I'll tell you how much.' She thrust a finger up inside herself, wriggled it around, and then pulled it down and out again. She held it under my nose. 'Does that smell good to you?' she asked. Before I could reply, she said 'Suck it, honey. Have a free taste. It tastes good, too.'

I sucked the cunt juice off her wet finger. She was right. It did taste good. 'I'll have to move on now,' she said. 'I'll stop here again the next time around. We can talk more then. Ciao.' And she was off, prancing along the catwalk-type bar top, flaunting her all. She had a fabulous ass. She had a fabulous everything. I wondered, idly, why she was trying to sell it. She had to be pulling down at least two hundred bucks a day. Probably a great deal more. There was always a reason. A sick mother. A no-good brother. An expensive drug habit. A sister in hospital. Who could tell? At least she was better off where she was, for all the objections that you and I can think of, than working the streets downtown for some pimp who would beat her up if she didn't bring in what he thought she should bring in every night.

I wondered if she knew Dee Dee. But what with her, Katrina, the girls from the brothel (whom I still had to telephone) and one thing and another, I didn't really want any more problems. The next time around, when she squatted down for my ten, I said to her, 'I'll take a rain check this time, sweetheart. OK?' 'OK, baby,' she said. 'Shall I tell Dee Dee you were in?' She saw my mouth drop as she stood up, and she grinned down at me as she danced away. 'I'll still be here, the next time you're around,' she said. 'See you.' And she was gone.

I wandered slowly back to the office, feeling better for the steak sandwich and the couple of large scotches that I had consumed. When I got back, I phoned June again, and this time I got through. 'Tony, my love,' she said. 'Where've you been? My girls have been pining for you. When are we going to see you?' I told her that I'd been pretty busy since I came back from Puerto Rico with Annabel, but that things were settling down now, and how about this evening? 'Great,' she said. 'We'll expect you when we see you. Terrific. I'll let the girls know that you're coming. See you, baby.' So that was settled. There was a message form Pauline, my Pan Am hostess (whom I had met originally in Daly's Dandelion, the singles bar a few blocks up the road from the office) telling me that she was back in town. I made a mental note to get in touch. She was always good news. At that point Dave, the art director, came into my office.

'Hi, Tony,' he said. 'I've just done a first edit on the trannies of the Lucy and Dee Dee shoot. They're pretty hot stuff. I wondered if you'd like to come along and have a look at them? Can you spare some time?' 'Sure, Dave,' I said. 'I'd like that.' I got up and followed him back through the art department to his office at the far end. He had a screen and a carousel set up there, and the blind was down, keeping out the bright afternoon sunlight. The pictures of Lucy and Dee Dee making simulated lesbian love were a tremendous turn-on, and at the end of the review I congratulated Dave on his edit. The photographs of the black, six-foot-tall, bald-headed, shaven-pubed Lucy, contrasting with the pale, white-skinned Dee Dee from the topless/bottomless bar that I had visited only that morning, were quite fabulous.

'I would think we could put an extra twenty-five thousand copies onto our print run for that issue, Dave,' I said. 'Will you have a word with production? That'll be, what? The October issue?' 'November,' he said. 'On sale October. I surely will speak to production,' he said. 'I'll do it right now.' 'Thanks,' I said.

CHAPTER THREE: MOSCOW MISCHIEF

It was Charlene who opened the door to me at the entrance to the apartment that was June's brothel. She literally hurled herself at me, flinging her arms around my neck and her tongue down my throat. 'Tony, baby,' she said, when she at last withdrew her pinkly wet tongue, and allowed us both to draw urgently necessary breath. 'How are you, honey? Where have you been?' I mumbled something about Puerto Rico.

Charlene stood back and took a good look at me, which allowed me to pay her the same compliment. She was wearing a transparent pink silk teddy, through which her large breasts stood out boldly, the nipples erect, pleading to be sucked. I could see her blonde pubic hair clearly through the silken crotch of her pink creation. Her long legs were encased in almost white, almost transparent stockings, held up by wide pink garters, and she wore white, high-heeled court shoes. Vogue would not have approved, but her appearance said one thing: 'Fuck me.'

She must have read my mind. 'Are you going to fuck me, Tony baby?' she asked. 'My pussy's getting wet at the thought of it.' I kissed the end of her nose, and grinned at her. 'It's lovely to see you, Charlene,' I said. 'I'm going to fuck all of you, darling. But I have to fuck Andrea, Louise, and Victoria before I can fuck you, because I haven't fucked them at all yet, and I promised, the last time I was here, that they would be next. And a promise is a promise. You do understand, don't you, sweetheart?' Charlene pouted her adorable lips, and pretended to sulk. She looked up at me through her dyed blonde lashes. 'Can't I even give you a quick blow job?' she asked. 'Out here? Right now? Nobody need ever know.' Nobody need ever know what, Charlene?' said June's voice from farther down the entrance corridor to her apartment. And then, 'Put that man down at once. You've had him, the last time he was here, and there are other girls who haven't had that pleasure. Tony, darling. How are you?' June came up to me, and gave me a big kiss. Then she smacked Charlene lightly on her bottom. 'Ooh, nice,' said Charlene. 'Do it again.' 'You're so naughty,' said June, laughing at her. 'I guess that's why you're so good at your job. Now run along, and leave this poor man in peace.' 'I'd rather leave him *a* piece,' said Charlene, 'but somehow I don't seem to be getting anywhere with that thought.'

She tottered down the corridor in front of us on her high heels, her pretty little ass swaying away from me, its deep cleavage doing things to my prick. I'd have happily settled for a time with her and forgotten about the others. As she disappeared into the brothel's main room, she must have said something to the other five girls, for suddenly there were excited screams, and the five of them came running, jostling each other to get near to me, and five mouths and five pairs of hands bade me welcome in a number of pleasurable different ways.

I didn't know who was doing what, but apart from kisses on my mouth and face, someone unzipped my fly and gave my cock a friendly, welcoming squeeze. I looked down, and saw that it was Louise. 'Hey, Tony,' she said. 'How are you?' Before I could reply, she said 'I'm ready.' She squeezed my cock again, and then tucked it back into my trousers, and zipped me up. 'Are you?' she asked. 'Yes, I am, sweetheart,' I said, taking her by the hand,

and leading her down the corridor. 'But let's just have a quick glass or two of champagne first. And then I'm all yours.' 'Wow,' she said. 'It must be my birthday.'

Louise, like Charlene, was a blonde, but Louise's hair colour, I think, was natural. It was a sort of soft, gentle, honey blonde, cut short around her chin, rather like a Greek helmet, and just slightly streaked, as opposed to Charlene's blatant, peroxided, almost white mane. Louise was short, about five six, and slim, with pert, pretty young breasts, their shape plainly showing through the thin cotton T-shirt that she was wearing over a pair of black silk hot pants. Over her shapely legs she was wearing a pair of seemingly self-supporting black silk stockings, the tops about six inches below the bottom of her shorts, leaving a sexy band of firm, tanned flash deliberately exposed between the two. She was wearing black patent leather pumps. The only other noticeable thing about her person was a tiny red rose tattooed on her left shoulder, its green stem and leaves a contrast to the deep red of the petals.

We got to the bar, and I was surprised to see there were two middle-aged men, who patently had to be customers, already sitting on two of the bar stools. They were chatting to each other in a way that indicated that they knew each other well. June didn't make any kind of an effort to introduce me to them, or vice versa, but Victoria and Rita waved fingers at me, and went over to keep the two men company. I remembered some of the sexual things I had experienced with Victoria and Rita, and wondered idly if the two men would have the same kind of fun. I doubted it, somehow, but that was probably just sheer arrogance on my part. June took me aside for a moment and whispered in my ear that the arrangement this time was exactly the same as on my first visit: anything that I cared to enjoy was on the house. I tried to argue, but she just put a finger over my lips, and said,' Shut up,

Andrews. If the girls want to give it away, who are you to argue?' It was a fair point, and I shut up.

Someone – Gloria, I think – had opened a bottle of champagne and June passed me a glass. 'Here's to you, Tony, darling,' she said. 'Please don't stay away so long next time.' 'I won't,' I promised. 'Cheers, everyone.' I told them then that I was soon to be situated permanently in New York, and mentioned my upcoming trip to London to sort out my affairs there. 'Oh, do me a favour, darling, will you please?' asked June. 'Of course,' I said. 'What?' 'Bring me back some kippers, will you?' she said.' Real kippers. Isle of Man ones if they still produce them. I can't remember when I last ate a kipper.' She smiled at me, and said 'Frankly, I'd sell my soul for a real Isle of Man or Aberdeen kipper. Does that make you laugh?' 'No,' I said. 'But as a matter of interest, what else do you miss from home? What else can't you get here that you really care about?'

'Oh, that's easy,' she said. 'Potted shrimps. They simply don't exist here. I ought to write to Young's and ask them if I can be an American franchisee. But then, of course, they probably aren't available here because there's simply no demand. And then smoked salmon. Proper, Scottish, oak-smoked salmon. That doesn't exist here, either. You can get Newfoundland smoked salmon, called lox, but it's an entirely different thing. Real smoked salmon you can't get here. And the other thing, of course, is bacon. Real, home-grown, proper English, lean back bacon. Or Irish, or Welsh, or whatever. Danish, even. Anything other than the awful streaky bacon that you get served everywhere her. It's disgusting. I don't think it's even American. I don't believe that they grow bacon. I think what you get here comes from Canada. I'd send my share straight back, frankly. And another thing. Runner beans. They simply don't exist here in New York. Don't ask me why. I don't know. But they don't. Green beans, yes. Runner beans, no.' She stopped for a moment, and took a deep draught of champagne.

'But don't misunderstand me, Tony,' she continued. 'I didn't come here all those years ago, thinking that living in New York would be like living in South Kensington. I'm not quite that stupid. And there are a million things here that are magical that you can't get in England.' 'Name one,' I said. 'Decent, really fresh orange juice,' she said, without stopping to think. 'It's just that, after a while, after you've had time to absorb the excitement, experience the differences, discover where the really worthwhile things are, then you begin to hanker for just one or two tiny things that aren't always readily available here. And of all those things, the main thing that I do sometimes really miss is kippers. OK?' 'Of course it's OK, darling,' I said. 'Whatever turns you on. One large box of genuine Manx kippers will soon be winging it's way across the Atlantic to you, with my compliments. That's an absolute promise.'

Louise was standing close to me. I could smell her perfume. She was silent, seemingly quite relaxed. I looked at her. She smiled up at me. 'And where are you from, Louise?' I asked her. 'What do you miss most from the days of your youth?' 'I'm from just down the road a little ways,' she said. 'I was born here in New York, in Little Italy. My mother was Swedish, my father New York Italian. I've got his physique and her colouring. Since you ask, I think the only thing I miss from my childhood is my innocence.'

She smiled at me. 'But that's a bit heavy, isn't it? As far as practical things, physical things, are concerned, I don't think I miss anything, in that it's all still here all around me. Both my parents still live where they did when I left home. I visit with them most Sundays. They don't know how I earn my living, of course. They think I'm a secretary. To June here. That's what I trained for, originally. And I actually really do undertake some secretarial work for her, whenever she needs it. It's just that I discovered my pussy soon after I learned shorthand, and I find it more fun, and infinitely more profitable, to pound my pussy instead of a typewriter. Does that make sense to you?' 'It surely does, Louise,' I told her. I drained my glass. 'And speaking of pussy, shall we go? Is this a good time?' Louise nodded, drained her own glass, and led the way. None of the other girls said anything as we left the room.

She took us up to the same bedroom where I had previously experienced such varied sexual pleasures with Rita, Victoria and Charlene. Whether by chance, or whether the others had told her that this was my preferred room of those available, I didn't ask. 'Charlene tells me that you're a pantie freak,' she said, conversationally. The smile which accompanied the statement removed any embarrassment that I might perhaps have felt had it not been there. 'By which I mean that panties, and anything and everything to do with them, turn you on. Especially recently worn panties,' she said. 'Warm, fragrant, damp-at-the-crotch panties.' 'That's right,' I said. 'She also tells me that you Brits call them knickers,' she added. 'Yes,' I said. 'The English word for panties is knickers.' 'How quaint,' she said. 'Here in America, knickers are something that sportsmen wear.' 'So I understand,' I said. 'How very kinky.' She laughed.

'But going back to being a pantie freak,' Louise said, 'I can relate to that. I love the taste of my own pussy, when I suck a cock that's recently been fucking me. It's the same sort of thing, isn't it? It's simply straightforwardly sexual. The scent of cunt. The taste of cunt. The smell of cock. The taste of cock.' 'I guess so,' I said. 'I've simply never thought of it in that way.' 'Whatever,' she said. 'But when June told us this afternoon that you were going to visit with us this evening, we girls got together to see how we could think up something that would be fun for you, You know; something that little bit more amusing?' I couldn't think of anything to say, so I said nothing. 'And what we came up with,' she said, smiling an enormous smile, 'is over on the bed there. Shall we go and have a look?' We walked over towards the bed. I wondered what these lovely girls had been up to. When we got to the bed, I could see six pairs of knickers laid out upon it.

'It works like this,' said Louise. 'We all looked out a pair of panties that we thought were our very sexiest. Then we put them on, and we spent quite a long time feeling up each other's crotches. You know, playing with each other's pussies from outside the actual panties. Squeezing and pushing up through the material. And playing with ourselves too, of course. And now here they are, with the crotches still all damp and sticky, with each one giving off the unique aroma of its owner's pussy juices. What you have to do is bury your nose in the crotch of each pair of panties and identify to me, from your assessment of each individual scent, which of the six of us girls each pair of the panties belongs to. What do you say? You've fucked three of us, but that was a while ago. But if you're the cocksman that the girls say you are, it shouldn't be too difficult. Should it?'

I laughed. Mostly from sheer amusement at the trouble the girls had taken to pander to my favourite fetish. But what had she said? 'It shouldn't be too difficult?' I looked at her. 'Not too difficult?' I repeated. 'I think that it's bloody nigh impossible. But I'm happy to have a go.' I went over to the bed, and picked up the nearest pair of knickers.

I noticed that each pair had a number pinned to it. This pair was made of pretty little white muslin inserts into plain, white silk material, with tiny blue ribbons here and there. Very sweet. Innocent, basically, but depending upon who was wearing them, I could imagine that they could be very sexy too. I buried my nose in the cotton lining of the gusset, and inhaled deeply. And then I suddenly realized that it wasn't going to be as difficult as all that after all. The damp crotch certainly carried the tangy aroma of freshly deposited pussy juices. That was for sure. My John Thomas almost leapt to attention at the first sniff. But overlaying that delightful scent was the far stronger, completely unmistakable smell of Charlene's perfume. I drew a second breath, partly to make certain that I was right, partly for the sheer, sensual pleasure of inhaling the heady mixture. I looked around at Louise, who was standing there, watching me. 'These are Charlene's,' I said, looking at the number pinned to them. 'Number three.' I handed them to her. Louise took them, and looked at the list she held in her hand. 'Fantastic,' she said. 'And right. Damn right.'

She looked up at me again. 'Luck,' she said. 'Beginner's luck.' I grinned back at her, and picked up another pair. I chose the tartiest pair that I could see. They were minuscule. More of a sort of tiny pouch, attached to two thongs, than anything that could properly be described as knickers. They were shiny red nylon, adorned with tiny black roses, and there was a slit where the wearer's pussy lips would be. I looked closely, and yes, that *was* a tightly curled, auburn pubic hair that I had thought I could see stuck to the thin material. I inhaled the scent from the tiny cotton gusset, and yes, I had been right from the start. Victoria's perfume. Victoria's pubic hairs. I looked at the number pinned to them as I gave them to Louise. 'Number six,' I said. 'Victoria's.' Louise looked at her list. 'Shit,' she said. 'It's uncanny. I don't believe it.'

The next choice wasn't going to be so easy. Charlene and Victoria both wore quite strong, fairly heavy, individual-style perfumes, and I had, in any case, been as close to them as anyone can get, even if a while ago. But I hadn't been that close to Louise, or Andrea, or Gloria, and nothing in my memory gave me any kind of clue as to what kind of scent they wore. Rita's I thought I could remember, just about. So I decided to cheat, in as far as I could. First I went over to the drinks cupboard that I remembered from my first visit to this room, some weeks ago now. 'I seriously fancy a drink,' I said to Louise. 'Champagne, probably. Do you fancy a glass of champagne, or would you prefer something else?' 'Oh, what a good idea,' she said. 'Champagne would be perfect. Thank you.' I opened a bottle from the small fridge that was inside the cupboard, and poured two glasses. 'Cheers,' I said to Louise, as I gave her glass to her. Then I leaned forward, and kissed her cheek.

I did it slowly, and at the same time I inhaled – as quietly as I knew how. Thus I was able to get a good sniff of her perfume whilst so doing. It was light and flowery, with a definite lilies-of-the-valley content, and slight overtones of something lemony. A reasonably easily distinguishable scent. I stood back, and we chatted for a few minutes whilst we sipped our champagne. Then I put my glass down, and I went back to the bed. 'It's definitely getting more difficult,' I said. 'I think I've picked out the easiest, so far.'

I picked up the four pairs of knickers left on the bed in quick succession, sniffed them, and put them down again. My recent whiff of Louise's scent immediately enabled me to pick out her panties. They were listed as number one, a pretty pair of pale lemon-coloured panties, both feminine and sexy. The crotch, I noticed, was particularly wet, indicating a freely lubricating lady. It augured well for my forthcoming fuck. It would, I thought, have been too obvious to select them straight away, so I picked up the next pair that my nose told me were Rita's. They were gold satin, with delicate embroidery in gold silk all over them. They were number five. I revelled in my inhalation of Rita's mixed scent and cunt odours, the latter very strong indeed, with just a whiff of the gamey smell of urine in the background, to which, to my surprise, my cock immediately reacted. I handed them to Louise. 'Number five,' I told her. 'They're Rita's. Right? She looked at her list. 'Right,' she said. 'The girls simply aren't going to believe this.'

No, they're not, I chuckled to myself. So what if I was cheating? There wasn't any money involved. It was only a game. It was time to pick up Louise's knickers, leaving just two pairs to follow, Andrea's and Gloria's. I grabbed hold of the pair marked number one, the pale lemon-coloured ones, and made a great performance of sniffing, inhaling and, finally, licking the cotton gusset. 'Mmmm,' I said, licking my lips theatrically. 'Delicious. Real gourmet stuff. This has got to be a class pussy. Number one. These have to be yours, Louise. Yes?' She just looked at me and shook her head. 'Yes,' she said. 'Right,' and marked them off on her list. She looked up again.' Oh, and thank you for the pretty compliment,' she said. 'I really appreciate it.' 'My pleasure,' I said.

So, four down, and two to go. Nothing here to help me. Whichever I chose, I had a fifty/fifty chance of being right. Or wrong, of course. I wondered if I could extract a clue from the material, and style, of the panties. One pair – identified as number two – was a pair of skimpy white knickers, with a transparent panel in the front, and tiny, baby frills down the sides and back. The other – number four – was a pair of cotton all-over flowery patterned knickers, plainly but well cut, with the emphasis on comfort and practicality, rather than on any kind of sensual statement. They indicated a confident wearer, someone who didn't need to prove her sexuality, either to herself, or to anyone else.

When I first met them both, black-haired Andrea, I remembered, had been wearing satin hot pants, and a white T-shirt. Little Gloria, with the plain brown hair in an urchin cut, had been wearing a white bra and knicker set. Was that a clue? Did white knickers then mean white knickers now? Did a T-shirt and hot pants mean a confident sexuality? God knows, I thought. I might just as well flip a coin. Well, here goes, I said to myself. I picked up the flowery knickers, and, crossing my fingers, I looked at Louise. 'Number four,' I said, confidently. 'These are Andrea's. Which means, of course, that this other pair,' I turned around and picked up the frilly white ones 'these, marked number two, are Gloria's. Am I right?' I waited, expectantly.

After a moment, she said 'Yes, you're absolutely right. I can't believe it, but I've seen you do it. There was no way you could know. But you're one hundred per cent right. You couldn't even bloody *guess* a hundred per cent correctly. I'm staggered. Absolutely staggered.' I was genuinely delighted. Well, I'd only cheated a *little* bit! 'So where's my prize?' I asked Louise. 'Oh,' she said. 'I got so involved, I quite forgot about your prize. Here I am,' she volunteered. 'I'm your prize.' She went over and picked up the champagne bottle, bringing it back over to me and pouring us both a fresh glass. 'Congratulations,' she said. We clinked glasses. 'Thank you,' I said. 'May I have my prize now please?' I asked. 'Of course you can, honey,' she said. 'How would you like me? Did you have anything in particular in mind?' 'Yes,' I said. 'As a matter of fact, I did.' 'Tell Aunty Louise all about it,' she said. 'I'm into anything that doesn't cause me pain.'

'Well,' I said, 'I think you will understand when I tell you that one of the major attractions for me about this delightful establishment is that it seems to be designed to function solely for the pleasure of its gentlemen guests.' (I used the word guests, rather than customers, since I hadn't personally spent a penny here since I became aware of its existence.) 'And those pleasures centre, largely, on sexual matters.' Louise nodded, but she didn't say anything. So I went on. 'So, in accepting my hard-won prize, may I now ask that we do that which we came in here to do originally – i.e., fuck? Make love? Have sex? Get our rocks off? Copulate? You know what I mean? It is simply that the charming, extremely horny contest which you dear girls lined up for me has rather distracted me from our original intention. Now that we are ready to continue, may I ask, please, that I may simply lie back and enjoy it? In other words, that *you* fuck *me*, and not vice versa? I would just love to lie there and have you do all the exciting, sexy, lovely things to me that you can think of. Is that a possibility?' She came over and took me in her arms, and gave me a very sexy kiss. It was lovely. My cock paid full attention to what she was doing.

'It's not only a possibility,' Louse said. 'It's a reality. Just stand there, will you?' She undressed me as I stood there. Slowly and carefully. When she got down to my underpants, she pulled them down, very slowly, and as I stepped out of them, she took my almost totally rigid prick in her hand, and spent some time examining it. She pulled the foreskin back, gently, and kissed my prepuce, wetly, lovingly. 'What a lovely big cock,' she said. 'I'm going to enjoy myself with that.' She put it in her mouth, and took it almost all the way down into her throat. But only for a moment. It was, as it were, a foretaste of things to come. My cock reacted exactly the same way as yours would, and sprung fully erect, the blood pumping into it, causing it to throb in her hand. 'Very impressive,' she said. 'I like big cocks. But tell me a girl who doesn't.'

She let go of it, and stood up. 'Just go and make yourself comfortable on the bed,' she said. 'I'll be right with you.' I went and sat on the edge of the bed, watching her as she undressed. Louise took almost everything off (which wasn't actually very much, when you got down to it). Her T-shirt, her black silk hot pants and her patent leather pumps, in fact. But she left the self-supporting black silk stockings on, and her stripping had revealed a pair of tiny, black-lace bikini panties which she also kept on. Thinking back, I wondered if the hot pants belonged to Andrea, or if they were, in fact, Louise's own? Or perhaps the girls used a communal wardrobe? The thought gave a new dimension to the concept of mix 'n match.

Louise walked over to me and stood in front of me. As she stood there, she ran a hand down over her pudenda. I could see her black pubic hair through the transparent panties, and I thought I could smell the scent of freshly aroused pussy as she stroked herself through the flimsy material. 'All women like to play with themselves, Tony,' she said. 'Did you know that?' I watched her fingers as she moved them over her cunt lips. Massaging, feeling, stroking. 'Yes,' I said, eventually. 'Yes, I did know that.' 'So I thought that you might enjoy watching me playing with myself for a few moments, before we start getting down to the serious business of fucking,' she said.

I didn't say anything, and Louise continued to stroke and massage herself through the thin material of her panties. Soon she began to move her hips in a copulatory motion, and her fingers moved faster and faster. Suddenly she pulled her panties down, and she thrust two fingers deeply into her wet cunt, her panties now stretched taut between her legs, just above her knees. I could see the wetness of the cotton lining, a darker shade where her juices had run. She was thrusting her fingers in and out so quickly, obviously stimulating her clitoris as she did so, that her digits moving in and out of the copious wetness of her liberally lubricated pussy were making rude little sucking noises as her vaginal muscles gripped, then were forced to release, the delightful invaders. 'Ooooh,' she said, suddenly. 'I'm going to come. I'm making myself come. I'm playing with myself in front of you, and now I'm going to come. It's lovely. I like it.' Her fingers moved even faster, and she was bent over, in a kind of almost foetal position, as she began to seriously masturbate herself to a climax.

'Oh, yes,' Louise cried. 'Ooooh, yeees. Here it comes. Here *I* come. Oh, fuck. That's fantastic. Oh, terrific. Oh, God.' Her fingers began to slow down, and finally stopped. She quickly straightened herself up, and looked at me. 'Forgive me,' she said. 'But there's nothing like a quick wank, as you British call it, is there?' She laughed as she pulled her knickers up. 'Now then,' she said, 'that should have got us both going a bit. At least, it has me. How about you?' 'Me, too,' I admitted, happily. 'Watching a woman masturbate herself is one of the most arousing things in the whole of the world for me. Especially when she knows I'm watching, and the fact that she knows exactly how best to bring herself off is exciting, too. And here's the proof,' I said, indicating my fully erect cock.

She laughed. 'Don't go away, honey,' she said. 'I'm just going to slip next door for a moment or two. But this should keep you amused while I'm away.' She went over to the wall and pressed a couple of buttons, at which a picture slid back, revealing a large screen and a small panel of controls. She pressed a couple more buttons, and a full-colour film came up. It was of two very pretty, very young, totally naked girls. They were in the *soixante-neuf* position. There was gentle music in the background, over which could be heard the grunts and sighs and moans of the two participants, as they set about each other, lovingly, and with great finesse.

The camera lingered on the couple from a short distance, and then dollied in to a tight close-up of the pinkly open vagina of one of the girls. Her pussy lips were spread like exotic wet petals as the other girl's tongue and lips laved and licked, kissed and sucked, while her long, elegant fingers spread her partner's pussy lips even wider as I watched. I was entranced. So much so that I didn't notice that Louise had left the room until I heard the door open, and she re-entered. What I saw completely distracted me from the erotic antics of the girls in the movie, and as I looked at her, Louise went over to the control panel. 'I'll leave it on,' she said, 'in case we fancy a little external stimulation. But I'll turn the sound down, so that it won't distract us.' She walked over towards me, stopping short about four or five feet away, and she performed a professional model's twirl, standing on her toes and pirouetting through 360 degrees.

She quite took my breath away. Louise was dressed in the classic little housemaid's outfit of every man's forbidden sexual fantasy. The basic item of her outfit – the black dress, covered by its tiny white apron – was absolutely minimal. The skirt of the dress, for example, was the mini-est of mini-skirts, and almost completely exposed her black silk knickers. It was pulled tightly over her full buttocks, and it also revealed her black elastic suspenders, stretching tightly down from a tiny nylon suspender belt which held up her black silk stockings, themselves revealing the statutory expanse of naked flesh between her stocking tops and her knicker hem. The white apron too was minuscule, and she also wore the obligatory white maid's cap, with its restraining band of black ribbon. She was carrying a feather duster, and as I watched, she began to busy herself about the room. Turning her back to me, she bent down to dust the legs of a table set against the wall, exposing her shiny black sexy knickers, pulled tautly across her buttocks as her skirt rose up behind her.

Keeping her back to me, she then spoke, saying, 'You can feel me up, sir, if you so wish. I am but a poor servant girl, here to do your every bidding. If you wish to put a hand up my knickers, and feel my tiny virgin cunt, then – as my master – that is your privilege. You can pull my knickers down and have your way with me, in any way that you wish. Or you may open up my bodice, and feel my firm young breasts, suck my perky little nipples, do anything to me that you like. I am your servant. I am here only to obey you. If you want to force me to suck your cock, then tell me to kneel down in front of you, and then thrust your swollen prick between my wet, subservient lips. Spurt your hot come down my willing throat. I will obey your every wish.

'Or you might perhaps prefer to deflower me. You may wish to begin by sucking and licking my virgin pussy lips, be the first man to taste the luscious, free-flowing juices that run down my legs when I play with myself. Play with my little clitoris, make me come, over and over again, until I scream for mercy. Or you may want to rape me anally. Force your huge, stiff, engorged cock into my tiny, tight little anus, while you squeeze my breasts. Make me cry as you spurt your come up my rectum. All these sexual pleasures are yours for the asking. Tell me now, my lord, what it is that you would have me do.'

'Hey, Louise,' I said. 'What a fantastic turn-on. Fabulous, baby. I love it. All of it. I want to do all of the things that you have suggested, right now. All at the same time.' She laughed. 'No, honey,' I said. 'I'm serious. But come over here, and bend over in front of me, and let me feel your pussy through those lovely, sexy black knickers. Perhaps that will give me some kind of inspiration. OK?' 'OK,' she said. And so saying, she came over to where I was still sitting on the edge of the bed. She then knelt on the bed in front of me, and bent over forward, away from me, so that her bottom was offered up to me. Her tiny skirt had ridden up, exposing her firm white thighs, with her taut suspenders stretched very tightly down them, and with her lovely black, shiny, silk knickers pulled tightly across her full buttocks, the crotch of them pouting wet up at me.

I could smell the scent of her wet cunt. I put out a tentative hand and, extending my middle finger, I ran it down the centre of that attractive, erotic target. I could feel the heat emanating from her cunt, and the clinging wetness of her as the pressure of my finger caused the silky black material to stick to her damp cunt lips. I looked at what must be one of the world's most sexually enticing sights: a beautiful woman's ass, with her bent over before you, already a sexual supplicant to your secret fantasies, with her skirt up in the air, her knickers wet at the crotch, her black pubic hairs curling erotically through the sides of her knicker legs, her thighs spread, and your cock rigid with the knowledge that you can do anything, but *anything*, to this willing sexual slave.

I took her knickers by their elastic waistband, and slowly, oh, so slowly, pulled them down her firm buttocks, exposing, first, her bottom cleavage. Next, I could see tufts of her anal hair, surrounding her brown, tightly puckered anus, offering itself to my rampant, rapist tendencies, and, finally, her wet, pink, sticky cunt lips, covered in the sexual mucus that indicated her need for penetration of one kind or another. I could see, smell, feel – and, I hoped, would soon be able to taste – her sexuality. Her act as the servile, subservient housemaid of yesteryear had struck a chord in my own sexuality that I hadn't realized was there. There she was, with her wet, sexy knickers pulled down and tautly stretched between her spread thighs, with both of her sexual orifices willingly offered up to me. What a delightful choice! I grabbed her around her waist, and pulled her towards me. As our bodies met, I put a hand down, and guided my throbbing cock towards her wetly open pussy.

Then I used the fingers of both hands to spread Louise's inner labia to their maximum, and I thrust myself down into that delightful, widely open, inviting hole. She clenched her pussy around me, and drew me deeply down inside her, her muscles working on me like a massage parlour girl's expert hand. She was tight, wet, welcoming, and very, very sensual. She had more feeling in her cunt than most women have in their whole bodies. I exploded into her, pumping my jism up into her with long, copious spurts.

When I'd finished, I withdrew and sank back onto the bed in sheer exhaustion. 'Hey, Tony,' she said. 'That was good. I enjoyed it.' 'So did I, darling,' I said. 'We must do it again, sometime soon.' 'How about now, baby?' she suggested. 'You're kidding, sweetheart,' I said. 'Promise me you're kidding. I couldn't fuck my way out of a paper bag, right at this particular moment. 'That's no problem, honey,' she said. 'We've got all the time in the world. Just relax.' I did as she suggested, and quickly fell asleep. When I woke, I was alone, and the room was in darkness. I reached out a hand towards the bedside table, and found what I was looking for. The telephone. But all I got from it was a dialling tone. I realized that there wasn't a switchboard, and not knowing any of the extension numbers, I put the telephone down again. Getting up off the bed, I started to make my way towards the door, in order to find the light switch. Just as I almost got there, the door opened, and someone put on the light. It was Louise. She had changed out of her fantasy maid's outfit, and was wearing a short-skirted, very contemporary, *décolletée* evening dress, in a pale shade of pink. She looked terrific. She was also carrying a heavily laden tray.

'Hi, baby,' she said. 'You were gone there, for a while, so I thought I'd let you sleep.' She looked at her watch. 'That was two hours ago.' 'What's the time now, for God's sake?' I asked her. 'It's a quarter after midnight,' she said. 'The place is just beginning to fill up.' She crossed over to one of the tables against the wall, and put down her tray. 'I don't know about you, darling,' she said, 'but I was starving. I thought a little sustenance might go down well. How about you?' I looked at the tray. She was quite right.

I was starving too. I just hadn't thought about it.

'Terrific idea,' I said. 'But where's yours?' She had the grace to laugh, even if it wasn't a very original joke. 'You'll find a robe that should fit you in that closet over there,' she said, nodding towards a pair of doors set into one of the walls. I went to the closet, and found a silk robe that might have been made for me. Looking at the contents of the tray again, I could see that it was laden with cold lobster, potato mayonnaise, and a variety of salad dishes. There was a bottle of white wine in a silver ice bucket, and crisp, starched, white linen napkins. There was all the necessary china, cutlery, and anything else that might be needed. Lobster crackers. Lobster picks. Condiments. Cut-crystal wine glasses. I picked up the bottle from the ice-bucket, and looked at the label. I couldn't believe what I read there. It was a 1971 Puligny-Montrachet. Delicious. It would have set you back at least sixty or seventy dollars in any decent New York restaurant. I reached for the corkscrew. Whilst I opened the bottle, Louise set up a table for us, laying out the china and cutlery, the napkins and the glasses, and she then helped both of us to generous platefuls of the food. She noticed me watching her, and smiled at me. 'Fucking always makes me hungry,' she said. 'Right now, I could eat a horse.' I grinned back at her. 'Right now,' I said, 'you deserve a horse.'

I poured us each a glass of white Burgundy. 'At the risk of being called a wine snob,' I said, 'do you know that this is one of the great white Burgundies, and that its year, the year of this bottle, 1971, is the best year for white Burgundy since before the last war? There were no vintage white Burgundies declared at all between 1945 and 1970, and this year, this 1971, is one of the best ever.' I grinned at her. 'Or so I'm told. And there hasn't been a vintage year for white Burgundy declared since then. So this is something of a rarity.' I swirled the wine around in my glass a little, and inhaled the rich bouquet. Louise sipped her wine.

'I don't actually know anything about wine,' she said. 'I know to ask for a Chardonnay when I go to a bar, or a restaurant, because I know that I like the taste of it. And I know that I prefer white wine to red. But that's about it. I normally drink American wine. I buy Californian Gallo wine by the jug. I don't know anything at all about French wine.' 'Nor do you need to,' I said, as I raised my glass to her. 'Enjoy.'

I'm not a wine snob. Really I'm not. I just appreciate the rare opportunities that I sometimes get to taste something special. And this was very special. 'As a matter of interest, Louise,' I said, 'who chose the wine to go with our food? Did you?' 'No, darling,' she said. 'I was out in the kitchen, talking to the chef while he got the lobster and salad together, and June came out into the kitchen, and she said "Is that food for you and Tony?" And when I said yes, she said "Hang on while I go and get a bottle of wine to go with it." And she went away, and came back with that. She obviously wanted to give you something that she knew you would enjoy.'

'You can say that again,' I said. 'It *is* rather nice,' said Louise. 'I think I could get used to drinking this. Do you think they keep it in the local liquor store?' 'Probably not, darling,' I said. 'If you really fancy some, perhaps you should ask June where she got hers.' 'Oh, I did,' she told me. 'At least, when she came back with that bottle, I said "What's that?" and she told me that an old customer, who died a year or so ago, had left her a case of this wine in his will. I thought, what a funny thing to do, I'd much rather be left money in someone's will, but she said she was very pleased with it, and that she knew you would enjoy it. Which reminds me,' she said. 'I'm sorry, I quite forgot. But June said, now that it is getting busy out there, to tell you that she was keeping Gloria and Andrea in reserve for you, just in case you fancied some time with them this evening, but she said that, should you not feel like that, would we let her know, and she'll put them to work with the other customers.' I had to laugh. After what I'd enjoyed with the lovely Louise, I doubted I could fuck anyone or anything. Not for a while, anyway, I was knackered. 'Louise, sweetheart,' I said, 'Tell June that I really appreciate what she's doing, but not to have Gloria and Andrea hang on for me any longer. I'll catch up with them another time, if I may. I'll speak to her myself on the way out, but just tell her that for now, will you, please, darling?' 'Sure I will,' she said. 'I'll go and do that now. I'll be right back. OK?' 'OK,' I said.

I sat down at the table, and sipped my wine until Louise returned from her errand. She joined me, and we ate our meal. The lobster was so fresh, it tasted as if it had swum up from Maine that morning. For all I knew, it probably had. The salad was crisp and equally fresh, the potato salad excellent, and the mayonnaise had been made with a light hand, one which plainly understood what mayonnaise was all about. And the Puligny-Montrachet? What can I tell you? It was the purest nectar. We ate and drank, mainly in silence, but in a very comfortable silence. Louise, either from her innate kindness or simply because she didn't drink that much wine, allowed me to consume about two-thirds of the Burgundy by myself. I didn't – wouldn't – argue with her. And then the miracle of its existence was over, and it was gone. One of the most memorable wine experiences of my life.

I got myself together, bathed, dressed, thanked both Louise and June for the pleasures of my evening (and June particularly for her gift of the wine), waved goodnight to those of the other girls who could be seen, and took myself back off to Fred's apartment. Fred was still up, and suggested a few quick games of backgammon, which I was happy to play, mellow as I was from the evening's sex, food and wine. We played for about an hour, ending up reasonably even, to our mutual disappointment. At which point Fred, thankfully, yawned, and said he thought it was time for him to go to bed.

The next morning I did some serious thinking about my forthcoming trip to London. Why exactly was I going, I asked myself? In theory, I was going to make arrangements about my Hampstead flat. And the Porsche. Everything else was already arranged. So what would I do while I was over there? I would almost certainly fuck Annabel, from a combination of old times' sake and selfishness, and probably Carla, *Tiptop*'s randy London production editor, for fun. But what would that actually achieve? Precisely nothing. I decided to telephone Annabel, and ask her if she would be good enough to make whatever arrangements were necessary to look after my flat on a more or less permanent basis, and to sell the Porsche for me. She had, after all, been looking after the flat all the time I had been in New York already, and selling the Porsche was no big deal.

I waited until mid-afternoon, which was roughly mid-evening in London, and rang her. It was the first time that I had spoken to her since her return visit to me here in New York. When I put my proposition to her, she didn't hesitate for a moment, bless her. Of course she'd look after everything. She'd work it all out, and let me know how much money to transfer to her. How would I like to do it? Monthly? Twice yearly? Quarterly? Monthly, I decided. When she gave me the amount, I would arrange with my New York bank to transfer that sum to her London bank on the first of each month. If she needed any more, for whatever reason, all she had to do was call or write, and I would transfer it by return. Had I the slightest interest in renting it out, she asked, should a likely tenant appear on the scene?

Absolutely not, I told her. And how much did I want for the Porsche, she asked? Whatever she could get for it, I said. It wasn't, in my opinion, worth the hassle of shipping it over to New York. There were too many problems finding anywhere to park in the Big Apple. But I was in no hurry to sell it. I suggested that if she were to take it to the garage in Lancaster Gate that serviced it for me, they would probably tell her what she ought to get for it, and possibly even sell it for her, on a commission basis. What about clothes, she asked me?

I didn't think I needed anything, I told her. Perhaps she'd spread a few mothballs about the place, if she had a moment. Fine, she said. And how was I? I took a deep breath. I was OK, I said. Missing her, of course. Was I, she asked? That was a surprise. I thought I'd let that go. And when would she see me, she asked, if I had no plans for going over at the moment? Well, I said, I wasn't sure, really. I mean, I'm sure there'll be a reason to come over, sooner or later, I said. And of course, she could always come over here and stay with me again, particularly when I'd got myself an apartment. Oh, yes, of course, she said. Then, if there was anything else I thought of, perhaps I'd give her a call? Yes, of course I would, I said. Goodbye, then, she said, and rang off. Goodbye, darling, I said. I was a frog once more. I reflected on the sadness of life for a moment, and then shrugged it off. What the fuck? Life's too short, I thought. I went through to Eileen's office.

'Hi, honey,' she said. 'Where've you been all day? I know you've been in, but I haven't heard a squeak out of you. How's life? What's new?' 'Life's good,' I told her. I then explained to her that I had decided not to bother to go to London on my proposed trip. I could do it all by telephone, I said. I didn't mention Annabel. 'So, sweetheart, now's the time to get the real estate people working, if you will. I'd like to get into my own place as quickly as possible. It's not that I don't appreciate Fred's kindness in letting me stay with him. It's just that I actually prefer to be on my own.' She grinned at me. 'I do understand, honey,' she said. 'But I haven't been idle. I've spoken to a number of real estate people, and they have been sending me wads of possibilities.' She hunted around on her desk, and found a pile of printed details of apartments. These she handed over to me. I began to look through them.

'I've crossed out the hopeless ones,' she said. 'They're either too expensive, or not worth looking at, or they've got something seriously wrong with them, or they're in the wrong part of town, or something like that,' she said. 'And I've marked with a tick a few that I think might appeal to you, accepting that I haven't actually seen any of them. Now then, there are any number of ways we can go about it. You can telephone the real estate people yourself, and make arrangements to view apartments with them direct. Or I can make the arrangements for you. Or I can make the arrangements, and also come with you. Unless you feel strongly about it, I would recommend that I come with you. That's because I can ask questions that wouldn't occur to you, like, how much do the utilities cost each month, and is there free gas, and is there a service charge? Things like that. How many references do you need, and do you have to be interviewed by a committee? And, of course, I guess I'll have a better idea than you will of whether or not the rent that they're asking is reasonable. Not,' she added, slightly acidly, 'that I think you care about that too much.' 'That's kind of you, sweetheart,' I said, ignoring the last remark. 'I'd love you to come with me, and I shall value your advice, of course.'

Over the next few days, we saw perhaps a dozen apartments. By London standards, they were all exquisite. I was, after all, going for fairly near the top of the rental market. Property values in New York in 1976 were, surprisingly, pretty close to rock bottom. We saw apartments in all the best areas, but I finally fell in love with one in Sutton Place South. It was a delightfully old-fashioned, pre-war apartment block. It was all about status and money, and it was distinctly Jewish, as opposed to some of the blocks we saw, which were distinctly WASP. New York, everyone tells me, has more Jewish people living in it than does the whole of Israel. There are times when one can believe that statement. This was one of them. I had to be interviewed by a committee of existing tenants, all of whom were Jewish. I had to give two bankers' references, two attorneys' references, and a personal reference from someone whose reference actually meant something. Fred's reference, for example, wouldn't have been any use at all. Money wasn't everything. Not in this block. The apartment was actually for sale, and had been for over a year. It was on offer for $30,000. For a one-bedroom apartment in a luxury block in one of the best addresses in Manhattan, it was dirt cheap. My company would have given me a mortgage, but at that stage of my career in New York, I didn't want to think about mortgages.

In the end, I lived in that apartment for six years. Seven years from the day I moved in, my landlord sold it for a million and a half dollars. But that's life. Failing any interest from anyone wanting to buy it back then, the owners were offering it for rent. It was $1200 a month, inclusive of service charge and gas. 'Take it,' said Eileen. 'It's cheap.' I took it. It came fully furnished, with decent, good quality antique furniture, and it was complete with linen, china, glass, and cooking utensils. It had a large sitting/dining room, a decent-sized bedroom, with *en suite* bathroom complete with both bath and shower, a balcony overlooking Roosevelt Island and the East River beyond Roosevelt Drive, a big, fully-fitted kitchen, and a guest washroom with lavatory and washbasin. It even had TV.

All I had to do was to get Home Box Office to come in and connect me up to their cable. It's not possible to get a TV picture in New York without cable, due to interference from the myriad skyscrapers. (Cable provided fifty-two different TV stations in those days.)

I moved in with one large suitcase, five backgammon boards, and my teddy bear, Henry. He sat on the marble mantelpiece, master of all he surveyed. There wasn't a fireplace, but that didn't seem important. There was central heating, air-conditioning, constant hot water, hot and cold running doormen and lift attendants, and a plethora of in-house repairmen. Whatever kind of a problem you might have, be it an electrical or a plumbing problem, or something needing a carpenter or an engineer, the solution came free, courtesy of the block. That's what the service charge was for. Fred's attorneys in New York provided – or rather, put me in touch with – the requisite two bankers, one other attorney, and a personal reference, all of which the apartment committee found acceptable. When they asked me what I did for a living, I simply said that I was in publishing, running a British publishing company in New York. They didn't, thank God, ask for any details of what I was actually publishing. I'm certain that, had they known, I would never have been allowed to rent the apartment, although later I believe that everyone in the block knew what I was doing. But by then it was never a problem.

I quickly felt very much at home, and I became a part of my local neighbourhood within weeks, something that I have never done in Hampstead in twenty-seven years. I very quickly came to know my butcher, my greengrocer, my fishmonger, my shoe repairer, my dry cleaner, my liquor store owner, and my neighbourhood bar and restaurant managers – and all their staff – by their first names. I suppose it's true to say that I stood out among my neighbours because of my accent, but even so, it was a much more friendly approach to commercial life than I had ever come across before or have encountered since. I loved it.

It was a joy to learn about New York shops and shopping. Everyone collects and delivers. The first day I took something to the cleaners, the guy behind the counter said, 'Do you want the regular or the de luxe service?' 'What's the difference?' I asked him. 'Oh,' he said. 'The de luxe service means I deliver it back to you later on this morning. The regular service, you collect it from me this afternoon.' Back home in Hampstead, you took it in one day, picked it up a week later. The liquor store, when you rang with your order, delivered it fifteen minutes later. The only differences between New York liquor stores and Hampstead off licences – apart from the instant delivery – is that you have to pay cash in New York. You may not, legally, buy booze on credit. No credit cards. No cheques. Only cash.

The apartment block had an amazing foyer. It was the size of the whole block, taking in what were in fact three separate wings on the ground floor level. There was an enormous fountain, a huge reception desk, six regular doormen day and night, and six lifts – sorry, elevators – to take you to the wing and floor of your choice. I was introduced by the head doorman to a delightful woman called Rose, who, for all the time that I lived there, did my daily cleaning, and all my laundry, which she serviced in the laundry room in the basement. It was fully equipped – at no extra cost to me – with washing and drying machines, ironing boards and irons. To my intense pleasure, we still exchange Christmas cards to this day.

Jamaican in origin, Rose had originally emigrated from Kingston, Jamaica, to London, where she married a New York black from Harlem. He had eventually returned to New York, taking her and their son with him, where he had very soon abandoned them both. When I met her, she was working all the hours God sent, putting her boy through college. Whenever I went back to London, whether it was on a business trip or on holiday, she always asked me to bring her back tins of Crosse & Blackwell's baked beans. So superior, she always said, to the Heinz baked beans that she could purchase in New York. A strange taste, I always thought, for a Jamaican lady. But why not?

Something that strangers often notice when they start to live in New York is the high rate of unemployment amongst blacks. In my early days there it was running at forty per cent of the population of Harlem, as against roughly ten per cent of the rest of the population of New York. Hence the high crime rate there, much of it revolving around the drugs trade.

One nice thing about living in Sutton Place that I discovered immediately was that I could walk to the office. It was just three blocks. Eileen helped me to move in. It was mostly a matter of a couple of suitcases of clothes, and then stocking up with food, drink and household goodies. Another great joy was discovering that the block seemed to be free of that bane of New York apartment life, the common cockroach. New York's cockroaches are famous for their virtual indestructibility. They are as big as any you are likely to see anywhere in the world, and are simply an appalling fact of life, even in the most expensive, most exclusive apartment blocks. God knows where they come from. Despite never seeing one in my stay in Sutton Place, the apartment was sprayed regularly twice a week to make sure that they were kept at bay. I remember, too, being amused about the time that it took to install telephones in my new apartment. All Manhattan telephones are the responsibility of the New York Telephone Company. When I called to order a phone, the man I spoke to was extremely apologetic. 'I'm afraid we're rather behind right now,' he told me. 'We've got something of a backlog.' Tell me about it, I thought, having recently left London behind me, where the GPO were taking around six months to install a new telephone. 'What's your address?' he asked. I told him. 'I'm awfully sorry,' he said, 'But there's no way I can get an installation engineer to you until about midday tomorrow.' Now that's American service for you. It also seemed strange to me then that it was cheaper for me to have three telephones in my apartment (one in the sitting room, one in the bedroom, and one, would you believe, in the kitchen?) than two. The New York Telephone Company's research told them that the more telephones a person had, the more calls they would make. It's as simple as that.

Eileen really was a great help, and by the end of the week, I was pretty much settled in. I took her out to supper at the Four Seasons as a big thank-you for all her hard work, which I know she appreciated, but I declined her offer to accompany me to bed in the new apartment, under the pretext of being too tired to do her justice. She wasn't greatly pleased, and I think she thought that I had someone else lined up for that evening, which I didn't. But I *had* made up my mind that the lovely Katrina would be the first young lady to grace my bed in Sutton Place. I'd called her again earlier in the week, and we had decided to spend the day together on Sunday, with Katrina arriving at around eleven thirty in the morning. We'd also decided to cancel our reservations at Oh Ho So and have lunch at my neighbourhood restaurant instead. I spent the Saturday putting the finishing touches to this and that, buying some up-to-date magazines, buying and arranging flowers, checking that I had a full range of drinks and mixers, putting champagne in the fridge, and, finally, I decided that everything was about ready. On Sunday morning I was up early. I put clean sheets on the bed, and then took a cab over to Zabar's, New York's finest delicatessen, at 2245 Broadway, where I bought lox (American smoked salmon), freshly baked bagels and cream cheese, all three an essential staple on New York Sunday mornings. I hadn't yet ordered newspapers to be delivered to the apartment, so I also bought the *New York Sunday Times*, a gargantuan publication, in all its many sections.

The doorman rang through to ask me if I was expecting Katrina, and, having confirmed that I was, I went out to the elevator to greet her. I was on the fourteenth floor of the block, and there were six apartments on my wing, all the same size as mine. The apartments got larger the higher you went in the building, with five-bedroom penthouses on the twentieth floor, studio apartments on the ground floor, and other variations in between. Mine was a one-bedroom apartment. The elevator arrived, the doors opened, and Katrina emerged. She looked absolutely ravishing. She wore a flowery-patterned, blue and white summer dress of some thin, gauzy material, which showed off her trim figure to perfection. Her long, exquisite legs were bare, and she wore high-heeled, navy-blue sandals with ankle straps. She had a wispy, dark blue scarf tied around her neck, and her gorgeous, long blonde hair hung loosely around her shoulders. She was carrying a tiny dark blue leather handbag. She looked like something out a picture by Monet.

'Darlink,' she said, and ran towards me. I grabbed her, and she lifted her legs up as I swung her around in my arms. It was as if we had known each other for ever, and had then suddenly met again after having been parted for a long time. I put her down, and she gave me a big kiss. 'What a smart address,' she said. 'Now show me your lovely new apartment.' I had told her that I had been sharing with Fred, until my recent move. We went into the apartment, and as she stood against the sunlight that was streaming in through the windows, it became blatantly obvious that she was wearing neither bra nor underskirt. I could see her small, pert breasts, tipped by tiny, erect nipples, standing out plainly against the light. Nothing, in fact, under her dress, bar the tiniest panties. I wondered how she had escaped being raped on the way over. She lived, she had told me, in an old apartment on the Upper West Side, which she shared with three other girls from the ballet.

'Are you very rich, Tony darlink?' Katrina asked me, as she looked around the place. 'They tell me that Sutton Place is probably the most expensive address in New York. How much does it cost you to live here?' Her curiosity was so innocent, I couldn't possibly take offence at her questions. I laughed, and put an arm around her. 'Come and have a look around,' I said. 'No, I'm not rich. I earn good money, but I'm not what you would call rich. Although I hope to be, one day. As to how much does it cost me to live here, the honest answer is that it doesn't cost me anything, because my company picks up all the bills. The rent, the utilities, the telephone bill, and so on. So this is all free, if you care to look at it that way.' I steered her around the place on a short, guided tour.

Katrina stopped, and swung around to face me. '*Free*, darlink?' she said. 'My God, all this is *free!* That makes you as rich as Croesus! Do you know how much I earn?' 'No, sweetheart,' I said. 'I haven't the faintest idea. Tell me.' 'Well, no,' she said. 'I wouldn't want to embarrass you. Except to tell you that when I have paid my share of the rent, here in New York, I have no money left for food. None at all. That's why I work at the restaurant. I make a little money there, and tips, which helps me with clothes, and make-up, and travel. That sort of thing. And I can beg scraps of food from the kitchen. Left-overs. Otherwise, as far as eating goes, it is often only what I can scrounge. Like today. Where is the food, darlink? I am starving. *Starving!*' 'Sit down, sweetheart,' I said, and as she did so, I went into the kitchen and soon brought back a tray with the lox, cream cheese, bagels, and butter.

'My God, darlink!' Katrina cried, and almost knocked me down getting at the tray, snatching a bagel, and thrusting it into her mouth, followed by a spoonful of cream cheese, and a large piece of lox. 'Mmmmm,' she breathed through her full mouth, chomping away like a starving animal. Perhaps that was what she was. Literally. A starving animal. I tried hard, but I couldn't actually remember when I was last seriously hungry, with no chance of obtaining food, or sustenance of any kind. I served up champagne, without any of the attendant fuss and ceremony that people who drank it less frequently than I often use, and I was delighted to notice that she accepted it in the same vein, as if there was no other way to serve a drink on a Sunday morning.

When I could drag Katrina away from the lox and its accompanying goodies, we went off to lunch at my neighbourhood restaurant, where they served – like most neighbourhood restaurants on a Sunday – my favourite corned beef hash, with hash brown potatoes. A magical, truly New York dish of such delicacy, the likes of which you are unlikely to be offered – properly made – anywhere else in the world. People tell me that I exaggerate the culinary importance of corned beef hash, but it is, for my money, a dish worthy of kings. Utterly without parallel. Katrina chose to have the same as me, and we sat there in silence, the two of us munching away steadily, until our plates were clean. Katrina managed some apple pie and cream, and then some cheese, before announcing that, since her period had started – and finished – earlier than she'd anticipated, it was probably time to go back to the apartment and fuck. She was obviously amused by my expression, as she announced this fact to the restaurant customers in general.

'You look shocked, darlink,' she said. 'Have I upset you? Do you not wish to fuck me? In Russia, all young girls are brought up to fuck. We are taught that it is our duty. Soon, it becomes much more than duty. It becomes a pleasure. At first, when I began at ballet class, I was, what? Eight years old. By the time I was ten, I had learned to hate the old harridan who taught us little girls in class. She was a, how do you say it in English? A ditch? No, no. Sorry. A dyke. That's it. A dyke. She liked me, especially.' Katrina looked deeply into my eyes with those startlingly blue eyes of her own. 'Am I embarrassing you, darlink?' she asked, seemingly completely unaware of the fact that the entire restaurant was hanging onto her every word. She went on. 'When I was about sixteen, the old harridan told us that some very high up, very important Party members were coming to our neighbourhood for a meeting, and that we young girls were to be offered to them for their pleasure at some stage of the evening. We were taken to the hotel where the meeting was taking place, and we were kept waiting for what seemed like hours, in a room in the basement. Then the harridan came and fetched us, and took us up to the vast dining room, where there were about twenty or so old men, all very drunk.

'There were fifteen of us girls, and when we got up there, the old woman made us take all our clothes off. We were all grabbed by one or another of the old men, and some of us were raped, and some of us were made to suck them off, and others were encouraged to masturbate them. All in all, we each one of us had everything done to us – including anal rape – and we all had to do everything to the men. We were there until the small hours, by which time most of us were bleeding. After that, we were offered to all and any Party members using the hotel near which our ballet school was situated, every time there was any kind of an overnight meeting. So it was physically demanding ballet training all day, every day, and rape and sodomy almost every night. Many of the teenage girls became pregnant, and we were taken to have abortions. I myself have had four. Birth control is not taught in Russia. And then things began to improve a little, in that, as we got slightly older – you know, nineteen, twenty – we began to lose our appeal to the old men, who only want the really young girls, and we were downgraded to servicing athletes.

'For us, of course, it was an improvement. Not a great improvement, for there is no one as arrogant as a Russian athlete, but an improvement of sorts. Every Russian athlete thinks he's God. There is no love, or gentleness, or kindness about any of them. They just like to fuck young girls. But they were marginally more attractive than the old drunks. To start off with, they were at least sober. They could all get an erection. And how! So we didn't have to spend hours trying to get them into a state where they might, just possibly, reach ejaculation. They fucked like, what do you English say? Stoats. That's it. Like stoats.

'The down side, for me, was the women athletes. Did you know that many of the Russian women athletes are lesbians? No? And we had to service them too, when required. But at least the women athletes were young, fit, and clean. And some of them were actually quite kind. They were gentle with us. They loved to kiss and be kissed. Mouths, cunts. Both. And they would do it to us, whether we wanted them to do it to us or not. I think that a large part of me, simply from repeated lesbian activity, is now seriously lesbian, although if you were to ask me which I prefer, it is always men. Never women. Not voluntarily.' Katrina paused.

The diners in the restaurant paused too, waiting breathlessly for her to continue. 'Now that we are grown up,' she continued, 'most of us in the chorus prefer men. But there are still a couple of girls who like to make love with each other. They are continually touching each other in rehearsals. You know the sort of thing? Putting their arms around each others' waists, holding hands. That sort of thing. Kissing, sometimes. Little quick, furtive kisses. They are such pretty girls that I must admit that sometimes I think it looks rather nice, seeing the two of them together. I once went into their room when they were doing it to each other, you know, lying there naked, both with their legs open, eating each other. Isn't that what Americans call oral love? Eating each other?'

I didn't say anything. I just shrugged. I was, I admit, embarrassed. Not by the conversation, but by the audience. 'But they didn't stop what they were doing,' Katrina continued. 'They went on as if nothing had happened. I was fascinated, and I just stood there, watching, for a few moments. It made me all wet. It was quite involuntary. I wasn't wanting to join in, or anything like that, but suddenly my panties were all wet. It was almost as if I had peed myself.'

She laughed, a merry tinkling little laugh. My cock stiffened at the thought of her wet panties. 'And then I just went out, and shut the door quietly behind me. But they had known I was there. Perhaps *they* wanted *me* to join in. I went back to my room to change my panties, and I was standing there with these wet panties in my hand when I realized that I could smell the scent of the dampness, and I suddenly felt very sexy, and I had to play with myself – you know, masturbate – and I put my hand down there, and rubbed myself until I came. Do *you* masturbate, Tony?' She paused again, obviously expecting an answer to her question. I looked around at the other people in the restaurant. They too, appeared to be waiting to hear whether or not I masturbated. Or whether or not I would admit to it. I looked at Katrina. She had finished eating.

'Let's go, sweetheart,' I said, waving at the waitress for the check. 'We can continue this conversation back at the apartment.' Katrina looked a little surprised, but she didn't argue. 'Sure,' she said, pushing back her chair, and standing up. The waitress brought the check, and I paid it. I could almost *feel* the disappointment from the other diners as we left. I personally felt considerably relieved, once we were outside once more. I took her hand in mine. 'To answer your question, yes,' I said. 'I masturbate, sometimes. I think everybody does.' 'Do you like girls to do it for you, Tony? she asked. 'I'm very good at it. I like to do it. Would you like me to do it for you? I like to suck cock too. Do you like that?'

This girl was too much. Her transparently straightforward honesty was beginning to tell on me. I was having difficulty walking without bending over to relieve the pressure in my now almost rigid cock. It was time for a little straightforward honesty from me. 'Yes, sweetheart,' I said. 'I love all those things, and I love having all those things done to me. I love sex of all kinds. But I'm getting such an erection thinking about you doing them to me that I soon will have to walk on all fours. Or you'll have to carry me. Can we change the subject, at least until we get back to the apartment?' Katrina looked at me, and then she stretched out a hand and felt my erection through the material of my trousers. She laughed. Really laughed. 'How lovely, darlink,' she chortled. 'You've got the hots for me. Keep it. Don't lose it. Don't let it go away.' And she laughed again. 'Let's hurry, darlink,' she said. 'I know just where you can put that.' She practically doubled over with laughter at her joke. Fortunately I *did* lose sufficient of my erection for it not to be noticed by the doormen when we got back to the apartment block. Katrina was chuckling and giggling all the way back, and all the way up in the elevator.

As we got inside the door she grasped my cock through my trousers again, and then said 'But it's gone, darlink. Never mind. Katrina will find it for you again.' She led the way into the bedroom, and undressed with a seeming completely natural nonchalance which I assumed came from years of dressing and undressing in front of the other girls with whom she lived and worked. Her body was so beautiful, it almost defied description. It will forever be the most beautiful body that I have ever seen. It was slim, and totally fit. Not exactly muscular. Lithe describes it better. Her breasts were as pert as their outline had portended, earlier. Her nipples also were small, but prettily defined, upon roseate areolae. Her legs were long and slender, and beautifully shaped, with clearly defined thighs, calves and ankles. She had pretty toes, too.

Her buttocks were firm, the skin stretched tautly across her well-defined muscles. She wasn't shaved, as I had wished her in my fantasy, but her pubic hair was blonde, light and fluffy, around well defined, pouting, pink outer labia. I could see a trickle of moisture issuing from between them. I too undressed in what must have been record time, and my erection bloomed once more, rapidly. 'Oh, darlink,' said Katrina, coming over to where I stood. 'What a lovely big cock. Russian girls love big cocks.' She took hold of it in a way that I can only describe, rather self-consciously, as admiringly. 'Just wait until I tell the girls in the chorus about this,' she said. 'They'll all be round here, knocking on your door. Will you like that?' I laughed. 'One at a time is fine with me,' I said. 'Let's start with you.'

I put my arms around her and hugged her closely to me. Somehow her hand found my cock, which she squeezed, gently, to its intense pleasure, whilst I kissed her. Her mouth tasted of cherries. Her tongue was sweet and fresh, and it explored my mouth, hungrily. I guided her over to the bed, and laid her down carefully on her back. She spread her legs as she lay there, and I put down a hand between them, feeling her wet lips open up in welcome to my fingers. I slid two inside her, and felt her wet, lubricated warmth. She felt elastic, her muscles gripping my fingers, and I couldn't wait to replace them with my cock. The hell with foreplay, I thought. I wanted to fuck her. In any case, her wetness signalled that she was more than ready to be fucked. I withdrew my fingers, and I pulled back sufficiently to guide my rampant prick towards her pretty pussy.

'Yes, darlink,' she sighed. 'Oh, yes. Fuck Katrina now. Please. Now.' I used my fingers to spread her outer lips, and then I put the knob of my cock at the entrance to her inner lips, and pressed forward. My cock felt as if it were being sucked in, and then I was deep inside her, feeling the pulsating of her vaginal muscles as she worked them around me. I began to thrust and delve, working up a steady rhythm, fucking her slowly, deeply, wonderfully. I couldn't remember when I had felt like this before. It was almost like my first fuck. It was intensely pleasurable. I put my head down and sucked a tiny nipple as I fucked. First one, then the other. They were hard, like little baby bullets. Katrina began to talk dirty.

Somewhere, a million miles away, something in my head wondered which of the dirty old men, or dirty young men in her youth – or dirty young women, come to that – had started her off down that particular track. It was one that I was happy to travel myself. I wondered, next, who had started *me* off down that track too, and I couldn't remember. It wasn't important. 'Your huge cock is fucking me,' said Katrina, throatily. 'It's splitting my cunt open. It's making me cry. It's fucking my cunt. You're going to come up my cunt. You're going to spurt hot spunk up my cunt. Oh, God, you're fucking me. I'm coming. I'm coming. I'm coming nowwwwww.' I could feel her cunt spasming as she orgasmed beneath me. I fucked harder, more quickly, as she rose to a peak, and then it was over.

It was a pattern that she repeated almost continuously for the rest of the time that I continued to fuck her. I was in no hurry to ejaculate. I was enjoying myself too much. But finally, inevitably, I felt my ejaculation begin to build, and then, suddenly, it was upon me, and I began to spurt my jism into her in long, sustained spurts, which brought her once more to orgasm, loudly, noisily, and happily. And then, at least for the moment, it was over. Katrina cuddled up to me like a little puppy to its mother. 'Oh, darlink,' she said. 'That was a lovely fuck. I think maybe you have fucked one or two girls before. I change my mind now. I shall not tell the other girls about you. I would never be able to get near you, for other girls lining up for you to fuck them. I shall keep you for myself. You shall only fuck me. Is OK?' 'Is OK, sweetheart,' I said. 'You are very kind. It was good for me too. It was beautiful. It was out of this world. Wonderful. Exquisite. The best ever. I thank you.' We lay there, in each other's arms, and soon we both fell asleep.

I awoke a while later. Looking at my watch, it showed nearly four p.m. I disentangled myself from the still sleeping Katrina, and got up off the bed. I stood there, looking at her. She looked like an angel, her long, blonde hair awry, her eyes closed, her small, perfect breasts standing out from her chest, her flat stomach. I looked lower. My jism was dribbling out of her cunt lips, shining wetly over the pink of her labia, and running in a small stream down her naked thigh. Looking at that small, wrinkle-folded altar to sexual pleasure, I felt my cock stiffening as I stood there, and I was suddenly taken with an insane urge to rape her, hurt her, force my now fully erect cock up her, make her cry.

She stirred as I looked at her, and opened her eyes. She saw my erection immediately. 'Oh, darlink,' she said. 'Are you going to fuck me again? I am ready, now. Right now.' She lay back and spread her legs wide, then reached down and opened up her cunt lips with her fingers. She looked down. 'I am still sticky with your love,' she said, smiling. 'Do you mind? Shall I go and wash it off?' I thought of the delight of seeing that gorgeous body in the shower, water running down those glorious curves. 'Let's both go and have a shower,' I said. 'That might be fun.'

She leapt up off the bed and, taking me by the hand, she took me to the bathroom, which was right next door. She got into the shower, leaving the glass door open, and ran the water until it was at the temperature she wished. 'Come and soap me, darlink,' Katrina cried, over the noise of the spray. She bent down, took her right foot in her right hand, and lifted it up straight, until she was standing on one leg, with the other leg vertical in the air in front of her. She was virtually doing the splits standing up. 'Soap my fanny, darlink,' she said. 'I would like that. Soap it very slowly, please.' I got into the shower with her, picked up the soap, and did as I was asked. I rubbed slowly, enjoying what I was doing, loving the feel of her slippery, fleshy cunt lips beneath my fingers.

After a while, Katrina took the soap out of my hand and, putting her leg back down, she took my cock in both hands and started to soap it. Also very slowly. It grew in size as she massaged it, until it was eventually fully erect. She then eased herself forward and, standing on her toes, she fed my cock into her soapy cunt and began to fuck me, moving her beautiful little ass backwards and forwards, slowly and delicately. 'I'm making your cock dirty again,' she said, biting my earlobe. 'Do you mind?' 'Mind, sweetheart?' I said. 'I love it. You can make my cock dirty any time you like. Feel free.' She began to move faster. 'This is a quick fuck,' she whispered in my ear. 'A quickie. That's what Americans say, isn't it? I'm coming now. Right now. Oooohhhh. Yes. Nowwww.' She wriggled about, humping and bucking as she came, enjoying her orgasm to the full.

'Have you come yet, darlink?' she asked. 'I didn't feel you come.' 'Not yet, sweetheart,' I said. 'But I'm not in any hurry.' As I said it, she pulled away from me, and suddenly my cock was waving freely in the air. But before I could complain, she had knelt down on the floor of the shower and taken my swollen, engorged penis in her mouth. I looked down at her, seeing the water glancing off the top of her blonde head, and watched it bobbing up and down as she sucked me off, quickly and expertly, swallowing my ejaculate as I pumped it down her throat.

She sucked me until I had finished coming, milking me of every last drop, before taking me out of her mouth and standing up again. 'I can see why they say it's rude to talk with your mouth full,' she said, giggling. I patted her bottom in a pretend spank, and wondered, as I did it, whether being spanked or caned had been part of her Russian sexual schooling. She went out of the shower and, grabbing a towel, began to dry herself. I turned off the water, and followed her out. She was rubbing her nipples briskly with the towel. When she had finished, they stood out, obligingly. She saw me looking at them. 'Do you like them, darlink?' she asked. 'I'm afraid they're very small. I'd make them bigger for you, if I knew how.' I crossed over to her, and kissed them, in turn. 'They're beautiful, my darling,' I said. 'I love them exactly as they are.' 'You're sweet,' she said. 'But are you sure you're not saying that just to make me feel better? If you really like big breasts, I can arrange for you to fuck my friend Greta. She's not a ballet dancer. Her tits are too big for that. She'd fall over. But she works in the company offices. Would you like me to arrange that? I could watch you, and play with myself while you fucked her. And then you could fuck me. She and I could take it in turns. And you could fuck her breasts. She tells me that men like to fuck her breasts. You know, she squeezes her breasts together, and they put their cock in between, and she masturbates them with her breasts, and they come all over them. She says they love it.

'It doesn't do anything for her, she says, but they like it so much that she doesn't mind. She's a big country girl. She's got a big, fat cunt too. I've seen it. What do you think?' I laughed at the enthusiasm with which she offered me her friend's sexual involvement, and I wondered what her friend would say if she could hear Katrina offering her body to me. 'Right now, sweetheart,' I said, 'I am more than satisfied with you. I think you're beautiful, and I love your breasts. I do not need your big-breasted friend's mammary assistance. I enjoy our sex together, and I don't feel the need for anyone else. For whatever reason. But perhaps another time. I'm all for fun, and sex, and excitement, and if your friend would like to join us one day, that would perhaps be amusing for all three of us. But for now, I am happy. OK?' She grinned back at me.

'Of course is OK, darlink,' she said. 'That is good. But, you know, all Russian girls like to fuck. And suck. And be fucked, and be sucked. And all kinds of naughty things. And, you know, now that we are not in Russia, and we do not have to fuck old men, or be forced to fuck anyone at a moment's notice, now that we can choose who we fuck, and when we fuck them, I have to tell you somethink.' 'What's that, my darling?' I asked. 'We probably fuck even more now than we did then.' She giggled. 'That's very naughty, isn't it?' 'Yes,' I said. 'Naughty, but nice.' By this time we were both dry, and I took Katrina by the hand and led her back into the bedroom. She lay on the bed on her back, and spread her legs. 'Here I am, darlink,' she said. 'I am all yours. Do anythink to me that you would like. Or tell me what you would like me to do to you. My body is yours to play with. To amuse yourself with. Take me, any way you like.'

I looked at her, and wondered how any man could be so fortunate. Here was this beautiful young girl, with her long, blonde hair, her startlingly blue eyes, her perfect skin, her exquisitely formed breasts, her wispy blonde pubic hair, and her pretty little pink-lipped pussy, with her gorgeous, slim hips, her rounded bottom, and her long, long legs spread wide, and she was behaving like a whore. "Fuck me any way you want," was what she was saying to me. I was tempted to stand there and simply jack off, just looking at her, and thinking about some of the things that I could do to her. Or have her do to me.

But what I actually did was lie down on the bed beside her, and put an arm around her beautiful body, and pull her close to me. She put her arms about me too, and then I began to kiss her, gently, and tentatively, and my kiss was returned in similar loving fashion. But slowly, and without rushing, we both seemed to mentally gather momentum, and our kisses gradually changed from loving to lascivious, from tender passion to lewd sexual excitement. My cock became erect and, putting a hand down between Katrina's legs, I could feel that her pussy lips were wet with sexual desire. I took my arms from about her and, moving down her body, I used my hands to spread her legs even more widely, placing myself so that my mouth was positioned immediately over her sex.

I looked at it closely, fascinated, as I have always been, by the fact that every woman in the world has her own, totally unique, individual pussy. Each is different as its owner's fingerprints. To some men, I'm told, cunts are but holes that they stick their dicks in and – to all intents and purposes – masturbate in. To me, pussies are beautiful in exactly the same way that other parts of the body are thought to be beautiful. As beautiful as breasts, or hands, or faces, or feet. Yes, you're right, of course. Occasionally, one comes across a face that, at best, can only be described as plain. Or breasts that proclaim their years of good service. Feet that have seen better days. Hands that are careworn. But usually, these fractionally less than perfect parts of the body belong to someone of great character, whose inner peace, or experience, or worldliness, outshines all else. And as is the way with bodies, younger pussies are, usually, prettier than older pussies, just as young cocks are physically more attractive than old ones. That's life.

Katrina's little pussy was very neat. Her pale pink outer labia were minimal, and closed tightly over the entrance to her inner lips, which were also small by comparison with those of many other women. When both sets of lips were held open, her inner vagina was smoothly wet and shining, blue-veined beneath the slippery outer skin, and smelling sweetly of her fresh, girlish secretions. Her inner lips were a slightly darker colour than the palest pink of her outer lips, but only fractionally. Both sets of lips were more like well-formed little ridges, than the clearly defined, often loosely hanging lips that can sometimes be seen. And right now, both sets were swollen with passion, inflated with sexual desire, the same emotion that was causing her to produce the freely flowing, erotically scented clear liquid that was oozing copiously from out of her as I examined her so closely.

I bent down and licked the length of her outer lips, slowly, carefully, lovingly, enjoying the taste of her, wallowing in the sensual feel of her warm wet flesh beneath my lips. She wriggled beneath me as I did so, pressing her pubic up against my mouth, so that she might increase the pressure of my lips and tongue upon her cunt. 'That's nice,' she murmured, throatily, huskily.

'I like it. All Russian girls like men who kiss pussy.' Good, I thought to myself, but I was too involved in what I was doing to reply to her. In any case, I don't think that she was expecting me to say anything. Not right then. I lifted my mouth up, for a moment, and slipped a finger down inside her wetness, searching for her clitoris. I quickly found it, standing to attention as it was, a well-drilled, experienced little soldier. She used her muscles to suck my finger down, squeezing it firmly but delicately, and I knew now what it was that felt so deliciously good for my cock whilst I was fucking her. Her vaginal muscles were as well trained as were the muscles of any and every kind of Russian athlete. Somehow, until now, I'd never thought of a seriously trained sexual athlete. Male or female. But that, undoubtedly, was what Katrina was. Lucky me!

The close proximity of aroused female sexual organs has only ever had but one effect on me: that of encouraging a rapid, and raging, erection. It's one of the reasons I enjoy sucking pussy. The sight, the taste, the aroma, sends the blood coursing into my penis in quantities that threaten its demise by simple explosion, if not used quickly and effectively. It is something that I have always found useful, for it matters not how much I have had to drink, nor how tired I might be, nor – in different circumstances – how many times I have recently performed. I can always rely on raising the finest of erections, provided that I can see, suck, and scent prime pussy.

I had by now reached, with Katrina, the point of no return, and it was becoming increasingly necessary to put Percy to work. I pondered – still paying lip service to her parts – the question of how best to accept her invitation to do anything to her that I wished. Or vice versa. I ran through a quick mental list. I had already fucked her, and been fellated by her. I had performed cunnilingus upon her. Which didn't leave an awful lot, really. I would be more than happy to enjoy any of those things again. I could always ask her to give me one off the wrist, but that seemed something of a waste at this stage in our relationship. Her tits were too small, as she had said herself, for a French necklace, but that was not, in any case, something that was high – in terms of priority – on my list of sexual activity. So what did that leave. Ah, yes. Of course it did. Anal sex. Anal rape. I tucked my hands beneath her as I continued to suck and tongue her, and felt those beautiful, slim, muscular buttocks, squeezing them in my hands as my cock expanded even further at the very thought of what I was going to do. I realized that I had already taken the decision.

I raised my head, and looked up at Katrina. It is a lovely viewpoint from which to look at a woman, as I'm sure you know. Along her flat stomach, up over her breasts, surmounted, as they should be, by erect nipples, to her relaxed face, lying there, as she is, enjoying what you have been doing to her pussy. Katrina lifted her head and looked down at me. 'That was very beautiful, Tony,' she said. 'Thank you. Are you goink to fuck me now, darlink?' 'Yes, sweetheart,' I said. 'If it's all right with you, I'm going to fuck you up your bottom. Is that OK?' 'Oh,' she said. 'How lovely. 'Yes, is OK. I like to be fucked in the ass. All Russian girls like it in the ass. Is good. Do you have lubricant? Is better with lubricant. Is not nice dry. Butter will do. Anything greasy.' 'Don't worry about it,' I said, and I went off to the bathroom to find the essential KY jelly that I always kept handy. Just in case.

When I got back to the bedroom, Katrina had turned over onto her stomach, and she was lying there, her beauteous, slim, muscled, trim bottom raised slightly. As I approached with the tube of KY, she reached behind her with both hands, and pulled her buttocks apart, revealing her tiny, puckered, pinky-brown little bumhole in all its sensual, cock-engorging glory. It was surrounded by pale blonde, fluffy anal hair that matched the hair around her pussy. 'Grease it well, darlink,' she said. 'It will repay you tenfold to make sure that I am well greased. Push the lubricant as far down as you can reach with your finger. And grease your cock well too, please.' She held her buttocks pulled as far apart as she could stretch them, exposing her anus to the seemingly welcome invasion of my finger, which now carried a generous dollop of lubricant. Having pushed that as far down her anal passage as I could reach, I took another dollop and spread it generously all over the full length of my swollen prick. And then I was ready. I slipped quickly into the bathroom to wash the grease off my fingers. When I got back, Katrina was kneeling on the bed on all fours, her legs well apart, her gorgeous buttocks facing me as I entered the room, her puckered anus winking at me.

'Here I am, darlink,' she said. 'Now you are going to fuck your first Russian girl in the ass. I'm ready for you. Please treat me gently, until you are properly inside me. Feed your cock into me slowly.' I knelt behind her, and placed the purple, shining knob of my cock against her tightly closed anus. I then took hold of her around her firm thighs, and at the same time I pulled her towards me, and pressed my cock, very carefully, against the forbidden entrance. To my surprise, it opened without any trouble, and my rampant cock slid inside, up to its full length.

It might have allowed me in easily, but Katrina's bumhole was exquisitely tight, and it gripped my cock enticingly, seductively. I began to move slowly, and Katrina said 'Oh, that's good. So good. I like it.' I took this as an indication of her approval, and began to fuck her properly, quickly building up to a rhythm which gave me intense pleasure as my cock thrust in and out of her asshole. Nothing that felt as good as that felt, or that gripped my cock as tightly as that did, was going to last for very long, and it seemed only a matter of moments before I was spurting my ejaculate up inside her. 'Aaaah,' moaned Katrina, breathing hard. 'Aaaah,' I groaned, as I came. Ecstatically. Torrentially. Gratefully. I kept at it until I was spent, after which I withdrew. I went into the bathroom to clean up, after which I went back to the bed and lay down, and fell asleep.

When I awoke it was nearly seven. Katrina was still asleep, snoring gently, her mouth open, her long, blonde hair all about her face. She looked like an angel. As I looked at her, she woke up, saw me looking at her, and smiled at me. 'Hello, darlink,' she said. 'What time is it?' I told her. 'What do you want to do, sweetheart?' I asked her. 'Are you hungry? Do you want to have a drink here, and then we can go out and find somewhere to eat?' 'What is the alternative?' she asked.

I thought for a moment. 'I could knock up something here,' I said. And then we could watch television. Or go and catch a movie. Or fuck. Whatever. I'll go look in the fridge, and see what I've got in the way of food.' When I got there, it didn't amount to much. There were eggs, milk, cheese, salad, bread. That was about it. I went back to Katrina. 'I could make us an omelette,' I said. 'A cheese and tomato omelette, with a side salad. Bread and cheese afterwards, if we're still hungry. Good wine. Nothing exotic. But I make a decent omelette.' 'Done,' she said. 'Drinks, omelettes, side salad, television, and bed. How does that sound? Oh,' she said, putting her hand to her mouth, as if embarrassed. 'What's the matter?' I asked. She looked at me. 'I don't know whether you want me to stay the night,' she said. 'I'm so sorry. I didn't mean to be rude. Just for a moment, there, I assumed that you would want me to stay with you overnight.' 'For a moment there,' I said, 'you assumed exactly right. I *do* want you to stay overnight. How about some champagne?' She jumped up off the bed and came over and gave me a big kiss and an even bigger hug. 'You are such a darlink,' she said. 'I think I love you.'

We drank our champagne, and Katrina watched me put together the omelette and salad. When it was ready, we ate our meal in the kitchen, accompanied by a second bottle of champagne, chattering away like an old married couple. Katrina told me about her life in the chorus of her ballet company, which sounded like a combination of excruciatingly painful hard work and utterly dedicated sex. Russian girls, it would seem – or, at least, *these*

Russian girls – were completely amoral, due largely (and in fact unsurprisingly) to their use at an early stage in their young lives as free prostitutes for elderly Party members and successful athletes of both sexes. These activities had ceased with their freedom to work in the United States, but the enforced sexual habits and tastes of their youth stayed with them. One fact came out of that conversation which, on reflection, I found rather surprising.

It was that, although these young ballet dancers were paid so little for their dedicated dancing – so little that all of them, like Katrina, had other, part-time jobs – not one of them had ever considered selling their considerable sexual charms commercially. I reconsidered my statement that they were totally amoral, and mentally withdrew it. After supper, we watched television for a little while, and then took ourselves off to bed, where we made gentle, caring love, before falling contentedly asleep.

I dropped Katrina off at her apartment on my way to the office the following morning. On the way figuratively speaking, of course. I was three blocks from the office. She lived way over on the Upper West Side. I had settled down to go through my mail with Eileen – who seemed in good spirits – when Fred popped his head around the door. 'Can you spare me ten minutes, Tony?' he asked. 'No hurry. When you're ready.' 'Of course, Fred,' I said. 'I'll be with you in a moment.' I finished what I was doing, and asked Eileen to hang on. I didn't think I'd be long.

'Good weekend?' asked Fred, when I got to his office. He didn't know about my Sunday arrangements with Katrina. 'Not bad, thanks,' I said. 'How about yours?' It didn't always do to tell Fred everything. 'Oh, OK,' he said. 'I went out to Atlantic City, played the casinos. A little roulette, a bit of blackjack. You know the sort of thing. Good fun.' 'Did you win?' I asked. He hesitated. 'Er . . . I guess I broke about even,' he said. That probably meant that he had lost. Probably heavily. When he was drunk, or high, or both, he tended to throw money away. But what the hell. He could afford it. Add to that the cost of the limo to take him out to Atlantic City, the suite in the best hotel in which he almost certainly stayed, and the expense of ladies – amateur or professional, they both tended to be expensive in Fred's life – and he'd probably spent quite a few thousand dollars. Oh, well, I thought. It's only money. His money. 'I've been thinking, and I've had an idea,' he said. 'Tell me what you think of it. Now that *Tiptop* has been running out here for as long as it has, I think we need to expand its horizons a bit. You know, keep ahead of the competition. We cover sexual happenings in the States pretty well, and of course our coverage of London, and through London, Europe, is good too. But there's an awful lot of sexual things happening in other places around the world that we don't touch. The Far East, for example. We haven't got anyone out there. Nor has anybody else, I hasten to add,' he said. 'But it's vital to keep ahead of them. I think that, for a start, we should produce a Far East issue, if only to see how it goes. What do you think.'

I didn't actually need time to think, because what Fred had said made complete sense to me. 'It's a terrific idea,' I said. 'When you think of what is going on in Thailand, in Hong Kong, in Manila in the Philippines, all around there, it's got to be a doddle to find enough terrific stuff to fill an issue. More.' Fred looked at me. 'I had in mind more than one issue, really,' he said. 'Not all at once, though. Perhaps every third issue. Maybe every fourth. Something like that. Depending a bit on how the first one went. But I thought Hong Kong would be a good place to start. They've been selling sex there for centuries. There are brothels, sex shows, a street full of transvestites that apparently look like some of the most beautiful women in the world, God knows what.

'You name it, if it's sexual, they'll sell it to you. At a price, of course. Not like India, where in some of the busier ports they keep women in cages, and sell them to sailors for five rupees a go. Or is it annas? But it's not the cheap end we're after, is it? *Tiptop* readers want their sex at the top end of the market. And, of course, *Tiptop* readers don't pay for it anyway. They get theirs for free. They just like to read about how other people have to pay for it! Am I right?' he laughed. 'Anyway, I'm glad you agree in principle, because I thought I'd send you out there to bring it all back. What do you say?'

Now that *did* surprise me. I had thought that it was a genuinely good idea, but I had also thought that Fred saw it as an opportunity to get away himself from New York for a couple of months and swan about the better hotels in the Far East, getting a few sexy features together and himself well laid. Not that he wasn't good at getting features together. He was. Always providing that he didn't have to write them himself. But then, the world is full of hungry freelance journalists. I know. I used to be one. But it hadn't occurred to me for a moment that he was thinking of sending me to Hong Kong. 'Fantastic, Fred,' I said. 'I can't think of anything I'd rather do. When shall I go?'

'As soon as you can arrange it,' he said. 'I can give you a couple of names out there that might be useful, but basically you'll be on your own. Eileen, of course, will set up the travel for you. Stay at the best hotels. Travel Club. It's important in that part of the world to show that money is no object. Take plenty of cash with you. Have you got an Amex card?' I said that yes, I had. A gold one. 'Oh, good,' said Tony. 'The best kind.' (Platinum ones hadn't been invented in 1976.) He stood up, and held out a hand. 'Good luck, then,' he said. 'Don't do anything that I wouldn't do. Come and see me any time before you go if you want to talk anything through. But you know that anyway. Tell me if there's anything that I need particularly to keep an eye on while you're away. How long do you think you'll need there, to get an issue together?' 'Will that include girl sets, or not?' I asked. 'Probably not, I thought,' he replied. 'It sounds reasonable, if you say it quickly, but when you think about it, it's not a question of finding the girls to model. I'm sure there are plenty of those. It's finding the right kind of photographer, as you well know. I don't see the point, frankly, of paying to fly out one of ours from here, with all his equipment. I think the answer is to look for Thai or Chinese or Malaysian or Asian model girls here. I can do that while you're getting the facts together. You'll obviously want some local photography, but not girl sets. Does that make sense to you?' I said that yes, it did, and left it at that, and I said that I felt I should be able to do everything necessary in four weeks.

CHAPTER FOUR:
THE HOUSE OF A THOUSAND DREAMS

Three days later I landed at Hong Kong's Kai Tak Airport. It is situated in the centre of the mainland part of the city, and your plane lands on a runway that has been built out into the harbour, skimming down between the skyscrapers of Kowloon so closely that you can see the laundry hanging like flags, on bamboo poles jutting out from every room. It is probably safer than it looks, but that's no help the first time that you experience it. It's on a par with landing in Vienna, Malta, Gibraltar or Singapore. Something to be avoided if you possibly can.

Most of Hong Kong's hotels are in Kowloon, and I had been strongly recommended to book in at the five-star Peninsular, allegedly the doyen of Kowloon hotels for more than fifty years. My stay with them began by my being picked up at the airport by one of their fleet of Rolls Royces. My room on the top floor had a balcony with a great view, looking out across Victoria Harbour to Hong Kong Island beyond. I felt pretty weary after the long journey, but I also felt enthusiastic about what I was there to do. So, after a shower and a change of clothing, I took the Star Ferry across Victoria Harbour to Hong Kong Island, where Ho Ming Chan, a Chinese publisher who Fred knew, had his offices.

It was only a seven-minute journey, but it must be one of the most romantic in the world. If it should bring to mind the Staten Island Ferry, forget it. The Star Ferry is a huge green-and-white vessel, crewed by Chinese sailors in blue, naval-type uniforms. Shrill bells ring just before departure to announce that imminent happening, and the two hundred or so first- and second-class passengers jostle each other to stand by the rails for a good view as the ship weaves in and out of the thousands of small craft that mill about in the harbour.

Hong Kong is a city of contrasts, a mixture of old and new, of wealth and poverty, and nowhere is this more noticeable than in crossing the harbour, with ageing, decrepit junks and houseboats jostling cheek by jowl with multimillion-dollar yachts. But, despite the crowded waterway, the ferry eventually makes it to the other side, tying up at the ferry terminal before repeating its journey back to the mainland. It is also possible to take an ordinary taxi from Kowloon to the island, driving across the causeway, or through one of the many tunnels, but the Star Ferry is probably quicker, and it is certainly cheaper than any of the alternatives. It's certainly more fun.

Outside the terminal I took a rickshaw, showing the driver the address that Eileen had given me the previous day. He grunted something that sounded like *tai-pan*, which I discovered later is simply Cantonese for 'successful businessman'. I sat back against the rickshaw's cushions, and watched the scene around me as we progressed along narrow, dingy streets, dominated here and there by tall skyscrapers that match anything that Manhattan has to offer. There were cars and people everywhere, and my driver had his work cut out as he weaved in and out of the traffic, sweating and cursing as he went along. We went up in the general direction of Victoria Peak, the hill that is the centre of the island, and which is the site of the main residential area – provided that you're rich enough to afford the rents there.

We passed Connaught Road central, Des Voeux Road, and Queen's Road Central in quick succession, turned right into Wellington Street, and eventually drew up outside a small block of offices in a fairly quiet little street just off Hollywood Road. I gave the driver the five Hong Kong dollars that he had earlier indicated would be the fare, and I added an extra dollar as tip. Whilst there was absolutely no sign of pleasure on his face, he must have been satisfied, for he grabbed the handles of his rickshaw, and started off down the street at a positively enthusiastic lope. And for a twenty per cent tip, I should bloody well think so, I thought.

I turned towards the office block, which had a large sign in – to me – totally indecipherable Chinese characters, beneath which, in English, it said 'Ho Ming Chan, International Publishers'. I pushed through the swing doors to find myself in a small reception area. I could see no sign of anyone and, as my eyes became more accustomed to the dim interior, I could see that the place was indeed empty. But even as I stood there, a beautiful young Chinese girl came through a beaded curtain at the rear of the reception desk and, smiling at me, said 'Good afternoon, sir. May I help you?' 'Please,' I said. 'I'm hoping that Mr Ho Ming Chan is in, and that he can spare the time to see me. I've just arrived in Hong Kong from New York. I work with a friend of his, from Tiptop Publications.' I gave her my card. 'Do please sit down, sir,' she said. 'I'll check whether Mr Chan can see you.' She left me with a memorable glimpse of her black silk, embroidered *cheongsam*, which revealed that it was indeed split to her thigh as she turned to go back through the bead curtain. She was wearing silk stockings, for I could see the flash of pale skin at the top of her thigh. I wondered if Chinese girls wore traditional Chinese or modern underwear, and what the difference might be.

Moments later the curtain parted again, and an elderly man of anywhere between sixty and eighty years, dressed entirely in Chinese apparel, came through. I wondered if we were going to have a language problem since, like most Westerners, I speak none of the Chinese dialects. But it was not to be so.

'Good afternoon,' he said, in perfect English. 'I am Mr Chan. Or, to be more accurate, I am Mr Ho, since we Chinese have the quaint habit of putting our last names first. But that is no matter. You are Mr Tony Andrews, and I was expecting you, although I wasn't too sure when. Fred cabled me. How are you? Did you have a good journey?' He didn't wait for an answer, but held out his hand, which I shook. He had a firm grip. 'Do please come through,' he said. 'Shall I lead the way?' He turned and led me back through the bead curtain. I followed him along a narrow passage way, through another bead curtain, and into what was obviously his office. He waved me to a chair in front of his desk. 'First, let me offer you some tea,' he said. 'It is the custom of my country.' He clapped his hands, and said something in Chinese through yet another bead curtain behind him. I couldn't see anything through it, but I could hear the sound of cups clinking. After a moment or two, the young Chinese girl who had first greeted me came through the curtain and set down a silver tray, upon which were two handleless cups with saucers and a small pot of tea. She filled the tiny cups with green China tea, clasped her hands together in front of her, and bowed. I smiled at her, and she turned and vanished through the curtain again as silently as she had appeared.

We drank our tea, and I told Mr Ho in some detail of Fred's idea for a Far Eastern, or Hong Kong, edition of *Tiptop*, and asked for his advice as to the best way to go about my task. He was silent for a while, and I began to realize what people meant when they referred to Orientals as inscrutable. Eventually he looked at me, and said that he would find for me the best person to guide me to the various places that he believed would be what I was looking for. Right at this particular moment, he said, he didn't know who that would be. But if I would tell him where he could contact me, he would, within the next twenty-four hours, put me in touch with the right person. He stood up when he had finished talking and bowed, to indicate, I assumed, that our meeting was at an end. I told him that I was staying at the Peninsular, and gave him the number of my suite. I thanked him, and he said something again in Chinese, at which the young girl came once more through the curtain. 'Let me show you out, Mr Andrews,' she said, and she crossed the room and held the beads of the other curtain aside for me. I bade Mr Ho a final farewell and followed the girl back down the corridor, out through the entrance door, which she held open for me, and into the street. I could remember the way that I had come earlier by rickshaw, and I decided to walk slowly back to the Star Ferry pier. I aimed for the 52-storey Connaught Centre, towering up just in front of the General Post Office, which in turn was right by the ferry terminal.

A little way along Hollywood Road on the return journey, I came across Ladder Street, a street running downhill so steeply that the roadway is formed of stone steps. Better down than up, I thought, as I negotiated my way along it. I caught a ferry once again, and fifteen minutes later I was back in the comfort of my air-conditioned hotel suite. Having pushed the reason for my visit along as far as I could for the moment, and still tired from my journey, I decided to shower and then sleep away the rest of the afternoon, before deciding how best to spend my first evening in Hong Kong.

I was awoken by the telephone. Looking at my watch, I saw that it was just after six p.m. I picked up the phone. 'Mr Andrews?' said a woman's voice, with an attractive Chinese lilt. 'Yes,' I said. 'My name is Guai Tim Bun,' she said. She giggled. 'It means Expensive Dessert. I am friend of Mr Ho. He tells me you look for guide to sinful things in Hong Kong. My friends call me Cherry. I know all fun, naughty places. May I help you?' She sounded dead sexy. 'You certainly can, Cherry,' I said. 'Where are you now?' 'Downstairs, in Peninsular bar,' she said. 'Give me fifteen minutes,' I said. 'I'll be right down. How will I know you?' 'Just ask barman for Cherry,' she said. 'He know me. I'll be here.' She put the phone down.

When I got down there, precisely fifteen minutes later, and the barman pointed her out to me, she was even more attractive than I had fantasized her to be. She was tall for an Oriental, about five eight, with typical blue-black Chinese hair, deep brown eyes, a pretty face, breasts at least big enough to be visible beneath the material of her dress, and a big, welcoming smile. She was wearing an expensive-looking silk evening *cheongsam*, with the traditional, thigh-length split down one side, revealing slim legs wearing black silk stockings and ending in black, patent leather, high-heeled sandals. As with the girl over on the island earlier, I could see an inch or so of naked thigh at the top of the split in her skirt as she sat there. I wondered if she fucked. I hoped so. 'Cherry,' I said, putting out a hand. 'Tony Andrews. Please call me Tony.' She took my hand in a firm, dry clasp and held on to it slightly longer than was strictly necessary, which I liked. She didn't get up. 'Tony,' she said. 'How nice to meet you. Mr Ho didn't tell me your age. I was expecting an older man.' 'I hope you're not disappointed,' I said, smiling. 'Not at all,' she replied. 'Quite the opposite.'

I ordered myself a scotch and water, no ice, and Cherry asked for a dry martini on the rocks. When the drinks came, she raised her glass to me. 'Cheers,' she said. She asked me if I wanted to start to see some of the things in Hong Kong that might make amusing or interesting stories for *Tiptop* tonight, or wait until tomorrow. I told her that I was happy to begin this evening, but that I would like to eat before doing anything else. It was, I suggested, in any case a bit early for any serious night life to have started up, with which she agreed. We discussed some of the possibilities, and after listening to her, I decided to give the big hotel cabarets a miss, at least for this evening, and go look at some of the honky-tonks and topless bars of the Tsim Sha district, apparently an easy stroll away from the hotel. All one needed to do, apparently, was follow the neon glare.

To start with, Cherry recommended that we eat at a restaurant in Nathan Road, Kowloon's main street, and when we had finished our drinks we went out to join the throngs of tourists and local inhabitants window-shopping and bar-hopping along the length of this wide, tree-lined avenue. The Chinese, Cherry told me, as we wandered slowly along, take their food seriously. So much so, she said, that the everyday Cantonese greeting is *'Nei sik jo fan mai a?'* which, freely translated, means 'Have you had your rice?' The majority of restaurants in Hong Kong serve Cantonese cuisine, although there are a good half-dozen other cuisines from various regions of mainland China. The restaurant that Cherry took us to was serving Chiu Chow, from the Swatow region of southeast China. The menu was in Chinese characters, so I let Cherry choose for both of us.

What arrived was a dream. Little dishes kept coming, each one more delicate and interesting than the last. Two things stand out in my memory of that culinary delight: the tiny cups of a particularly bitter China tea called Iron Buddha that were the constant accompaniment to the food, and the main course, which consisted of minced pigeon meat, ground and fried with herbs, and eaten wrapped in crisp lettuce leaves, together with something called *congee*, a sort of rice porridge. It may not sound amazing, but it was all absolutely delicious. After we had eaten our fill, we resumed our promenade, but this time

Cherry took us off down a side street, away from the glittering golden mile of Nathan Road, and walked us past the hostess clubs and topless bars that are such a feature of this area. She eventually entered one which, as far as I could tell from the outside, seemed to combine an air of respectability along with the advertised sexuality of the show.

We went inside and sat at the long bar, along the top of which gyrated six pretty young Oriental women. They were clad only in minuscule G-strings, so small that tiny wisps of black, curly pubic hair were erotically visible, peeping around the edges as the girls bumped and ground to the Western music of a live group, playing on a small stage to the rear of the bar. Their gyrations were entirely sexual, to the noisy approval of the sailors of various nationalities who made up the majority of the customers.

The Chinese girl on the bar almost over my head looked as if she had just left school, her pert breasts – the nipples rouged – bouncing with the firmness and enthusiasm of youth. Her G-string was semi-transparent, and I could see her pussy lips clearly outlined beneath the flimsy, damp material. Whether wet from the sweat that was trickling down her slim body, or from a more interesting source, I could only guess. She saw me looking up at her, and moved directly over me, her legs splayed and bent until her protuberant crotch was almost brushing my face. I could savour the sexually titillating scent of clean young pussy, and I could tell, from that close, that it wasn't sweat that was dampening the material that I could now see was drawn up tightly into the lips of her sex: it was the juices that her sexually oriented movements were producing. She smiled at me as she fucked the air in front of my face, and I smiled back, aroused by her blatant sexuality. She lifted her hands and started to squeeze her nipples as she danced, occasionally running her fingers down her sweat-filmed body, almost – but not quite – into the top of her G-string.

She left very little to the imagination as she danced. It was not so much a dance, in fact, more of a prelude to the sexual act. And I was under no illusion as to what that act would be. Should I have been tempted, it would have commenced with my mouth around that pouting little pudenda, and sooner or later, those lips would encompass *my* sex. At that moment the tempo of the music increased, prior to the end of the set, and the girl's movements became equally frenzied as she kept time, her breasts shaking, her thighs swaying backwards and forwards and, as the music hit a final, high-pitched note, her right hand slipped all the way down inside her G-string and, I could see quite clearly, several fingers ended up inside her pussy lips.

As the music stopped, the girl squatted down and pushed two fingers, clearly wet, and strongly scented from their insertion into her cunt, between my lips. Nothing daunted, I sucked them for the few seconds that they were there. Then, with a giggle, and a final waft of the aroma of sexual excitement, she was gone. The lights went up, and I turned and smiled at Cherry, who smiled back. I ordered us another drink each and sat back, waiting to see what would happen. If I wasn't very much mistaken, the girl, slightly more properly dressed this time, would arrive and sit on the bar stool next to me. I wasn't wrong. About five minutes later she returned, but this time on our side of the bar. She had obviously showered, for her black, glistening hair was still damp. She had changed into a low-cut, almost backless dress, and her full-length skirt was, inevitably, split to her thigh. As she sat down on a stool between Cherry and me, I could see no evidence of panties as the slit opened. Just pale brown skin, all the way up. 'Hello,' she said, as she took a cigarette from a pack in her purse, and held it between slim, brown fingers as she waited for a light. 'My name's Juanita.' I gave her a light from a book of matches on the bar. 'Hello, Juanita,' I said. 'I'm Tony, and this is Cherry,' indicating the girl on the stool behind her. Juanita turned around. 'Hi, Cherry,' she said. 'Are you working here? I don't think I've seen you here before.' Cherry laughed. 'No, honey, I'm not working here,' she said. 'Tony and I are just good friends.' Enough was enough, I felt.

'That was quite a performance you were putting on up there on the bar,' I said to her. 'What can I get you to drink?' 'Thank you, Tony,' she said. 'I'll have a glass of champagne, please. It isn't real champagne, but it's drinkable, and I get more commission on that than on a glass of white wine, which is what I'd really like.' I waved to the barman, caught his eye, and ordered the glass of champagne.

'What brings an attractive Englishman, and with a girlfriend, to a go-go bar?' asked Juanita. I explained to her, briefly, that I was looking for material that would lend itself to words and pictures for *Tiptop*, and I promised that yes, I would certainly consider her as a possibility for photography. Which I genuinely would. But I needed to see more of Hong Kong's night-life before making any kind of a final selection. I refused Juanita's offer of a free fuck as politely as I could, but I took a card from her which had both her home and the club's telephone numbers on it, kissed her lightly on the cheek, and said goodnight.

We picked up a cab and drove, at Cherry's instigation, to the Hong Kong Central district on the main island, through the Cross Harbour Tunnel. Once there, she directed the driver to a street just off Gloucester Road, in the Wanchai area, and we eventually ended up outside a slightly garish-looking entrance. I paid off the cab, and we entered through a bead-curtained doorway. Inside it looked like a perfectly ordinary Hong Kong night-club,

THE HOUSE OF A THOUSAND DREAMS

with a long bar all the way along one wall, booths along the opposite wall, and a dancing area between the two. There was music from a jukebox, and a few couples were dancing. We sat up at the bar.

There were far more girls than men, but there's nothing unusual about that in an area which, like Tsim Sha Tsui on the mainland, caters largely to sailors from the merchant ships that dock in the harbour. The girls were almost all exceptionally beautiful. We ordered drinks and when they arrived I asked Cherry what was the particular reason for bringing me here. I didn't want to be critical, I said, but it all looked very ordinary indeed, and not all that exciting. 'Exciting, probably no,' said Cherry. 'But interesting, yes.' 'Interesting?' I queried. 'But why, especially?' Cherry smiled at me, leaned forward and dropped her voice. 'Because every "girl" that you can see here, apart from me, is a transvestite,' she said. 'One or two of them have had the operation, but most have just had hormone injections, or implants. Those who haven't had the operation are bisexual. Mostly they're homosexual, but they'll go with girls for money, if necessary. They're all prostitutes.'

I nearly fell off my seat with surprise. I looked around me, taking in the low-cut necklines, the transparent evening blouses, all designed to expose the maximum amount of breast. And what a selection of breasts there was! Full, firm, rounded, dark-nippled breasts were everywhere. And even the faces were feminine. Every 'girl' present was either Chinese, Asiatic, or Eurasian, with perfect skins, exquisite make-up, feminine shoulders, those breasts, and tiny hands and feet. I would have fucked any one of them on sight, given the opportunity, had I not known that beneath many of the slit evening skirts all around me were cocks and balls, nestling – presumably – in silken panties. And here and there, if Cherry was correct, the occasional surgically manufactured vagina. I remembered the old joke about the transvestite who was suing her surgeon, because her cunt kept healing up, and shuddered at the thought. I wondered too about the few men at the bar. Were they *all* homosexual? They certainly didn't look it, but I knew that didn't mean a thing.

If they were straight, what did they do with the 'girls?' Did they want to be sucked, or did they want to fuck the 'girls' in the ass? It was all very confusing. I turned back to Cherry, and asked her exactly who did what to whom, and with which. She laughed. 'Well,' she said. 'I can't speak for all of them, obviously. But take that girl over there.' She pointed to a beautiful, black-haired young girl in a plain green *cheongsam*, slit, as ever, to the thigh, the colour setting off perfectly her pale brown skin. 'Do you see the one I mean?' she asked. I said that yes, I did. 'Well, I know him reasonably well. He's called Cora. He'll basically do anything and everything. He'll suck cock, and suck pussy. He'll fuck girls, or men. He's not fussy. He's clean, and he's got a good body. Very pretty breasts.' 'Could I talk to him?' I asked Cherry. 'But don't misunderstand me. I don't want sex with him. Or her. It's just that, if he looks as good at close quarters, I'll ask him if he'll let us photograph him for the magazine. And take some shots of the whole place. For money, of course,' I added, hastily.

Five minutes later, Cora was sitting beside me. Very close beside me. I could feel the warmth of 'her' thigh against mine, and breathe the scent of her musky perfume. I was more than pleasantly surprised. 'She' had a pretty, sexy smile, and her voice was soft and feminine. I could see the soft swell of her breasts, and admire her flawless facial skin, which showed no signs of ever having been near a razor. Even at these close quarters, if I hadn't known, I would have sworn that she was a beautiful young Oriental girl of maybe twenty or so. And yet, according to

THE HOUSE OF A THOUSAND DREAMS 131

Cherry, there was a large masculine appendage between her legs. She smiled at me, revealing two rows of small, but perfect, teeth. 'You like me, Tony?' she asked.

Yes, I said, I did, and then I explained why: that I would like her to pose for the magazine. She was delighted, and we quickly agreed a fee. She also said that she would get the owner of the place to agree to some general shots – also for a fee. That, she assured me, would be no problem. I told her that either Cherry or I would be in touch to arrange dates and times. I thanked her, and we left. 'Fantastic,' I said to Cherry, outside. 'Unbelievable.' But then I suddenly remembered back to Crysis in New York, and I realized that it wasn't the first time I hadn't been able to tell the boys from the girls. Extraordinary!

We found a cab and Cherry gave an address over in the Happy Valley area of the island. 'Have you ever been to a brothel?' she asked me. 'Not in Hong Kong.' I told her, which of course was true. 'Then with your agreement,' she said, 'I shall take you to The House of a Thousand Dreams. It is owned by a man called Billy Chang. He runs brothels, makes sex movies, and produces and sells pornography. Hong Kong of course has been in the sex business for more than two thousand years. What Billy Chang has done is to organize that industry. In doing so, he has become a multimillionaire. He has established decent working conditions. Made sure that the girls profit, as well as him. In his brothels, the girls are well paid and well looked after. He has a waiting list of girls wanting to work there. Many of them have university degrees. Why do they want to work in Billy's brothels? Because they'll make more money doing that than doing practically anything else in this chauvinist centre of cheap female labour. And most of them are supporting whole families, not just themselves. Big families of twenty or thirty people, in many cases, are suddenly eating every day.

'It's not so long since female children here were sold as

ten-year-olds into brothels, and into sexual slavery. They were worked almost literally to death in a few short years, and then were often strangled, and their bodies thrown into the sea. Billy has changed all that. What he does may be immoral, but it's a whole lot better than what went on before.' Put that way, it was a pretty convincing argument. I had to agree.

We drove out of Gloucester Road, still in Wanchai, which made sense, since this is the area of Hong Kong Island which caters to every sexual appetite you can think of. We drove along Hennessy Road, the main thoroughfare, and then turned off right, up Morrison Hill Road, where we turned yet again, driving away from the main honky-tonk area. We were now in the Happy Valley area that we had been aiming for. After about another five minutes, we turned into the driveway of what appeared to be a large, well-maintained, residential home, its garden well trimmed and manicured. The building was of white stucco, and of elegant proportions. There were lights at almost all of the many windows, and the sound of Western music could be heard softly as we got out of the car and walked up to the front door.

I was impressed by the fact that the door opened just before we reached it. It was obviously someone's job to keep an eye on arrivals. A Chinaman in a white tuxedo and black evening trousers bowed to Cherry, then to me. 'Good evening, Cheng,' said Cherry. 'Tony,' she said, 'this is Cheng, Billy Chang's manager here. Cheng, this is a friend of mine, Tony Andrews.' He bowed to me, and offered me his hand. 'Welcome to the House of a Thousand Dreams, Mr Andrews,' he said, and stood back, waving us inside. It was another world. It was entirely Oriental. There were silk wall hangings, rice-paper pictures, low-slung but comfortable-looking damask-covered Oriental couches, intricately carved ebony tables with marble tops, and everywhere the heavy scent of incense.

THE HOUSE OF A THOUSAND DREAMS

As I looked more closely, I realized that every picture, every carving, every piece of patterned material, was on one single theme – that of sex. As we stood there, a Chinese woman appeared, beautifully dressed in a pale blue, heavy silk *cheongsam*. She could have been any age between eighteen and fifty, so heavy was her traditional Chinese make-up, but I guessed that she was probably around thirty. She bowed low to Cherry and to me, then turned to Cheng. 'What is your pleasure, sir?' she asked.

'Take these two people to the private balcony,' said Cheng. 'Make them comfortable. Serve them with anything they wish.' The girl bowed low again, and turned away, beckoning us to follow her. She led us through a curtained doorway which led to a lift at the end of a passage. She pressed the button, and the whine of an electric motor heralded the arrival of a small elevator, just large enough for the three of us. We got in and she pressed the top button. After a short journey, the door slid back and we got out of the lift to find ourselves standing in a corridor, off which was a long row of white-painted doors.

The girl walked along to the first door and opened it, motioning us to follow her into the room. It was small, but comfortably furnished. There were armchairs around the walls, a few small pictures here and there, again of an erotic nature, and a number of small tables, upon one of which there was a telephone. 'Please sit,' said the girl. 'What can I get you to drink?' Cherry looked at me. I raised an eyebrow. 'Champagne?' she suggested. 'Excellent,' I said. The girl picked up the telephone, pressed some buttons, and spoke in Cantonese. When she put the telephone down, she looked at the two of us and said, 'Miss Cherry knows what this private balcony is about, because she has been here before. But let me tell you, sir,' she said, 'how it works.' I nodded at her, but I didn't say anything.

'This floor duplicates the floor below,' she said. 'Each room here is situated exactly over a similar room below. The entire floor below is exclusively for the richest of Mr Chang's customers. In these rooms they play out their fantasies. You name it, Mr Chang sells it.' 'At a price,' murmured Cherry. 'Indeed,' said the girl. 'As Miss Cherry says, at a price. Be that as it may, the main difference between this floor and the one below is that the floors up here are made from two-foot-thick glass and incorporate a complicated optical system which, at the flick of a switch, turns them into one-way mirrors.'

She went over to the wall, and pressed a switch. I gasped. The entire floor of the room had become transparent. We were sitting immediately over a huge double bed upon which lay a naked Chinaman of around forty. He was lying on his back, his huge erection disappearing and reappearing into and from the mouth of an equally naked, very beautiful Chinese girl of maybe eighteen or nineteen. She was kneeling between his spread thighs, her buttocks raised towards us, her long black hair falling over her face as she sucked the man's cock. His head was resting on a pillow, his eyes were wide open, and he appeared to be staring straight up at us. 'Don't worry,' said Cherry. 'He can neither see nor hear us. He doesn't know that we exist. He is simply watching himself and his activities in the mirrored ceiling. All he knows is that the young lady who is attending to his needs is his for however long he wants her for. She will do anything that he wants. Absolutely anything. This particular girl is famous for her ability to give head. Her house name is Heavenly Mouth. She will do anything, but this is her speciality.' I was saved from having to reply by a soft knock at the door.

The Chinese girl went to open it and admitted another young Chinese girl, this one carrying a tray, with champagne, an ice-bucket and glasses, which she put down on one of the tables. She didn't appear to notice what was going on beneath her feet. She opened the bottle with consummate skill, poured two glasses, and gave them first to Cherry and then to me. She then bowed deeply, and left. At this point the first Chinese girl said 'If you are comfortable and have everything that you need, I will leave you to enjoy yourselves. If you need anything, anything at all, just use the phone, and call me on extension 23. OK?' We thanked her, and she left. I looked down again, fascinated.

The girl was still sucking the man's cock, and she had increased the momentum of her bobbing, black-haired head considerably. The man was beginning to move his buttocks against the bed beneath him. Then he suddenly put his hands over and behind the girl's head, pulling her down onto his cock. He began fucking her mouth with an increasing frenzy. I could tell that he was about to come, and I could feel a growing response in my own groin. Suddenly the Chinaman pulled his rampant cock out of the girl's mouth and, holding her in position in front of him, he started spurting come all over her face, the white gobs running down her forehead, eyes, cheeks, and mouth. She seemed happy to accept them, her tiny pink tongue licking at those gobs near enough to her mouth for her to reach. As the spurts subsided, she took his still-rigid cock into her mouth again and sucked him gently, giving him the maximum amount of sensation that she could suck out of his ejaculation. She kept sucking until he pulled out of her mouth once again, and this time his cock had shrivelled back down to its normal size. As he did so, she used her hands to rub whatever was left of the come deeply into her face, almost as if she was using face cream.

She then started to rub her still sticky hands over her breasts, and I could see her tiny nipples burgeoning under her ministrations, their dark brown, almost black pigmentation assuming a starkly pointed stance beneath her fingers. Finally she put her fingers in her mouth, first one hand, then the other, sucking them clean, apparently enjoying the taste and flavour of the man's come. As we watched her, she got up from her position between his knees and lay down beside him. She spread her own legs, and we were treated to the sight of her masturbating herself madly, her delicate little brown fingers strumming her equally delicate-looking little cunt, like a skilled musician playing a mandolin. Her fingers moved faster and faster, and as the man watched her his shrivelled cock began to grow and rise, at which he reached down a hand and started lazily to masturbate himself.

Then the girl started bucking her slim body up and down, jerking against her busy fingers, and we could see that she too was coming now, her fingers an almost invisible blur, her cunt spread open, the juices from it shining and glinting in the light from the room, the wetness reflecting back in the subdued glare. The man's cock was now properly erect again, and suddenly the girl noticed it. Like a true daughter of the Orient, she at once abandoned her own pursuit of pleasure and started once again to pleasure the man. This time she climbed on top of his rampant erection and lowered herself slowly down on top of it, using her hands between her legs to spread her swollen pussy lips apart in order to give him easy access to her wet but obviously pleasantly tight cunt. He thrust up against her, impaling her upon himself, and I watched, fascinated, as the girl worked at him until he once more shot his load. This time it spurted up the girl's pussy, rather than all over her face. I looked at Cherry, and saw that she was laughing quietly to herself. 'What's so funny?' I asked. 'Life,' said Cherry. 'Life, and people. And sex too, viewed from this angle.' It didn't look particularly funny to me, but I let the remark go. Cherry stood up. 'Let's take our champagne and try another room,' she suggested. 'I think our friend below will probably be resting for a while. That's if you are agreeable?' I was, and I said so. I put everything on the tray and picked it up, following Cherry through into the next room. It was identical to the one that we had left behind. We settled ourselves down, and Cherry pressed the floor switch.

The scene thus revealed was rather more crowded than the previous one. I counted *five* young women with the middle-aged European man who was lying on the bed beneath us. Two of the girls were entwined together, their mouths applied with what appeared to be genuine enthusiasm to each other's almost hairless pussies, sucking and tonguing each other energetically. The man was watching and, as he lay there, a third girl was sucking his cock, slowly, lovingly, its wet length slurping in and out of her mouth, making her cheeks bulge as it filled her mouth. The last two of the five naked girls were arranged on either side of the man, masturbating themselves with practised fingers. Whether this was for their own or for his pleasure was not immediately obvious.

'That man is one of the bastions of our present legal system,' said Cherry. 'He's one of Hong Kong's top attorneys. He's probably relaxing after a hard day's work as the prosecuting attorney for the government in a case of prostitution. But that's life, I guess. Hypocrisy flourishes everywhere, not just here in Hong Kong. In any case, his future here is obviously extremely limited. When the Chinese take over, the legal system as we know it will almost certainly disappear.' I watched the attorney and his youthful ensemble with renewed interest. 'Is he married?' I asked Cherry. 'Oh, yes. He's married. But I doubt his forty-five-year-old wife can serve him as well as these girls can. And there's only one of her. How can she possibly compete with these young beauties?' I looked at them rather more carefully, and I could see exactly what she meant. Their bodies were perfect, their skins flawless. Their pert breasts were firm, their buttocks taut. Not a line, not a wrinkle, could be seen anywhere upon any of them. They were exquisite.

As I watched, the man said something to one of the two girls beside him and she clambered up and straddled his face. She then used her fingers to spread open her cunt which she then lowered over his mouth, settling herself down as she did so. He lifted up his hands and grasped her buttocks, kneading them as he pressed her pussy against his mouth. She began to wriggle her ass and, as she did, the girl who was sucking his cock took it out of her mouth and then sat down upon it. She began bouncing merrily away as soon as it was fully, deeply inserted.

The two girls sucking each other's pussies were still thus engaged, seemingly oblivious to the fact that their prime audience was now otherwise occupied, and the one girl left masturbating herself continued with her task. The European was obviously soon going to ejaculate, stimulated as he was by the ministrations of the two girls, one working at his cock, the other grinding her cunt into his mouth. Even as we watched he arched his back, lifting the girl impaled upon his cock up into the air as he did so, and I could see the spasming base of his prick as he pumped his semen into her. She put a hand down between her legs and squeezed his penis as it shot off into her snatch. Cherry switched off the glass floor as the girl squeezed the last drop of semen from his now wilting cock. We finished up the champagne, and then made a tour of the remaining rooms of the private balcony – all of which were empty. We didn't stay too long in any of them. Just long enough to take a quick look at the activity below. Cherry told me to let her know if I wished to spend more time in any one particular room. I promised that I would.

In the next room we visited we saw an elderly gentleman with his aged body stretched and manacled painfully across a wooden horse, being thrashed with evident pleasure by a statuesque Negress of twenty-five or so. His wrinkled buttocks were bleeding profusely as the almost naked girl wielded a long, thin cane with professionally vicious strength. Cherry told me that this particular customer paid dearly for this service, and complained bitterly if his backside was not cut to ribbons during the exercise. I say 'almost naked' advisedly, for the Negress was attired only in thigh-high patent leather boots, upon which her client's blood was splashing. I suggested that we move on forthwith. Giving and receiving pain, even watching its receipt and administration, isn't sexually pleasurable for me. None of Billy Chang's staff, Cherry told me, ever needed to entertain more than one client per working session, unless they especially wanted to. If they did, they earned extra money. We moved on.

The next room was occupied by a European man, and three young women of eighteen or so, and as we 'switched on', I could see that we had arrived at the ultimate consummation of this gentleman's desires. As we watched, the girls lined up to stand over him and squat on his face as he gulped and swallowed greedily at their young cunts, simultaneously masturbating himself.

In quick succession, we watched an elderly man being fellated by another girl, and an attractive man, who looked to be in his early thirties, being spanked. While the pretty Chinese girl, fully dressed, spanked him as he lay across her lap, he jerked away at his engorged cock, each stroke encouraging him to greater efforts, until his creamy come spurted down her black silk dress. His performance was followed by an abnormally normal young man, who was fucking a very pretty young Eurasian girl in the missionary position. We next watched an aristocratic-looking man, whom Cherry told me was a Russian, fucking the ass off a beautiful young black girl. Because of her face-down position, I couldn't guess at her country of origin. Wherever she hailed from, I could see that she was enjoying every moment of the anal fucking that she was entertaining.

The last room that we visited revealed, in the room below, a Chinaman of indeterminate, if advanced, age. He was sitting in solitary splendour in the centre of the room's king-size bed, surrounded by a trio of young ladies, all three of whom were fucking themselves with three of the biggest dildoes that I think I have ever seen. Each dildo stretched the sexual orifice of the girl who was forcing it up herself to the point where I would have thought that it was distinctly painful. But the girls gave no indication of suffering pain. Far from it, in fact. As they worked diligently away, their faces gave every sign of considerable sexual enjoyment.

The room lights glistened on the wet shafts of the dildoes, indicating that each girl was lubricating freely as she hand-fucked herself with the huge rubber cocks. I realized, of course, quite quickly, in fact, that the wetness could well be some kind of regular sexual lubricant that the girls had used before commencing their task rather than being the product of their own natural resources. The Chinaman was fully dressed, and made no movement of any kind. He didn't seem to want to touch either the girls or himself, and when I asked Cherry about the man's specific sexual proclivities she told me that she didn't know. The man had apparently been a regular client for many years. All he ever did was to pay for three girls – always different ones – to perform in front of him in this manner. After an hour of watching this activity, he left. He never laid a hand, or anything else, on the girls or on himself. He always tipped well, and paid in cash. Oh well, I thought. Whatever turns you on. Watching the three girls assaulting themselves with the dildoes was certainly turning *me* on. I thought that I had probably seen enough of the brothel for one evening, and said so to Cherry.

We went downstairs again in the tiny lift, and as we

dropped down to ground level, I couldn't help but laugh to myself at the thought of the reaction of the people we had been spying on had they known that they were performing to an uninvited audience. I wondered if there was any monitoring equipment recording the evening's activities as they happened, possibly to be used by Billy Chang either to blackmail his customers or to protect himself from the attentions of the Hong Kong police. I decided that there almost certainly *was* such equipment, but I was unable to decide exactly how the resulting film would best be used. Probably simply to safeguard Billy from having his brothel closed down, I finally decided.

Cheng was on hand to bid us farewell as we left the brothel, and he refused any money when I tried to pay for our evening's entertainment. He also insisted that we were driven back to the Peninsular Hotel in one of Billy's fleet of chauffeur-driven Rolls Royces. Or to the *Boob do jau dim*, as the Peninsular Hotel is known in Cantonese. In the car on the way back, Cherry asked if I would like to have a nightcap in a bar that specialized in showing porno movies. Why not, I thought, and I said that yes, that might be fun. Cherry redirected the driver, and we ended up back on the Kowloon Peninsular, not more than a couple of blocks from the Peninsular Hotel, which was convenient. As we drove back to the mainland, I thanked Cherry for introducing me to the places that we had visited. Billy Chang's brothel would make a tremendous feature for *Tiptop*, I told her, but it would have to be an exercise in descriptive words, probably illustrated by an artist. There was no way we could take any kind of photographs there, for all sorts of obvious reasons.

When we arrived at the bar, it was air-conditioned and plentifully supplied with attractive hostesses, whom Cherry said were all on the game. They left the two of us alone, however, probably assuming that we were lovers, rather than friends or – more truthfully – the business acquaintances that we were. I've always been something of a blue movie buff, provided that the bodies are young and beautiful, and also that the actresses and actors are doing what they're doing because they want to, not because they're being forced to, be it physically or financially.

I don't mind much about the story line – or lack of it – because if one's going to the movies to be serious, one simply doesn't go to blue movies. Pornographic movies, whether you watch them in a movie theatre or on a videotape machine, have only one purpose: to turn their audience on. The movies in the bar did exactly that. The stories were rubbish, but the bodies were young and fresh. The films alternately had Chinese sound-tracks and English subtitles, and vice versa. The photography was clear and in focus, homing in on boobs and bottoms, cunts and cocks, pussies dripping with love juices, and cocks spurting jets of creamy come. Every nipple was rigid, every breast full and bouncy. All the cocks were enormous, all the cunts pinkly, wetly tight. Shakespeare it wasn't. Horny it *was*.

At one stage, I had to excuse myself to go to the men's room, right in the middle of watching a beautiful young girl losing her virginity to six car park attendants, simply because she'd left her credit card at home and they wouldn't take her on trust. As I left, they were simply taking her. I relieved myself, washed my hands and combed my hair. I wondered if Cherry was available. She was certainly very fuckable. I decided that there was no harm in asking. She could always say no. And common sense told me that she had to be as sexually aroused as I was. She'd been watching the same catalogue of sexual acts as I had all evening. She had to be as horny as I was.

I slipped back into my seat beside the object of my desire. As I did so, up on screen a pretty young white girl was deep-throating a large black cock, and it seemed an appropriate moment to lean over to Cherry and whisper in her ear, 'Does that suggest anything in particular to you, Cherry?' She looked at me, and smiled. 'It certainly does, Tony' she said. 'Then why don't we give the rest of this movie a miss, and go back to the hotel, and make our own movies? Or something?' I said. 'What do you think?' 'I think that's a great idea,' she said. I waved for a check for our drinks, and over-tipped in my excitement. I was going to have my first Chinese fuck. We hailed a cab, and made it back to the hotel in good time. 'Would you like a drink at the bar?' I asked Cherry, 'or would you like to drink in my suite?' 'Your suite is fine,' she said. 'Thank you.' The view from the balcony of the suite was spectacular, even by Hong Kong standards, looking out as it did from the top floor of the Peninsular Hotel across Salisbury Road and out over Victoria Harbour to the island that is Hong Kong Central. The myriad lights twinkling everywhere were reflected in the sky as silver stars against a deep black heaven. The night was cool, and I opened up the glass sliding doors. Cherry sat herself down outside whilst I ordered a bottle of Crystal from room service. While I waited, I checked that the bedroom door was shut and that the air-conditioning was functioning in there. We would need its coolness fairly soon.

The waiter came with the champagne and I thanked him, signed his chit, tipped him, and told him I would open it myself. There is for me something ritually enjoyable, almost physically anticipatory, about the act of opening a bottle of champagne for a pretty girl that you know you are shortly going to fuck. This was no exception and I took my time, cutting the foil with my penknife, untwisting and removing the wire, holding the cork with the napkin and twisting the bottle slowly with my left hand, until the cork came loose with the tiniest 'plop', spilling not a drop. Let the Hooray Henrys of this world make unnecessary noises, and shoot corks in the air. If it amuses them, why not?

I poured two glasses, sniffing the unique aroma, in which I always told myself I could scent ripe strawberries and a whiff of the sea breeze on the Côte d'Azure (both probably totally imaginary) and carried the drinks out to the balcony. 'Cheers, sweetheart,' I said. She smiled up at me from her chair. 'May you be blessed with many male children,' she said. 'It is how we say "cheers." But don't worry. Like most young Chinese girls, I'm on the pill.' I laughed at her honesty, and we drank.

'Mmmm,' she said. 'Nice. I can tell it's vintage, but I don't recognize it. But it's not Dom Perignon, is it?' I was impressed. Not many girls of my acquaintance would know Dom Perignon from Lucozade, frankly. 'It's Louis Roederer,' I told her. 'Crystal. It's always been my favourite.' 'I've not knowingly had it before,' she said. 'But I shall certainly have it again. It has a distinct taste all of its own. My own favourite, up to now, has always been Mumm. Most Chinese businessmen who can afford vintage champagne order Dom Perignon. It's something many men do. It's all a matter of personal taste, I suppose.' She drank again, and I went and got the bottle from its ice bucket. I brought it out onto the balcony and then filled both our glasses.

'Did you know that here in Hong Kong we are the largest per capita consumers of French cognac in the world?' she asked me. I had to admit that I didn't. 'I think it has something to do with the fact that Chinese men believe that it has aphrodisiacal properties,' she said. 'I wouldn't have thought that was anything you needed to think about. Are you going to take me to bed now? I feel really horny. It's all that sexual action we've been watching all evening. It has really turned me on. I'm making my panties wet just thinking about you.' 'I'm ready when you are, darling,' I said. 'Let's go.' I picked up the champagne bottle and my glass, Cherry picked up her glass, and I ushered her before me to the bedroom. I wondered idly if she was going to charge me, as I watched her buttocks moving beneath the silk of her *cheongsam*. Frankly, I didn't much care. She would simply go down on my expenses. And on me, I hope, I thought to myself. The bedroom was cool after the evening air on the balcony, but not unpleasantly so. Cherry began to undress.

I watched her as I took my own clothes off. Her *cheongsam* simply unbuttoned all the way down the front. When she took it off I could see that she was bra-less, and that her breasts were nicely rounded in a most un-Chinese way, as I had earlier anticipated. The cold air in the bedroom made her nipples stand stiffly to attention. The black silk stockings, I could now see, were held up by a tiny black satin suspender belt, over which she was wearing black satin bikini panties. I remembered her saying that she was making them wet. She bent down and pulled them down her – for a Chinese girl – long, slim legs, and when she had stepped out of them, I could see her soft, wispy black pubic hair, hardly covering a plump little *mons veneris*, at the centre of which pale pink labia glistened wetly in the light from the bedside lamps. I could smell the musky, sexual scent of healthily aroused young woman. My cock stood firmly erect at the sight and scent of her.

'Do me a favour, Cherry, please,' I said. 'Keep the stockings and suspender belt on, will you?' 'Ooooh,' she said, smiling. 'Kinky. How lovely. Come and fuck me.' She got onto the bed and lay down on her back, her legs spread. It was then that I noticed that she had a small flower tattooed on her left inner thigh. It was a chrysanthemum. A pale, golden brown chrysanthemum, with a green stem and leaves. It was very pretty. I knelt on the floor bedside the bed, and positioned myself so that I could suck her pretty little Chinese pussy. Now that I was close to it, I could see that her juices were indeed trickling plentifully down her thighs. For what reason I know not, I suddenly remembered that at school we used to tell each other that Oriental girls – Chinese, Japanese, Eurasian, whatever – had horizontal cunts, as opposed to their European sisters' vertical ones. Since none of us, to my knowledge, had ever seen either a European or an Oriental cunt, I cannot imagine where that thought came from. But I now *knew* that it wasn't true!

I leaned forward and took those beautiful pale pink cunt lips in my mouth and sucked them. They tasted delightful. Her cunt had a delicate scent of incense overlying the more usual fragrant smell of freshly aroused pussy, and I inhaled deeply as I sucked and tongued with enthusiasm. I delved with my tongue for her clitoris and found its hard little nub standing erect. I concentrated all my oral efforts upon it until Cherry was wriggling frenetically, and almost screaming with sexual desire. I tongued more rapidly and she raised her hips off the bed and thrust herself against my mouth as she reached her orgasm, panting and grunting with release as she spasmed and jerked and writhed upon the bed.

Then she slowly relaxed and when she had finished climaxing she looked down at me and smiled. 'Thank you, darling,' she said. 'That was good. Really good. Now come and fuck me. Please.' I needed no further bidding, and I climbed up onto the bed and mounted her. She guided my rigid cock into her tight wetness, and I could feel her vaginal muscles sucking me in. She squeezed the base of my cock with her right hand, and she thrust herself up against me until I was deep inside her. 'Oh, that's good,' she breathed. 'That's really good.' I leaned down and took her rigid nipple into my mouth and sucked it, then the other one. They were hard and erect, and she moaned as I suckled.

I began to fuck Cherry with long, slow, relaxed strokes,

and the sweat of our exertions started to mingle, our bodies slapping together as we fucked. The noise that this created as our flesh met in mutual heat added to my sexual excitement. Her stomach was flat against mine. We neither of us had any excess fat, and the noise was that of our torsos slapping together wetly. After a while, Cherry seemed to be in continual orgasm, the contractions of her pussy muscles squeezing tightly around my cock. It was tremendously exciting. I felt as if I was raping her, violating her, breaking her membrane for the very first time. She felt submissive beneath me, and this excited me even further. I wanted to savage her, and then I was coming, spurting my semen against the wall of her womb, jetting it into her, filling her with my seed. I pulled out of her and fell back on the bed, panting with my efforts. My cock was still almost fully erect. She leaned over me and took it in her mouth, and started sucking me, gently. My penis quivered as she drew the last drops of warm semen from it. She continued to suck until it was finally all over, and my cock started to shrivel.

She took it out of her mouth, and smiled down at me. 'I can taste my own pussy, mingling with your spunk,' she said. 'It's naughty, but nice. I like the taste of my own cunt.' I smiled back at her, frankly too tired to think of anything appropriate to say, and we fell asleep, content, at peace with the world, our mutual desires fully gratified, at least for the moment.

I awoke a while later, and Cherry was curled against me, her buttocks against my prick, her back against my chest. I put down a hand, and felt her pussy through her closed legs. It was still wet, still emanating juices, my come and hers mixed, presumably. What goes up must come down. My erection stretched out stiffly, and I felt for and found her pussy lips. I spread them, and eased my cock gently in. It slid into her. She was slick, and warm, wet and tight, and I began to fuck her from the rear. Her buttocks were soft and full as I bucked against them, my prick deep inside her, and the feel of the silk stockings that she was still wearing rubbing against my knees as I fucked her was intensely sexual.

And then she was awake, and she was thrusting her buttocks back against me in time with my thrusts, signalling her enjoyment of my invasion. She was telling me that she was awake, and ready for anything that I wanted to do to her. Seeing that she was awake, I pulled her up from behind until she was in a kneeling position, her ass in the air. In that position I could thrust more deeply into her. I watched my cock as it spread her labia, enjoying the sensations that it was sending to my brain. The act of sex was in full flood. I was ravaging her again. She was tight and wet, and her muscles gripped me with a savage enthusiasm. I began to increase my momentum, gripping her thighs as I fucked her, and I suddenly found myself looking at her pinkly puckered anus. The thought of fucking *that* brought me immediately to my ejaculation, and as I once more spurted my jism into her, I fantasized that I was spurting into her tiny rectum. The excitement of that thought kept my cock bone hard. I felt her literally shuddering beneath me as I jetted into her, and then it was over. I didn't withdraw, I just lay there, my cock still impaling her until it slipped out in its own good time. I put my arms around her and eased her back down onto the bed, where I felt her slip a hand between her legs and start masturbating herself. I brushed her hand aside gently, and began to manipulate her myself, and as I did so she reached a hand behind her and took my cock in it and began to pull my foreskin up and down, masturbating me with what felt like a very experienced hand. We lay there, jerking each other off, the excitement mounting slowly as we both metaphorically lay back and enjoyed it, and soon we were both coming together once more.

CHAPTER FIVE: FOOD FOR THOUGHT

When I finally awoke, the sun was streaming through the curtained windows. I checked the time. It was three o'clock in the afternoon. Well, it *had* been a strenuous night. Cherry was fast asleep, her blue-black hair spread around her face on the pillow. I stretched lazily, and yawned. I felt well and truly fucked. Well, *that* made sense! I crawled out of bed carefully, so as not to awaken Cherry, and took myself off to the bathroom, where a lengthy session under the needle-point shower began to make me feel a little more alive. I thought of Cherry's lovely little Chinese pussy as I soaped my cock, and the combination of my soapy fingers and the memories of last night started me off using my fingers with a sudden enthusiasm, and the resulting ejaculation set me up for whatever the coming day – what was left of it – might bring. I washed my cock clean once more, and dried myself with one of the hotel's giant-sized fluffy bath towels. As I was thus engaged, Cherry came through the bathroom door, looking enchanting, naked but for her mini-suspender belt and black silk stockings, her hair precisely in place as if she had just emerged from the hairdresser. Have you ever looked at a Chinese girl's hair? It is always immaculate. Never a hair out of place. 'Good afternoon, sweetheart,' I said. 'And how are we this lovely day?' 'Well fucked,' she said. 'Very well fucked indeed, thank you.' 'Well, that's good to hear,' I said.

'Why don't you now have a good, long shower, after which I guarantee you'll feel like a million dollars. When you're through that, we'll ring room service and order some breakfast, which we'll eat out on the balcony, watching the world go by, whilst we plan what to do today. How does that sound to you?' 'That sounds terrific,' she said. 'I'll be with you in about fifteen minutes. OK?'

I dressed myself, and went out onto the balcony to look at the day. It looked pretty good from where I stood. The harbour was packed with small craft, jostling for position alongside the sampans the millionaires' yachts and the ocean-going liners, whilst the ferries sped back and forth like giant water beetles, in and out of the constant traffic.

Leaving aside the enjoyable sex with Cherry, I felt I'd had enough of commercial sex for a while, after the selection of places that we had seen the previous evening. In any case, if I followed up all the leads I had, and made the arrangements for the photography, I probably had more than enough to put together a Hong Kong issue of *Tiptop*. I would of course include Cherry in my writings, but not under her own name, and in any case I probably wouldn't tell her of my intention. What the head doesn't know, as they say. It also seemed likely that she wasn't going to ask me to pay for the sex with her, in that, if she were, I reckoned that I would have heard about it by now. But I did expect to pay her a reasonable fee for her expert guidance around Hong Kong's sex spots. So, I thought, let's go somewhere nice for dinner today. Let's relax and enjoy ourselves at *Tiptop*'s expense. Let's play tourists.

All the guide books will tell you that the Chinese invented *haute cuisine*. Certainly they care about food with an enthusiasm of which the French would approve. They use only the freshest of ingredients – from both land and sea – and put them together with skill and imagination. There are something like a dozen different regional cuisines, and literally thousands of restaurants from which to choose. But with Cherry to advise me I had a positive advantage, as well as some extremely attractive company. Over our late English breakfast on the balcony, I put forward my suggestion. 'Oh, yes, I'd love that,' she said. 'Where would you like to go?' 'I rather hoped that you would suggest somewhere,' I said. 'You know, somewhere that would be fun to go to, as well as with a good restaurant for dinner.' 'Macau,' she said, straight away. 'Have you been to Macau?' I told her that I hadn't. 'Then you'll love it,' she said. She was right.

I hadn't, of course, been anywhere outside Hong Kong and Kowloon. Later that morning we took the jetfoil to cover the forty miles from Hong Kong to what Cherry told me is the last outpost of Portugal's 16th Century empire. These days it is officially described as Chinese territory, under Portuguese administration. Three hundred thousand people live in the six square miles of mainland Macau and its two offshore islands, a density of population that exceeds even that of Hong Kong. Situated at the mouth of the Pearl River, it is an entrancing mixture of old and new, East and West, European and Oriental. But despite the enormous population, Macau lacks Hong Kong's skyscrapers, its traffic jams, and its crowded sidewalks. More importantly, Macau is the capital of Oriental gambling, famous throughout the East for its casinos, all of which are open twenty-four hours a day, and in which you can play Chinese gambling games like *fan tan*, *keno* and *dai-siu*, as well as the more familiar roulette, blackjack, and craps.

On arrival at the jetfoil wharf, immediately opposite the modern Jai-Alai Palace, Macau home of the frightenly fast Basque ball game (also played in Miami), we took a taxi ride around the mainland part of the city, looking at such contrasting sights as the contemporary Hotel Lisboa, with its 600 rooms and two floors of gaming; the 17th

Century Barra Fortress; the A Ma Temple, Macau's oldest shrine; the Macau Palace, a floating casino on a barge, moored off the Western waterfront, and the Leal Senado, the Macau Senate building. We ended our drive around with a visit to the ruins of St Paul's, originally a 17th Century Baroque church, of which now, sadly, only the façade remains.

From the ruins of St Paul's, where we paid off our taxi, we walked a couple of blocks to an attractive-looking Chinese restaurant on the ground floor of an old, peeling, pink stucco building on the Rua do Almirante, a long, palm tree-shaded avenue, almost in the middle of mainland Macau. The tremendous advantage of eating Chinese food in Macau, explained Cherry, was the availability of a whole range of delicious Portuguese wines, at extremely advantageous prices, by comparison with those prevailing in Hong Kong. The speciality of this particular restaurant, she said, was *linguado*, the delicately flavoured, local Macau sole, with which she suggested we drank *Vinho Verde*, a delightful dry white Portuguese wine, well-remembered by me from many a happy holiday along the Algarve coast.

I quickly discovered – to my surprise – that, whilst Cantonese is the language of the Chinese who live in Macau, English is the commonly spoken second language, rather than, as you might reasonably suppose, Portuguese. Despite the fact, it seemed sensible to ask Cherry to select our food for us, which she did, with enthusiasm and much discussion with the waiter. We started with a seemingly endless selection of *dim sum*, the small steamed or stir-fried dumplings, with a tremendous variety of fillings, varying from pork to egg, from snake to sea-urchin. I do not know, specifically, the contents of all that I ate from the selection of *dim sum*, but I do know that every single one was absolutely delicious.

Next came the *linguado*, served steamed, with ginger,

spring onion, soya sauce and garlic. It came with fried rice and mixed green, stir-fried vegetables. Mouth-wateringly good. We then had Beggar's Chicken, a traditional Shanghai dish, according to Cherry. Legend tells that a starving beggar stole a chicken, but had no means of cooking it properly. So, rubbing the bird simply with salt and onion, he then smeared it with mud – to prevent it burning – and roasted it in his fire. When the mud dried into clay, he broke the hard coating, and the feathers came off with the clay, leaving an exquisitely cooked bird. I know not how the restaurant that we were in cooked our bird, but certainly the end result was memorable. This was followed by the local version of hot-and-sour soup. Cherry explained that the Chinese eat their soup towards the end of a meal, rather than as we Europeans, who tend to start with it. It came with shredded pork, bamboo shoots, bean curd, spring onions, and mushrooms, all flavoured with seriously hot peppers. Excellent!

We enjoyed two bottles of the Vinho Verde with all this delightful food, and declined any thought of dessert at the end. But we did avail ourselves of the delicately flavoured, jasmine-scented green tea, with which most Chinese people accompany their entire meal. That and fermented black tea are the traditional drinks of China.

There are Chinese wines, but they are very sweet, by European standards, and some of them – specifically those fermented from wheat – are extremely strong in alcohol. They are best ignored. The grape- and rice-based wines, conversely, are not strong at all. Chinese beers, however, are excellent and there is a wide range of good beers on offer in most places. San Miguel, brewed in Hong Kong, is good, and cheap. Tsingtao, from mainland China, which comes in green bottles, is first class, and very acceptable to European tastes. European beers are available in most good restaurants. In Hong Kong itself, European and Australian wines are also available in the better restaurants, but the prices are phenomenally high. Which is what makes Macau's Portuguese wines such good value. My bill for the entire meal was half the cost (and, in my opinion, the meal itself was twice as delicious) of any meal I had eaten in Hong Kong. The owner of the restaurant came out at the end of our meal to greet Cherry and, through her, me. He kindly offered us glasses of Chinese plum wine which we accepted with much bowing and real pleasure.

After dinner, we spent a pleasant early evening, first of all wandering around the Lou Lim Ieoc garden, with its pagodas, ponds and bridges, not far from the house of Sun Yat Sen, founder of the Chinese Republic. From there we walked a couple of blocks north, along the Ferreira de Almeida, and then left along the Avenida do Coronel Mesquite, to the Kun Iam Tong, a 17th Century Buddhist temple, where local Chinese Buddhists worship daily. Incense was burning everywhere, and bells rang, gongs sounded, and the faithful recited their mantras, seemingly regardless of the tourists. We stayed away from the casinos, the main attraction for Chinese visitors from Hong Kong, finding the attractions of the city itself of more interest. Nor did we visit either of the two islands, Taipa and Coloane – connected to the mainland by bridges – which altogether make up the whole of Macau. Towards the middle of the evening we caught our jetfoil back to Hong Kong, where we returned to the Peninsular Hotel in Kowloon, and the welcome coolness of my air-conditioned suite.

Cherry joined me in a glass of champagne, before leaving me to go home and change her clothes. She had accepted my invitation for a light supper with me later that evening, and we had agreed to meet in the hotel bar, where I had first made her acquaintance. I passed some of the time in between telephoning Eileen in the New York office, telling her of the success of my visit and asking her to pass on various messages to Fred. I told her that I had basically only to set up the photography that I needed and wait around for it to take place, in order to ensure the quality of the pictures, and then I would be home. 'Are you getting plenty of Chinese pussy, darling?' she asked me. It's rather like that old joke about when did you stop beating your wife? 'You know me, sweetheart,' I said. 'Work is all. But there's a lot of it about. It's pretty much one of the major businesses out here. Which is why I'm here, of course. But although I've seen a lot — just wait until you see some of the pictures — I haven't actually sampled any yet.' If you'll believe that, you'll believe anything, I thought. Eileen laughed. 'Poor darling,' she said. 'You'll just have to make up for it when you get home.'

She changed the subject, and we chattered on for a while about the magazine. All, apparently, was well in the Big Apple. 'I'll see you soon, sweetheart,' I said, when we had finished. 'I'll call you and let you know when I'm getting back. Ciao for now, baby.' And I rang off.

I decided to fill in the rest of the time waiting for Cherry by enjoying the luxury of a long, languorous hot bath and I ran one, using a liberal amount of the expensive bath essence supplied by a thoughtful hotel management. I lay in it and soaked out all the tiredness ingrained in me by days of constant travel, followed by a night of strenuous sex. Please don't misunderstand me; I love both of those things. But if you indulge in them excessively, as I had, perforce, just done, they have a tendency to catch up with you. Having soaked away my tiredness, I then took a long, hot shower followed by a cold one, finishing with a brisk towelling, and I ended up feeling like a new man. (And yes, I've heard all those jokes.) I dressed slowly, enjoying taking my time in selecting a freshly pressed lightweight suit and an appropriate shirt and tie. I then poured myself another glass of champagne from the bottle that I had opened earlier and took myself out and sat on the balcony, watching the sunset fade away and the stars come out over Victoria Harbour. It has to be one of the more exciting sights in the world, comparable with your first view of New York at night, seen from uptown, looking downtown, and taking in the Empire State Building, the Chrysler Building, the myriad other skyscrapers, and the twin towers of the World Trade Centre.

My reverie was interrupted by reception telephoning to tell me that Cherry was on her way up, and I greeted her at the door to my suite with a glass of champagne and a welcoming kiss. She was wearing an attractive, embroidered, black silk suit this evening, rather than the *cheongsams* of before, and she looked stunning. She really was exceptionally beautiful, in a city of beautiful women. We sat out on the balcony, and I asked her what she had in mind for the remnants of this evening, and she said that she wondered whether I might like to eat in a famous, exclusive brothel to which she had access. She thought it would interest *Tiptop*'s readers.

The food, she said, was some of the best in Hong Kong, and it was served by pretty young girls, all of whom went about their duties completely naked. She – as a woman known to the owners – was apparently also welcome, and I could either indulge myself with the young ladies or not, as I wished. There was no pressure of any kind. But, she emphasized, if I *should* decide to become involved sexually whilst there, the place was expensive. As was the food. Would I perhaps, she asked, prefer to go somewhere more reasonably priced? She had by now, of course, as she well knew, aroused my curiosity, and since the money that I would spend, whatever I did or did not do, was *Tiptop*'s, the cost didn't really concern me too much. She seemed pleased when I said yes, of course I'd like to eat at the brothel. It was apparently called the Rainbow Palace, and was within walking distance of our hotel.

The Peninsular Hotel in Kowloon is on the junction of Salisbury Road and Nathan Road, Kowloon's main street built when Sir Matthew Nathan was Governor of Hong Kong, back in the early 1900s. At that time, most people thought that he was crazy to build a tree-lined avenue through what was virtually a wasteland, and it was then known colloquially as Nathan's Folly. Today, it is known – enviously – as the Golden Mile, and it is where all Kowloon's best hotels, shops, nightclubs, offices and restaurants are situated.

Cherry used the telephone to call the Rainbow Palace, and she made a reservation for nine o'clock. It was then just after eight-thirty. 'I guess we can make our way along there just as soon as you like,' she said. We finished our drinks, made our way down in the elevator and went out through the foyer. Nathan Road was thronged with people, mainly tourists, window shopping for watches, jewellery, jade, pearls, and ivory, and looking for the restaurant that would appeal to them from the dozens offering every possible kind of regional Chinese cuisine. It was a little early for the night-clubs, but the bars were doing a roaring trade. We took our time, walking slowly through the jostling, busy thoroughfare, watching the people, looking in the shop windows, stopping here and there to read the menus, most of which Cherry had to translate for me from the Chinese characters in which they were printed or written.

Eventually we arrived at the Rainbow Palace. From the outside, it looked like a residential home. A rich, well-kept residential home, set back from the crowded pavements behind a solid, pink-painted, stucco wall, with a manicured garden between the wall and the house. The house rose imperiously for five storeys, in crenellated, early Victorian splendour. Wide balconies graced each floor level, and the balconies were hung with baskets of flowers and backed by white-painted trellis work, up which grew carefully trained creepers. The whole façade was of expensively maintained elegance. We entered through a well-hung, white-painted wooden door, which opened noiselessly at a touch, swinging back easily upon well-greased hinges, and we then walked up a well-swept gravel path, and again up spotless stone steps to the entrance door. This was obviously hewn from solid oak, blackened by age and reinforced by steel bands and enormous, ornate metal locks and hinges. There was a spy-hole in the centre of the door, at about my height, and when we rang the bell the spy-hole slid open to reveal a brown, expressionless eye. The eye surveyed us both for a moment, and then the door swung back, as noiselessly as its streetside equivalent, and a white-uniformed servant bowed us inside.

We found ourselves in a large hallway, decorated in antique Chinese furniture, paintings and carpets, and with a large, lectern-style desk, beside which stood a huge, imposing major-domo, dressed in the classical Chinese manner. He greeted Cherry in Cantonese, and she replied to him in the same language, after which he looked at me, totally expressionless, and bowed, deeply. Failing any idea of what else to do, I bowed back, probably slightly perfunctorily.

'Shall we go to the bar for a drink, and then we can look at the menu, and decide what we want to eat?' suggested Cherry, to which I immediately agreed. She led the way down a short corridor to a door at the end which I opened for her, and through which we entered into a richly decorated bar area, composed mainly of small, almost totally enclosed, four-seater banquettes, but with a small curved bar at the far end.

There were a number of almost naked girls apparent about the place, their only gesture towards clothing being small, starched, white linen cuffs about their wrists, black silk stockings, and tiny black and white aprons that just about covered their pubic modesty but which left their tight little bottoms completely naked as they walked away. The place seemed about half full, mostly groups of men on their own, but the occasional woman guest was to be seen here and there. As far as I could tell, I was the only European in evidence. A very pretty girl came to greet us, and bowed low. 'Good evening, sir. Good evening, madam,' she said, in perfect English. She was perhaps eighteen years old. Certainly no more. Her tiny breasts were small but perfectly shaped. Conical, with matching, tiny nipples, which were standing erect in the air-conditioning of the bar area. 'Would you care to sit up at the bar, or would you prefer to sit at a table?' she asked. I looked at Cherry. 'Let's sit at the bar,' she said. 'We can see more of what is going on from there.' As the girl turned away from us to lead us to the bar, I could appreciate that she was wearing nothing behind her to interfere with the delightful, extremely attractive rear view of her tantalizing, taut young bottom. I was getting a serious hard-on, and I wondered if it showed. I didn't care if it did.

We sat on two stools at the bar, and I ordered champagne. They didn't have Crystal, but they did have Dom Perignon, so we had to make do. It was that, or non-vintage Moët. Well, it was only money, and *Tiptop*'s money, at that. You would have done the same. Cherry asked them for a menu, and in answer to her question as to what I fancied I told her that it was all entirely up to her. Why keep a dog and bark yourself, I thought? And in this particular situation, such specialized barking. Half an hour later, I knew I had taken the right decision. Cherry suggested that we eat our meal in a private room. There were, she said, certain advantages, although she didn't go into detail. Naturally enough, I agreed.

We were shown into a small but comfortable room, in which there was a table large enough for eight to sit around, but upon which only two places were set. The silver, glass, and napery were all of the finest quality. It was candle-lit, by a sufficiency of candelabra, which gave a romantic ambience to the room. No sooner had we sat down than our first course arrived. It consisted, Cheery told me, of individual oyster omelettes, made from eggs, oysters, and scallions (spring onions), all fried with sweet potato batter until crisp. They were served with tiny, delicious spring rolls, and were accompanied by a good French white burgundy. Cherry had ordered the wines too, since she knew what went well with what. Even the spring rolls tasted better than anything by that name I had ever eaten previously. When I asked Cherry what they contained, she told me that they were a Hokkien (regional) speciality, and that they were made from turnip, sprouts, prawns, egg, pork, chilli, and sweet sauce, all wrapped in a paper-thin pastry. It was a marvellous start to our meal, made all the more special by the two girls who served it, both wearing the almost-nothing uniform of the establishment. These two were additional to the one who had greeted us, and to the two serving behind the bar, but, like their colleagues, they were remarkable for their youth and their exquisite, unspoilt beauty.

The omelettes were followed by chilli crab. This turned out to be fresh crab in the shell, stir-fried with garlic, sugar, soya sauce, tomato sauce, chillies and egg. The crabs looked to be difficult to eat, particularly with chop sticks, but then Cherry told me, if I wished, one of the girls would sit beside me, extract the meat from the shell for me and feed me with it. This was a fantastic idea, to which I agreed immediately. After Cherry spoke to the girls in Cantonese, one of them sat at my right and delicately extracted the meat from the shell with her chop sticks. She then fed the meat to me. She didn't speak whilst occupied thus. We continued to drink the white burgundy with the crab. I wanted to reach out and touch the breasts of the girl who was feeding me, but I thought that this was perhaps neither polite to my guest nor likely to be appreciated at the meal table. But I was determined to have one of these delightful girls before the evening was out.

The crab was followed by a selection of dishes, which Cherry announced as our main course. There were stir-fried liver rolls (apparently a Teochew regional delicacy) served with a sweet black sauce; sliced salted goose meat, served cold, and flavoured with anise, cinnamon, and cloves; a mutton soup, a clear broth with sour tomatoes, ginger and parsley; and finally, plain steamed rice. For accompanying vegetables, we were served fresh bean sprouts, and water spinach cooked in shrimp paste, with chillies. With these mouth-watering dishes, we drank a good, fruity French red burgundy. For dessert we ate sweet mashed yams, a pleasant, if perhaps slightly cloying experience.

All in all, it was the finest Chinese meal I have ever eaten. The quantities were small, the flavours delicate, and the balance of textures, tastes, and colours most subtle. And all the way through the meal, the two charming girls were at hand to pass dishes, refill glasses, clear away plates, and generally contribute to making the experience the genuine gourmet pleasure that it most certainly was. Eventually they cleared the table, leaving us with green tea for Cherry, and decent espresso coffee for me. After a little while the two girls returned, stood together at the other side of the table, and bowed gracefully.

'Do you wish anything else, sir, madam?' one of them asked. They both smiled, charmingly. I looked askance at Cherry. 'They are asking us if we require their sexual services,' she explained. 'They will do anything that either – or both – of us might want. They won't do it here, of course, they'll take us upstairs. Or, rather, I should say, they will take *you* upstairs. If you so wish, now is the time to say. I have seen them in action and I strongly recommend them. If I may make a suggestion, whilst I know that you are a man of the world, and that your job offers you much in the way of sexual entertainment that many men probably do not get to experience, I do not believe that you will have seen anything quite as erotic as two of these girls putting on a private lesbian exhibition for you, as a prelude to anything else that you might wish. But it is entirely up to you.' Cherry spoke to the girls in Cantonese for a moment, and listened to the reply. Then: 'Both these girls speak English,' she said. 'Either or both would be happy to serve you. They ask me to tell you that they would be honoured to give their bodies to a *gaijin*. That means a foreigner. It would be a new experience for them.'

I looked at the two girls, who smiled sweetly, and bowed low again. I smiled back at them. 'Tell them, please, Cherry, that I too, will be honoured,' I said. 'But what about you? Shall I call you a taxi?' 'No, thank you,' she said. 'I am happy to wait here. I may go and play a little illegal *fan tan*. What is permitted – legally – in Macau, is not permitted – again, legally – here in Hong Kong.' She laughed. 'But don't worry. I shall find something to amuse me. Just ask for me when you're ready. Take your time. There is no hurry. I wish you happiness in your sexual adventures.' She got up, and left the room.

One of the girls held out her hand. I took it in mine and she led me from the dining room. The other girl came and took my other hand, and the two of them led me down a passage way and then up a large, sweeping staircase to the floor above. They took the third door on the left and opened it, standing back and motioning for me to enter. It was, essentially, a very large bedroom, dominated by an over-sized bed which was lushly upholstered and covered in silken sheets and pillows. I could see a bathroom through an open doorway. There were comfortable chairs, small tables, a sideboard with a good selection of alcoholic drinks and beside it a refrigerator, no doubt complete with ice, mixers, champagne and beer. We stopped at the end of the bed, and the girls let go of my hands. 'You Eng'rish?' asked one girl. 'Yes,' I said. I saw no point at all in saying no, actually, I'm Welsh. There are times to be patriotic but this wasn't one of them.

'Never fuck Eng'rish man,' said the girl. 'Onry Chinaman. Chinaman very sma'r cock. Eng'rish man, very big cock. Yes?' I grinned at her. 'Sure, sweetheart,' I said. 'You'll see. In time.' She grinned back at me. I had no idea whether she understood what I was saying or not. 'You rike us fuck ea'orrer fir?' she asked. I assumed that she was asking me if I wanted them to put on the recommended lesbian show. 'Yes,' I said. 'Yes, please.' 'Fir, we wash,' she said. 'You come watch.' Her almost total lack of properly pronounced English emphasized that the one doing all the talking now – as far as it went – was not the one who had earlier said, so eloquently 'Do you wish anything else, sir, madam?' at the end of our meal.

They went through into the bathroom, and took off their little aprons, their cuffs, and their black silk stockings, after which they ran a bath in the huge tub. There was plenty of room for me as well as for the two of them in there, once they got in, but I thought it might be more fun, right now, to watch rather than to take part. I looked longingly at their slim bodies, and at their almost bald little pussies. They were probably both in their early twenties but, to Western eyes like mine, their bodies looked rather younger. Their pubic hair, in both cases, was but a wisp, a tiny, fluffy line, barely discernible over the top of their *mons veneris*. Their pudenda were chubby, with fleshy, dark – almost black – little outer lips, the inner lips showing as a darkish pink gash in the hairless middle of the area. Their tiny nipples were the same almost black colour as their outer pussy lips. I had an erection that I could have used as a spade. I took my clothes off, and the girls shrieked with what I could only imagine was faked alarm, pointing at my swollen erection. I grinned at them again, and after a while they began to bathe each other.

They washed their bodies carefully, giggling constantly, spending much time thoroughly washing each other's pussies, with soapy fingers exploring and laving, after which they did the same with each other's puckered little dark-skinned assholes. They seemed totally oblivious to my presence, and seemed to be enjoying what they were doing to each other.

They didn't touch their faces which, reasonably enough, were not in need of soap and water, but which were, in both cases, quite heavily made up. They wore a kohl-like black eye make-up on their eyebrows and their eyelids, with the same cosmetic generously applied to their eyelashes, both top and bottom. They wore pink blusher on their cheeks and a powder base all over their faces, finishing off with dark pink lipstick on their luscious little lips. Their fingernails were well shaped, and quite long, and they wore nail varnish that exactly matched their lipstick. As I watched, one girl stood up, got out of the bath, and went over still dripping wet, to sit on the lavatory, where she noisily relieved herself, the sound of her pissing into the loo echoing loudly in my ears. Neither girl seemed embarrassed by this action but, not being a water sports enthusiast myself, the sight and sounds of urination do nothing for me. It is something I think that I would prefer happened in private, and not in my presence. But I digress. The girl who had used the loo splashed her way back into the bath again, and there was much demonstration of the re-cleansing of the offending parts, after which both girls emerged from the bath and dried themselves.

'Ready now,' said one of the girls. Even side by side, I found it difficult to tell the one from the other, but since I knew neither of their names, it didn't somehow seem important. They trotted through to the bedroom, where they pulled an armchair up towards the end of the bed – I judged that it was actually about three feet away – and sat me in it. They then both got onto the bed, and, wrapping their arms about each other's slim, completely naked young bodies, they began kissing each other. Their eyes were closed, their mouths were open, and their tongues entwined. I could have reached out and touched them, had I so wished, but it serves to show you how close I was.

They kissed passionately and then one girl lay down on her back, pulling the other girl down with her. The one on top put a hand between the supine girl's legs and prised them apart. She then started stroking and feeling her friend's pussy, which brought forth appreciative sounds from the first girl, who soon placed her hands each side of the second girl's head and guided it down between her legs. She then pressed her partner's face hard against her cunt. As she did so, I could see that her sex was exuding her love juices freely, the clear liquid glistening in the electric light. From where I sat, I could smell the sweet, slightly acrid scent of aroused young pussy.

The second girl started to kiss and lick and suck at her friend's sex, thrusting her tongue down inside it, and then withdrawing it and licking and slurping all around the outer lips before once more delving down inside. From time to time she raised her head a few inches from the source of her pleasure, licked her lips and swallowed lasciviously. The girl who was having the cunnilingus performed upon her next took both her own nipples in her hands and began to tweak and pull and rub at them, until they stood up even more stiffly than they had before she began this self-stimulation. She then reached down between both their legs, and began masturbating the girl who was sucking her off so prettily, sliding two fingers deeply into the other girl's cunt, massaging and manipulating until both of them were moving their hips in time with their obviously imminent orgasms. They began to move faster, gaining rapid momentum together.

It was, as Cherry had described, an extremely erotic sight, but it was more so because of the youth of the two girls, and the lithe exuberance of their writhing bodies, than from any particularly sophisticated or unusual sexual activity. But it was none the less enjoyable for that, and I was hard put to it not to start masturbating myself to a much-needed climax whilst I watched the two girls enjoying themselves. I was particularly aroused by the proximity of the top girl's tiny, tight little anus-eye which was winking at me from between her slim buttocks almost immediately in front of my face. It was but inches away, and it was, naturally enough, of the same dark, almost black pigmentation of both girls' pussies and nipples, and was entirely bare of any hint of anal hair. It was small, and I could imagine forcing my swollen cock into it, and the glorious feel of it gripping me tightly as I entered the forbidden place. It was, I realized, the second Chinese anus that I had fantasized about ravishing, the first, of course, being Cherry's. As I watched and indulged in wishful thinking – at least for the moment – the two girls came to a well-timed mutual orgasm, or series of orgasms, and their squeaks and moans and sighs denoted that they had both enjoyed themselves. Either that, or they were competent actresses. It was time, I thought selfishly, for a little fun for me. Watching is only for so long. Doing it is all.

I stood up, lifted the top girl off her partner, sat down

on the edge of the bed and, placing her between my spread knees, I pulled her face towards my cock, until she was in no doubt about what I wished her to do for me. She obligingly took hold of my prick and enveloped it with her small but capable mouth, and then she started, wetly, to fellate me.

I next turned to my left and pulled the other girl, still supine, backwards up alongside me, so that I could grip her about her hips, which I did. I then lifted her up, and, lying down myself, I placed her over my face, with her knees each side of my head, so that her wet, strongly-smelling little open pussy was immediately over my mouth. I set her down, and her soft wetness engulfed me. She tasted sensational. Fresh wet cunt is one of my favourite tastes, but this girl was a whole new experience. It's a difficult flavour to describe, but let me try. It's really very subtle. And every girl, of course, tastes differently. But there's an overall fresh fruit taste, akin to ripe melon. And just a taste of acidity. Lemon, perhaps. Add something over-ripe. Probably mango. And then the tiniest, *teeniest* touch of something just slightly fishy. Maybe anchovy. Mix them all together, and lick them from a pretty girl's pussy.

Magic! I sank my tongue into her, savouring her flavour with genuine relish. She moved about on my mouth, apparently enjoying the sensations I was producing in her pussy. Whilst all this was going on, I was mentally deliberating how best to enjoy the further company of these delightful young girls. It was, in all probability, a once in a lifetime opportunity. *Tiptop* or no *Tiptop*, I wasn't that likely to be in these parts again. So to speak. So it seemed silly not to take the utmost advantage of the girls. And in any case, the more I used them, the more I would have to write about for the magazine. Photographs I obviously couldn't get. But facts I could. I decided to go the whole hog. Having watched them at play with each other, there were now a number of options open to me. It was a question, really, of priorities. I didn't have too much time to decide. Unless I was happy to let the girl who was doing such a seriously professional job on sucking my cock take me all the way. She was terrific, and I knew that I wouldn't be able to hold out much longer. I took my decision. She could suck me until I came down her throat. Why spoil my fun, I thought? I'm enjoying it. Why stop?

Which meant that after this delight reached its inevitable conclusion, I would then (a) fuck one of the girls, and (b) fuck the other one. These difficult decisions taken, I relaxed, lay back, and endeavoured to enjoy it. It wasn't difficult. Having decided to relax and let events take their course, I concentrated on both giving and getting as much pleasure as was possible in my happy circumstance. The little girl who was fellating me was doing a magnificent job, and I was beginning to move my hips in concert with her slowly building rhythm. She had seemingly turned her mouth into a second pussy, and I was being fucked by it, slowly, carefully, lecherously, and intensely enjoyably. The suction that she managed to apply was sexually very exciting, and her mouth was warm and wet as it pumped away at my cock.

Meanwhile the other girl was riding my mouth with her fleshy, swollen-lipped little cunt as I tongued and licked and sucked at her, her juices running copiously into, and overflowing from, my mouth. I swallowed a great deal of these juices, with continuing pleasure. They were, as I have described, like nectar to me. I could feel my ejaculation gathering from somewhere deep down between my prostate and my balls, and I increased the rate at which I was fucking the receptive mouth between my legs.

As I did so, I could feel the girl sitting on my mouth increasing *her* rhythm, and then suddenly the two of us were coming together, writhing and groaning our pleasure, and I was spurting my load down the first girl's throat. She swallowed, and continued to suck my cock until all was finally spent, and then the girl on my mouth began slowly to lose momentum, until she too had attained her finally, dying orgasm of a series of multiple orgasms. She then lifted a leg and gracefully slid off my face and down onto the bed beside me. The other girl had not only sucked me dry, but she had sucked me clean, and she now went into the bathroom and returned with a warmly damp flannel with which she carefully and gently washed my face and mouth. She then used the flannel to do the same to her colleague's pussy, carefully wiping and patting until she was satisfied that it too was restored once more to its original fresh cleanliness. She then disappeared again into the bathroom, from which soon came the sound of teeth being cleaned. Cleanliness, to Chinese girls in Hong Kong, is obviously next to godliness.

I felt like a drink, and I got up off the bed to pour myself a scotch and water. Both were present with the other drinks and mixers on the sideboard. Scotch, in fact, was present in about half a dozen different brands. I chose Cutty Sark, and then I asked the girls – now both back together – what they would like to drink, if anything, and they said that I wasn't there to serve them, they were there to serve me. However, I insisted and, amidst much giggling, they both accepted orange juice. It was, happily, going to be a long night, and I wondered if I should send a message down to Cherry, telling her not to wait and saying that I would catch up with her in the morning. But then I realised that she was a big girl, and that she would do whatever she wanted to do, in the fullness of time. She was perfectly capable of calling herself a cab and leaving me a note, if that was what she wished to do.

I had a kind of obsessive fascination with the bodies of these two young Chinese girls and I wanted to examine them, without the distraction of sexual activity. I told them of my wish and one of them lay down on the bed, inviting me to examine her as closely as I wished. She was really beautiful. A real China doll. I touched her breasts, squeezing them carefully, and feeling how firm they were in their tiny magnificence. I pinched a nipple gently, and watched it burgeon.

I moved my hand down and stroked her flat stomach, her firm hips, and then the inside of her thighs, which led, naturally enough, to her genital area. I felt the softness of her wispy pubic hair, and touched the almost black skin of her outer vaginal lips which were presently closed. I used both hands to open them and expose her inner lips, which were a paler, more pinkish black. I slid a finger inside her, then two, and held her open. Inside she was pure pale, wet pink and, with my head immediately above her, I could inhale the rich scent of her. I felt my prick stiffening at the sight and smell of her. I took my hand away from her young girl's cunt, and, slipping it beneath her buttocks, I turned her over onto her stomach.

I stroked the nape of her neck and ruffled the luxuriant, blue-black hair with which she was crowned. I moved my hand down her shoulders, and then her back, feeling the taut muscles beneath the silken skin. I kept my hand moving down, past her tiny waist, to her small, beautifully rounded buttocks. I felt and squeezed them both in turn, and felt her wriggle beneath my hand. I slid my fingers down the crease in her bottom cheeks until I came to her tiny anus and I pulled her bum cheeks apart with both hands so that I might view it more closely. It too was the same dark, almost black of her outer vaginal lips, the skin wrinkled and tightly closed. I eased a finger inside her, and felt her beginning to relax her anal sphincter.

At this point the other girl, who had been sitting beside the two of us, watching what I was doing, got up from the bed and went into the bathroom. She came back with a small round jar of the kind that women buy face cream in and, unscrewing the top, she reached inside and took her finger out with a gob of some kind of jelly or lubricant on the tip. She used her other hand to extract my fingers from the first girl's anus, and, smiling at me the while, she began to lubricate her colleague's tight little bottom hole. I seriously got a hard on at this juncture. Whilst I had certainly been fantasizing about anal sex with one or other of these girls, I'm not certain that I would have actually moved to do anything about it. But here I was being given an open invitation. I mentally accepted it immediately, but did nothing to show my interest. I suppose, being realistic, that my throbbingly rigid cock said it all for me.

I watched, fascinated, as the one girl made a thorough job of greasing the other girl's anus. She thrust her finger, anointed with lubricant, as deeply inside as her small fingers would reach, using a reaming motion to spread the unguent as widely as she could. She then motioned me to stand up, which I did, and she carefully greased my erection, making sure that it was well greased all over. She then said something in Chinese to the other girl, who raised herself up on the bed onto all fours, presenting her bottom with its well-greased sphincter to me. The girl who had overseen the lubricating of us both now motioned me forward. I knelt on the bed behind the kneeling girl, at which the first girl took my stiff cock in one hand and, using the fingers of her other hand to open up the kneeling girl's anus, she fed me in. She eased me up into her friend's asshole slowly at first. Then, as my cock slid happily into the now oleaginous opening, she thrust me firmly in until I was sunk in up to the full length of my cock, my balls slapping against the girl's plump buttocks.

I grabbed her around her thighs, and began to fuck her, the tightness of her sphincter encompassing my prick. It was a joyous sensation to feel. I knew that I wouldn't be able to hold back from ejaculating for very long, what with the excitement of what I was doing and the beauty of the girl to whom I was doing it. Sure enough, moments later, I was spurting my come into her asshole, coming inside her, the tightness of her anus squeezing it out of me in hot, liquid spurts. I noticed, holding onto the girl's thighs as I jetted into her, that her friend was standing beside me, masturbating herself as she watched us, her fingers deep inside her cunt, no doubt rubbing her clitoris into a state of sexual frenzy, until she too was coming. She smiled a great smile at me as she came, suddenly noticing that I was watching what she was doing.

When all three of us were finished, the girl whose bottom I had been fucking grasped me by the hand and took me into the bathroom, where she ran a bath and stepped into it. Then she held out a hand for me to join her. I needed no second invitation. First she washed my cock, slowly, carefully and lovingly, after which I washed her asshole, in similar fashion. A few moments later the other girl came and joined us, and we spent some time fooling about in the bath, playing with each other, a sort of sexual adults' playtime. I began to get hard again, what with the proximity of these two beautiful young women, and the thought that I had the pleasure of actually fucking one of them in the quim still to come. After all this time, I could actually tell the one from the other, if only because of a tiny mole on the inner thigh of one of them. She was the one who had fellated me earlier and the one whom – if all went according to plan – I anticipated fucking.

As I thought about it, I was sucking the tiny, erect nipple of one of the girls and she was groping me with a lazy, half-masturbatory sort of action as I did so. With their thighs immersed in soapy water, I couldn't tell which was which. Eventually, however, we got out of the bath, and dried ourselves – and each other – with the huge, soft towels that were in the bathroom. When we were ready, we went back into the bedroom and I began to think seriously about my forthcoming fuck. As I thought about it, I wondered how one of these young girls would look other than completely naked.

I guess it was pretty perverse of me. Most men spend their time wondering how a particular woman – or women – will look completely naked. But having seen these two all evening in their birthday suits, I was curious to see how one of them would look in sexy lingerie. Nothing ventured, nothing gained, I thought, so I asked the girls if one of them could dress up for me, and explained what I wanted. I also said that I would prefer the one with the mole to do the dressing up. No problem, they said, straight away, and off they both went. They returned about fifteen minutes later, the one still naked, the other looking like something out of every red-blooded man's fantasy world.

She was wearing a beautiful, expensive-looking, black, transparent negligée in the sheerest nylon, beneath which she wore a tiny, totally transparent bra in a shade of the palest pale green, through which her nipples stood up, saying 'Fuck me'. She also wore matching knickers, with all but a small centre panel in the same see-through material, but with a tiny triangle in some sort of pale green lace hiding her pussy from immediate view. Beneath these she wore a minuscule pale green suspender belt, with long, pale green elastic suspenders running down her thighs to fasten onto pale green silk stockings, with the expanse of brown, naked flesh between her stocking tops and her knickers gleaming erotically, as if her skin were oiled. As she stood there, the other girl – still naked – took the nylon negligée and swept it off her friend's shoulders, leaving her standing there in her bra, knickers, suspender belt and stockings. On her feet she wore black, high-heeled, patent leather sandals. She smiled at me, and twirled around. I applauded, enthusiastically, and she bowed low. 'You rike?' she asked. 'I rike,' I said. I fucking *love* it, I thought. I could see that the naked one didn't have a mole on her inner thigh, so I knew that the one in the sexy undies was the right one.

I went over to her and, taking her in my arms, I kissed her passionately. She felt marvellous, all warm soft flesh through silk, and she smelt erotically of some heavy, sensual, musk-based scent. She thrust her sexy little tongue deeply into my mouth and explored my tongue. Her saliva as she kissed me was prodigious and ran into my mouth. My cock grew harder as I swallowed, with four of my five senses all working overtime; those of taste, sight, touch, and smell. All she needs to do now is fart, I thought, giggling quietly to myself, and I'll be using all five of my senses. She didn't fart, but she *did* whisper in my ear, bringing my sense of hearing into play. 'Are you going to fuck me now?' she asked, her voice throaty with what I hoped was desire. 'I want your big Eng'rish cock inside me. P'rease.'

'My pleasure, darling,' I said. I led her over to the bed and laid her down on her back. I then spread her legs wide and knelt over her, so that I might kiss and suck her pussy through the material of her pale green knickers, always one of my special enjoyments, combining taste, feel and scent. She was lubricating freely into the cotton lining of her knicker crotch. What with her sexual lubricant and my saliva, the two love juices were soon mixing in a wet, heady, exotically scented, erotically flavoured, sexually stimulating treat. After a little while, I decided that it would be good to suck her without the encumbrance of her now sodden knickers so I put my hands beneath her and raised her up. Then, using one hand to keep her bottom off the bed, I used the other hand to peel her knickers down her thighs, over her knees, and off, over her ankles and feet. I then buried my mouth and nose in her open crotch, inhaling her scent, tasting her cunt, licking, sucking, eating her. A gourmet sexual meal.

As I was thus occupied, she began to wriggle about a bit and, looking up, I could see that she was raising herself up sufficiently to reach behind her and unfasten the band of her brassiere, which she then dropped on the floor beside the bend. She took her nipples between the fingers of each hand and began to pull at them, pinching and squeezing, giving little moans of pleasure as she did so. Despite her breasts being more than well-developed for an Oriental girl, they were, by comparison to European or American girls' breasts, still tiny. But they were an exquisite shape: full – for their size – firm, pointed, and tipped with tiny, almost black nipples, mounted on equally almost black areolae, which were now fully erect from the fingering that they were receiving. At this sight I got very excited indeed, and I just had to suck one. I stopped eating her pussy and raised myself up, my cock finding the general area of her pussy as I rode up her body. As I took that delicious, small, hard nipple into my mouth, the girl took my swollen prick in her hand and inserted it into her waiting love-hole.

It was delightfully tight, delightfully wet, and delightfully active, and her vaginal muscles were working overtime as I thrust down into them. Her pussy felt as tight as had her friend's bottom, and pussies don't get any tighter than that. She was smiling up at me as she worked away at my cock, and I stopped sucking her nipple and leaned down and began to kiss her. She tasted of raspberries and cream, and I was aware of the fact that my mouth had to taste to her of her own love juices, which I had so recently been enjoying. Her tongue was all over mine, and she clasped my buttocks and thrust her hips and groin up against me as I fucked her, fucking me back with vigour.

I could feel her fingers squeezing and stroking the cheeks of my arse, and then I felt those fingers moving down into the crack between them, and feeling for – and finding – my anus, which she began to massage. It was a highly erotic sensation, which started off the beginnings of an all-consuming ejaculation, and as she slid a finger inside my arsehole and began to finger-fuck me there I shot my load into her welcoming, all-embracing pussy. I shouted out my pleasure aloud as I spurted into her, delving deep, holding her to me by her tight buttocks, and I was grinding away at her as I pumped her full of my semen, the intenseness of my ejaculation so great that I never wanted it to end.

But like everything else in life, it did, eventually. And you would be forgiven for thinking that was the end of my debauched evening with these two exquisite girls. At that moment, I too thought the same thing. But I am pleased to be able to tell you that, having been coaxed back into the bath by these two little sexual athletes to clean up (as I thought) before bidding them farewell, I enjoyed, first, an exquisite hand-job from one of them, while I watched the other one masturbating herself to climax. After which, with a decent interval for more whisky and what passed for conversation between the three of us, I had anal sex with the one that I had recently fucked in the cunt.

I had long since given up any thought of leaving the brothel before morning and after my last act of anal intercourse, I fell asleep on the bed, the two girls curled up, one each side of me. I'm proud also to be able to tell you that I fucked both of them once more the following morning, and if you think that's boastful, all I can say is, if you were where I was and in the company that I was in, you would have done exactly the same thing without the slightest problem. I bade the girls goodbye, tipped them extravagantly, and paid my bill. Thinking about the bill, thank God I had a gold Amex card. I won't embarrass you by telling you how much it was, but as I settled it, I wondered if I was buying a share in the business. But no; my receipt was just that. Not a share certificate. Well, Cherry had said that it wasn't cheap. 'Food and service,' it said. But what terrific service!

I shall long remember it. When I asked for my bill, one

of the staff in reception gave me a cheerful note from Cherry, simply saying that since I was so obviously enjoying myself she was going home to get some much-needed sleep, and asking me to ring her as and when. I couldn't detect any note of irritation in it anywhere, and breathed a mental sigh of relief. She had been so helpful to me that I didn't want to upset her, and I still needed her assistance. That wonderful night was, in fact, (if you will forgive the pun) the climax of my stay in Hong Kong.

I actually spent another ten days there, but all I was doing was arranging, with the help of Cherry (or Guai Tim Bun, to use her proper name), to set up and attend the shooting of the photographs of, first of all, Juanita and her colleagues in the pussy bar that she and I visited on the first night that we met in Hong Kong. I commissioned action shots of the girls at work on the bar, and a number of them posed individually for nude shots, which I would use in some cases where actual shots (in The House of a Thousand Dreams, or The Rainbow Palace, for example) were not feasible. I did not, as arranged with Fred before I left New York, bother with girl sets as such. You will remember that he was going to set these up himself in New York, using Oriental models. I spent the evenings with Cherry, extending my knowledge and appreciation of, and liking for, Chinese food, and I spent the nights in my Peninsular Hotel suite with her too, fucking her slowly, gently and exquisitely pleasurably. The pale, golden-brown chrysanthemum on her inner thigh is firmly imprinted in my memory, along with mental images of the two young girls from the Rainbow Palace brothel. I arranged for a plethora of exterior shots of the myriad hostess bars, topless bars, sex cinemas, sex shops, and other establishments devoted to selling the wide variety of sexual services that Hong Kong supplies for its visitors. Most of these were taken at night, the lurid neon lighting used by many of them providing more atmosphere than the same shots would have done during daylight hours.

Next I arranged for photography of Cora – and of some of the other men – in the transvestite bar in the Wanchai district that we had visited. I paid for shots of Cora naked, with and without her cock in evidence, and I have to tell you that, whilst the former were being shot, I was glad that I had my trousers on. It was the first time in my life that I felt worried about the size of my cock. But there's always a first time, isn't there?

I also managed to get one of the men who'd had the operation to pose, his legs well spread, showing what purported to be a vagina. It was just about acceptable, if you didn't get too close. He was very proud of it. I also had some general shots of the bar taken, making certain that no customers could be identified in them. We didn't take any shots of the exteriors of either of the two brothels, since our visits there had been on the understanding that they would not be recognizable in the pieces that I wrote about them in the magazine. But it would be fun, I thought, to mock up a picture in *Tiptop*'s New York studio of Cherry and me looking down through a glass floor at a scene of depravity set out below us, *à la* The House of a Thousand Dreams. Cherry allowed me to have some pictures of her taken fully – and flatteringly – clothed, wearing one of her charming embroidered, silken, evening *cheongsams*, but she flatly refused to pose for me nude, exquisite as her body was. She wouldn't even allow me to have a close-up photograph taken of the little golden-brown chrysanthemum tattoo. Not even for my own, personal, never-to-be-published photograph. Some you win, as they say.

One thing she did profess interest in, however, was my suggestion that, provided Fred agreed to an idea of mine that I hadn't yet had an opportunity to discuss with him (and that was always something of an if) she might like to become *Tiptop*'s first Far East contributing editor. Contributing in the sense of ideas. Suggestions for visual features, interviews, articles, anything that she thought might interest *Tiptop*'s readers around the world. It wasn't my idea that she should try and write anything. But if she put up an idea that was eventually agreed, then she could suggest possible authors or photographers, or both. She had provided the names of all the photographers that I had been using this particular week. And very professional they were too, although this was the first time that any of them had ever been commissioned to photograph women in various stages of undress. Most of them were usually either news or fashion photographers.

And then, suddenly, almost as though it had all been just a dream, something that hadn't really happened, I found myself on a plane back to the States, with the excitement and sexual enjoyment of my stay in Hong Kong fading rapidly with every mile the aircraft travelled towards New York, and Kennedy Airport.

CHAPTER SIX: KEEPING ABREAST

Eileen, bless her, met me at Kennedy, with the by now obligatory stretch limo, and filled me in on the gossip as we travelled into Manhattan. All was well, it would seem, and Fred had even been seen in the office fairly frequently during my absence. Sales of the magazine were still increasing, Wally seemed happy, and he apparently hadn't felt the need to visit New York. Eileen told me that she hadn't been fucked during my entire trip abroad, which didn't say much, to my mind, for the average Manhattan man. She said that she had hot – and wet – knickers for me, and didn't seem too pleased when I said that all I wanted to do when I got back to my apartment in Sutton Place was sleep. I felt as if I had been fucking non-stop for weeks. And thinking about it, that wasn't so far from the truth. She said, rather tartly, that she'd have to remember to buy a new battery for her vibrator on the way home. I didn't reply to that.

Speaking of fucking, said Eileen, taking a piece of paper from her bag, there had been calls for me from Pauline, my air hostess, and June at the brothel (who had said that Charlene, Victoria, Gloria, Andrea, Louise and Rita were all missing me). Jenny, from the S&M club, had also called, as had Lucy (Eileen's favourite bald, black model), not to mention Dee Dee from the topless/bottomless bar and, of course, the lovely Katrina, my Russian ballet dancer. In answer to my question, Eileen said that no, she personally wasn't aware of any messages from Annabel. And Fred had asked if I would join him for a drink at his apartment at around six this evening? I looked at my watch. It was just after noon, New York time. It felt more like midnight. I guessed that a long, hot shower, a large scotch and water, and a short sleep would probably work wonders. I told Eileen to tell Fred that, yes, I would be delighted to see him at six o'clock and, feeling mean about my earlier decision, I changed my mind and asked why didn't she come back to my place with me? I'd go and see Fred, and I'd probably fall asleep after that, but she was welcome to stay with me, if that was what she would like. I even said please. She seemed pleased, and said yes, thank you, darling, so everyone was happy again.

In fact, I was glad, eventually, that I had asked her back. The apartment seemed empty and cold, and I was grateful for her company. I unpacked, left my washing out for my cleaning lady, put the rest of my stuff away, and checked through my mail, almost all of which was either bills or junk mail. Nothing from Annabel. Not that I was really expecting anything, I told myself. Whilst I was unpacking, Fred rang and asked if I would mind holding the meeting over until the following morning, in the office, to which I happily agreed. I took Eileen out later that evening to eat at the little Italian neighbourhood restaurant that Annabel and I had gone to just before our trip to San Juan, and whilst the patron and his wife recognized me, and greeted me pleasantly enough, I got the impression that they disapproved of the fact that I was with someone other than Annabel.

We got back to the apartment at about ten and, after watching television desultorily for a while, we went to bed where I lay back and tried to enjoy it whilst Eileen worked out at least some of her frustrations on my cock. It, fortunately, was rather more responsive than I was. When

Eileen complained of my lack of enthusiastic participation, I admitted to it, and asked to be excused on the grounds of jet lag. She seemed a little soured by my lack of interest. 'I know there are something like two hundred million people in China,' she said. 'And even assuming that only half of them are women, you can't possibly have fucked *all* of them. What's the matter with you? Don't you enjoy fucking me any more? I can remember when you were actually keen to get inside my panties. I even thought that perhaps you were in love with me, just a little bit.'

I tried to ignore her, but it was difficult. I'm not sure about the 'in love' bit, but I *was* fond of Eileen, and I was quite certain that it wouldn't be too long before I was chasing after her with my dick in my hand, pleading with her to let me stick it up her. 'Be a sweetheart, sweetheart,' I said. 'I am seriously jet lagged, tired, knackered, and mentally and physically exhausted. It's been a long day, and all I want to do right now is sleep. I promise you, the next time that we go to bed together I'll fuck your socks off. OK?' I don't think she was particularly convinced, but at least she knew when she was defeated. So she said yeah, OK, if that was how I felt. And she got up, got dressed, and left. I turned over, gratefully, and went to sleep. I slept like the proverbial log.

I was up early the following morning, bright-eyed and bushy-tailed, and in the office by nine-thirty. When Eileen came in at ten, I made a point of apologizing to her for my performance the previous evening. She seemed to find my apology reassuring, and was very soon the same old Eileen that I knew and, well, loved. You know what I mean. We drank coffee together in her office until Fred came in. He looked well. Fit and happy. And he seemed genuinely pleased to see me. Eileen had told me that his personal habits didn't seem to have changed any, other than that he had been coming into the office pretty regularly, but he had the physique and stamina of an ox, and he seemed to thrive on late nights, too much booze, too much cocaine, and too much sex. 'Hey, Tony,' he cried, slapping me on my back so that I very nearly fell over. 'How goes it? How was Hong Kong? Did you get your end away? What are all those dolly little Chinese girls like anyway?' He didn't wait for an answer, but put his arm around my shoulders and guided me towards his office. Looking over his shoulder, he asked Eileen if she would bring us some coffee.

'Sit down, Tone,' he said. 'It's good to have you back. All these fucking gays are getting me down.' 'Which fucking gays are those, Fred?' I asked, curiously. 'Oh, you know,' he said. 'Dave, in the art department, and his lot.' Dave was the art director, and he did have two assistants, both of the same sexual persuasion as he. But I'd never found his homosexuality anything other than, when noticeable, extremely amusing. He tended to keep his sex life very separate from his work. I hadn't had too much to do with the other two, but they seemed pleasant enough.

'What's been the problem, then?' I asked Fred. Fred leaned back in his chair, looked across at me, and sighed deeply. 'Oh, I don't know, really,' he said. 'Perhaps I'm making it up. I think I'm getting old, or something. They just get up my fucking nose occasionally. I got used to you being here, and dealing with most of the shit, and then, while you've been away, what with Wally nagging me when I was in London, and one thing and another, I've tried hard to be a good boy while you were in Hong Kong. You know, get into the office on time, come in every day. That sort of thing. Remember to come back to the office after lunch. Try to remember not to try and fuck the telephonist. It's really been getting on my tits. I'm as depressed as hell. But I expect I'll get over it.'

'I'm sorry to hear that, Fred,' I said. 'Is there anything I can do to help? I mean, do you want me to have a word with Dave? Tell him to keep out of your way? Something like that? I can simply ask him to deal with me on a day to day basis, now that I'm back here, and not bother you unless it's really necessary. I'm sure that wouldn't bother him. He and I get on all right.' I looked at Fred. He really didn't *look* hassled. Whatever it was that was bothering him certainly didn't show.

'Nah,' he said. 'Thanks, but no, thanks. It's not really a problem. Now that you're back, I'm sure it will go away. And there's no point in my upsetting him. He's always been free to come and talk to me whenever he's wanted to. I'd be silly to try and stop that. But that wasn't what I wanted to talk to you about, Tony. They tell me that wet T-shirt contests are all the rage down on Florida's East Coast. On the beach, and in the bars and restaurants. Everywhere. There are apparently a few pretty girls with great tits who are cleaning up on the prize money down there. The money itself isn't that big. I gather that a hundred dollars is the usual top prize, at the level of competition that we're talking about. But if you can do that once at lunch time, and twice during the course of an evening, and perhaps four times a day on Saturdays and Sundays, you're not doing too badly. But it isn't the prize money that appeals to me. It's just got to be a great picture story for us, hasn't it? All those dolly little teenage girls with their tits poking through wet T-shirts. Hang on while I have a quick wank, will you?' 'It sounds good,' I said. 'It sounds a lot of fun. But how does it actually work?'

'Oh, it's very simple,' he said. 'The bar or restaurant, or whoever is running the contest, sticks posters and leaflets up all around town a day or two before the contest. There's no entry fee, or anything like that. The organizers are doing it simply to pull in the crowds, who are going to buy drinks – beers, mostly – while the contest is going on. Then, at the appointed time, the girls turn up. They're wearing just bikini bottoms and T-shirts. Usually plain white ones. And then, one by one, they get up onto a small stage, which has been waterproofed in some way, and someone throws a bucket of water over them. The winner is chosen by the amount of applause that each girl receives. It's pretty arbitrary, but it seems to work.

'Once the T-shirts get wet, you'll see why plain white ones are preferred to anything else. Because the girls' tits show through better. I'm told that when these contests started up, a few months ago, some girls took their wet T-shirts off, showing all they'd got, and often won simply by doing that. Now, I understand, that's banned by most competition organizers as being unfair competition, but the winning girl, so I'm told, still takes her T-shirt off after she's won, to show her approval to the guys who voted for her. It's using women as sex objects. It's chauvinistic, and disgusting. And the girls love it. Just as much as the men, apparently. They're only college kids, really. You know, late teens, very early twenties. That kind of age. If they've got good tits, they don't mind flashing them, particularly if they can pull in a couple of thousand dollars a week by doing just that. It beats the hell out of working. They tell me that a free feel before the competition to the guy who throws the water will guarantee you a bucket of warm water, but of course that doesn't make your nipples stand out as well as cold water does. I thought you should probably get down there, with one of our photographers, and see what you can get.

'You'll have to move about a bit, up and down the coast. Otherwise, if you stay in the same area, you're going to get basically the same girls all the time. You could start around West Palm Beach, and go on down through Boynton Beach, Delray Beach, Pompano Beach, and Fort Lauderdale, all the way down to Miami Beach. I don't think these competitions have got as far as the Florida Keys yet. It's still mostly fairyland down there.

But if the pictures are as good as I think they will be, we could run a *Tiptop* wet T-shirt photographic competition in the magazine, with readers sending in their pictures. What do you think?'

'It sounds good, Fred,' I said. And it did. At this time of year in New York, with September not so far away, and with the temperature already dropping noticeably at night, who would want to turn down a couple of weeks along the Florida coastline, spending all day looking at girls showing off their tits in wet T-shirts? Not me. 'Have you anyone in mind as a suitable photographer?' I asked Fred. 'Well, sure,' he said. 'Why don't you take Barbara Hartley? Have you used her?' 'No,' I said. 'I don't think I've come across her.' 'Oh, you'll love her,' he said. 'She's a very good, all-round photographer, but she's particularly good at things like this, where people aren't actually posing for you. You know, where you literally have to knock off your shots while whatever it is is happening. Not too many people are that good at that kind of photography, but Babs seems to have the knack. I've used her at discos, parties, that kind of thing. She's really good. Dave will dig up some of her shots for you to have a look at if you like. And Eileen will give you her number. But if you'd rather use someone else, feel free. I've got no axe to grind about Babs Hartley.'

He grinned at me. 'But speaking of grinding, now that we're on our own, tell about Hong Kong. Did you fuck a lot of Chinese girls? Their cunts aren't *really* horizontal are they? That's just an old wives' tale, isn't it?' 'Yes, of course it is,' I told him. 'Their cunts are just like any other girls' cunts. Round and wet and welcoming. Yes, I fucked a few Chinese girls. I could very easily become addicted, I tell you. I think it's something to do with that Oriental submissive bit. I didn't know I was into submissive women until I went to Hong Kong, but since I've been there, I'm all for it.'

Fred gave me a very old-fashioned look indeed. 'No, come on, Fred,' I said. 'Don't look at me like that. Think about it. Instead of them saying anything from "How dare you? What makes you think I'm that king of girl?" to "I'm sorry darling, but I've got a bit of a headache tonight," Chinese girls bow, and say things like "How may I pleasure you, my lord?" And they mean it. It's a whole new experience. I thoroughly recommend it. If I could afford to retire, I'd retire right now, and go and live in Hong Kong. Or maybe China itself. China's got to be all right, so long as you're not Chinese. But let me tell you some of the things I got up to during my trip to Hong Kong.'

I spent some time telling him about the various places I had been to, and some of the things that I had seen and experienced out there. I described my relationship with Cherry, but I kept the description of my night with the two young girls at the Rainbow Palace until the very end. He was fascinated. 'My God, Tone,' he said. 'Whatever did you come back for?' What was particularly nice was that he immediately agreed to my suggestion that we appoint Cherry as our Far East contributing editor, with a very reasonable annual consultancy fee and generous terms for any material she suggested that we actually used, including fees for the writers/photographers, and good additional fees for her. He also suggested that we pay for her to come over to New York for a week or so to see how we worked, and what we were all about, which delighted me. I told him, of course, that Cherry was the recommendation of his contact, Mr Ho Ming Chan, of International Publishers in Hong Kong, and he made a note to remind himself to write to Mr Ho and thank him for the introduction.

'Maybe I should go out to Hong Kong and have a look at the possibilities of producing a Far East edition of *Tiptop*, rather than sit around here messing about with a Far East issue?' he said. 'I don't think so,' I told him. 'By all means go to Hong Kong. You'll love it. But if you think about it, what is going to make a great American Far East issue for *Tiptop* are the fantastic, multitudinous sexual attractions of that part of the world. They have so much of the real thing out there – live, and cheap – that I don't suppose they buy girlie magazines. They don't need them. They actually buy girlies. For about the same price!' 'I guess you're probably right,' said Fred. 'But from what you tell me, I think I ought to go and have a look-see anyway.' 'So do I,' I said. 'And I think you ought to have a good look at Cherry's golden-brown chrysanthemum.' 'Not to mention her cherry,' said Fred, laughing. 'Good to see you, Tone. Let's catch up with each other socially soon. OK?' 'OK,' I said. 'And thanks.'

In the event, I didn't start off at Boynton Beach, I started off at Fort Lauderdale. I'd met Babs Hartley, and we'd got on like a house on fire, right from the start. She was shortish – about five five – brunette, attractive rather than old-fashioned pretty, and somewhere around the middle to late thirties, I would have said. She had a neat figure. Great legs. Good tits. And she was a lot of fun. She was one of those women who were always smiling. Plus the fact that she had an intriguing aura of sexuality. Nothing overt. Nothing you could put your finger on. She didn't come on strong, for example. But when she looked at you, eye to eye, you knew that she knew, if you know what I mean. It was definitely there, if you cared to chance your arm. But it wasn't for kids. It was for grown men.

We started off at Fort Lauderdale because Babs did some instant research amongst photographic colleagues who had already covered the story for the major newspapers and they said that Fort Lauderdale was where it was all happening. We flew down and rented a car at Fort Lauderdale airport. I fancied something flash, and so I chose a Camaro. Well, you're only young once, aren't you? When did *you* last drive a Camaro? Great fun, in the dry, in a straight line. If it's wet, stay at home. That's my advice, anyway. But Florida is essentially dry and sunny.

Babs had a minimum of equipment for a professional photographer. A neat little Nikon, a couple of extra lenses, and that was it. We weren't into a studio situation, and speed was of the essence. We booked into one of the better motels. As I parked the Camaro, and was about to get out, Babs said 'Hang on a minute there, Tony, will you please?' 'Sure,' I said. 'What's the problem?' 'No problem,' she said. 'But let's not fuck about. Or, rather, let's do just that. I like to be up front in what I do. What do you say we take a double room? You can always justify it on the grounds that it'll save *Tiptop* money.' She smiled across at me. 'I can't think of anything nicer,' I said. 'Thank you. I would rather justify it on the grounds that I've fancied you from the very first moment that I met you, back in the office in New York.' 'Terrific,' she said. 'That makes two of us.' It was about six in the evening by this time, so when we'd checked in, we thought we'd have a stroll along the beach front. Try a couple of bars, have a drink or two. Relax. Check out where the action was for the following day, perhaps. But enjoy ourselves, before we got too tied up with work.

We found more delightful, beach-side bars than you could throw a hat at. We drank ridiculous, vacation-style drinks. The kind of thing you'd never drink at home, wherever home was. Mai Tais. Sharks' Teeth. Pina Coladas. We ended up in a bar where there was a small but excellent group playing New York cocktail bar-style music. If you know what I mean, you'll know it's the sexiest kind of music to dance to that has ever been invented. Babs danced like a dream. We were both dressed in a manner that we thought would blend in with the kind of holiday-makers who would attend wet T-shirt

KEEPING ABREAST

competitions. For Babs, this meant a long, cotton, sarong-type skirt, knotted around her waist, and topped with what was known back in those days as a boob-tube: an abbreviated, elasticated, cotton bandeau top, which almost covered her boobs, and which left her sexy, flat brown stomach quite bare. I was wearing tropical-weight cotton trousers and an Hawaiian-style short-sleeved shirt.

All of which tells you that as we danced and ground our genitalia closely together there was precious little material between us to interfere with our intensely physical contact. The group was playing to a crowded house, and as the evening wore on I fell more and more deeply in love with Babs. You know how it is. She smelt divine. Her body was soft and welcoming, and fitted against mine like a well-made glove. I fancied that, over and above her musky perfume, I could smell the scent of wet pussy and, as I ground my erection against her pubis, I fancied that I could feel the heat of her cunt through the thin cotton of my trousers.

After a while, she said, 'If you don't mind, Tony, I think we should probably sit down.' 'Really, sweetheart?' I asked. 'Why is that? I was just beginning to enjoy myself.' She looked up at me from her slightly lower viewpoint and smiled. 'I'm enjoying myself, too, baby,' she said. 'But my cunt is so wet and your cock is rubbing against it so hard that I've come three times already. So I think the dampness is probably beginning to show through my skirt. If it isn't, it's only a matter of time. Like, maybe a minute. I don't want to embarrass either of us. So may we just get the check, and get the hell out of here? I expect we'll think of something to do when we get back to the motel. OK, honey?'

'Tremendously OK, darling,'. I said. I took her by the hand and led her through the crowd of similarly occupied couples, off the dance floor and back to our table. I waved to the waitress for a check, paid it, left a large tip, and

Babs and I went out into velvet Florida night. I was well over any country's drinking and driving limit so we left the Camaro in the parking lot and got a cab. We got back to the motel without any problems and found our way to our room. As I shut the door behind us, Babs took me in her arms, stood on tiptoe, pulled my head down to hers, and kissed me deeply. After a while, she pulled away, saying, 'Just one question, Tony, darling.'

'What's that?' I said, curiously. 'You're not married, are you?' she asked. 'No, baby,' I said, 'never have been.' I thought of Annabel and wondered what she was doing right now. I should by rights have been married to her, not fucking photographers down here in Florida. I wondered if I had made a terrible mistake. And then I looked at Babs, and realized that, mistake or not, it wasn't really that terrible. As an afterthought, I said to her, 'Since you thought fit to ask me, how about you?' Are *you* married?' She grinned at me. 'Not any more, honey,' she said. 'Now come to bed and suck my pussy. And then fuck me.' She walked over to the bed, dropping her long skirt on the floor behind her as she went and pulling off her boob-tube over her head when she got to the bed. She was bra-less, and she was wearing gloriously sexy, black satin, open-legged French knickers decorated at the hem with silver-coloured lace, and a tiny suspender belt, similarly decorated, with black silk stockings. 'Oh, baby,' I said. 'The full bit. How lovely.' 'Oh, God,' she said. 'Not another one.' 'Another what?' I asked. 'Another pantie fetishist,' she said. 'Or *knicker* fetishist, I should probably say, you being British and all that.' She looked at me and laughed. 'Don't worry, Tony,' she said. 'It doesn't bother me in the least. If it did, I'd be wearing plain cotton knit panties. Frankly, I love the attention. Why do you think I'm wearing these hooker's specials? And how do you like the stockings and garter belt?

They should get a rise out of you.' She looked down. 'Oh, good. I can see that they have already.'

I had stripped off while she was chattering away, and the state of my erection was plain for her to see. Babs bent down and, putting both hands between her legs, found the two little buttons that opened the cotton-lined gusset of her French knickers and undid them. 'The joy of these,' she told me, 'is that I can keep them on while you fuck me. That's good stuff to a serious knicker lover, isn't it? What do you say?'

I looked at her, but I didn't reply immediately. Her breasts were small but firm, tipped with pale pink nipples that were becoming erect even as I looked at them. They were mounted on similarly pale pink areolae which were raised and ridged above the surrounding smooth, pale brown, sun-tanned skin. Babs obviously spent a fair amount of time either sunbathing nude or lying naked on a sun bed. The black silk stockings gripped tightly around her slim, tanned legs, and they were stretched tautly by the suspenders. I could see the white cotton lining of her unbuttoned knicker-crotch, which was now hanging down, and I could see too that the white was stained a dark, damp grey where her pussy juices had been absorbed. I remembered that she had said, back in the bar beside the beach, that she had come three times whilst we were dancing, and that she was already then so wet that she was worried that it was going to stain her skirt.

I was somewhat preoccupied with the sexual excitement of all that these erotic signs portended when I remembered that she had asked me what I thought about the fact that I could fuck her whilst she was still wearing all her fantasy gear. 'Forgive me, sweetheart,' I said. 'I was in a little dream fantasy world there for a moment or two, appreciating you and your lovely, sexy lingerie. That you can keep it on while we fuck is indeed a special treat for me. And I didn't even have to say please. What more could a serious knicker fetishist ask? Now lie back on the bed, spread your legs, and let me suck your pussy for you. And since we're being so up-front about our sexual fetishes, how would you like to give me a slow wank while I suck you off? Not so much as to make me come, but just to keep me hovering on the edge. I'd like that.'

'For wank, read jerk off, in American. It will be my pleasure, baby,' she replied. 'Consider it done.' She climbed onto the bed, and spread her legs as requested. I lay alongside her, so that my cock was within easy reach of her right hand, and settled myself down comfortably with my mouth over her pussy. It was prettily framed by the moist flaps on her black silk, cotton-lined, French knickers, from which there issued a strong scent of sexually aroused woman and, in addition, I could actually feel the warmth emanating from her cunt. Her pubic curls were soft and silky, and were the same darkish brown as her hair. Her sex was a really attractive one, with medium-sized, neat little outer pussy lips, coloured pale pink, like her nipples, and glistening wet from her juices, which made them appear glazed. I used the fingers of both hands to open up these outer lips, in order the better to investigate her inner secrets.

Her inner lips were the same pale pink but, prising these apart, inside her vaginal orifice was a much darker pink, with pulsating dark blue veins showing through beneath the shiny, wet skin. I thrust my middle finger slowly down inside this holy of holies, and felt her vaginal muscles grip it, whether involuntarily or not I had no way of knowing. I gently removed my finger, and held it up to my nostrils, inhaling the freshest of fresh odours: hot, wet pussy, breathing it in deeply, enjoying the pungent, almost musky, fragrance. You will know by now that it is my most favourite perfume.

Whilst indulging myself in these fetishistic, hedonistic pleasures, I was also beginning to enjoy what we used to refer to, in the parlance of my early sexual experiences, as 'one off the wrist'. Or, more familiarly, a quick wank. She was masturbating me. Or – to use her term this time – jerking me off. Whichever description you prefer, it was a distinctly pleasurable experience. In my younger days, it was something that one either did for oneself, lacking a female partner to offer any kind of alternative, or it was a service offered by a steady girlfriend who, for one reason or another – from the onset of her period, perhaps, to the simple fact that she didn't feel like sexual intercourse – might be persuaded to perform this substitute for serious sex. Such girls were few and far between in those days.

Whatever the motivation, I am pleased to be able to tell you that Babs was obviously something of an expert. She had that grip that told me immediately that masturbation of a male partner was something that she had studied. When she commenced, she dug her fingers lightly down into the area between the base of my cock and the top of my scrotum, and massaged gently, just for a moment or two. The original male erotogenic zone. She then took hold of my cock and began to pull my foreskin slowly, oh, so slowly, up over the end of my cock-head, and then all the way back down again, as far as it would go without stretching the skin. It is a carefully judged action. Or it should be. Babs had it to a T.

She obviously judged my whole penile area to be too dry, for next she leaned over and took my cock-head into her mouth, not sucking it, but covering it with her saliva which she then spread over the whole area with her fingers. She then repeated her masturbatory action which, this time around, and with the added lubrication, she adjudged satisfactory – as indeed did I. But her expertise came in her ability to judge precisely just how far she could go in inducing exquisitely pleasurable sensations for me, without bringing me to the point of ejaculation. As I sucked and licked and stimulated her pussy, spending time on her clitoris – using both tongue and fingers – and trying to raise her up gently, gently, from her initial state of sexual enthusiasm to a point where she would, I hoped (if I was doing my job properly), plead with me to take her to, and past, the point of orgasm, I personally hovered right on the edge of my own ejaculation, relishing the eroticism of her manhandling of me (or should that be womanhandling, perhaps, more accurately?) while she managed to keep me well on the right side of coming. And leaving me, always, with a reserve that would see me through the inevitable climax of fucking her before I came myself. It showed that she had great understanding of the male orgasmic process, which implied considerable sexual experience of men.

In fact, I discovered shortly that there was to be no pleading for orgasmic release, for she simply started to reach her orgasm without the need for any such emotional entreaties. I guessed I should take that as a compliment. 'Oh, my God,' she said, beginning to move her hips up against my mouth as I tongued her clitoris. 'Oh, my God, that's good. That's *real* good. I like it. Don't stop. Do it to me. You're making me come. You're sucking my pussy and you're making me come. I'm coming. I'm coming now. NOW. Oh, Jesus, yes, I'm cooooming. Noooooow. Oh, God, yes. Oh, fuck. Yes. Now.'

She bucked and moved against my mouth, and as the final 'now' escaped her lips she raised herself up in the air, moving her whole pelvis in a fucking motion, until she suddenly collapsed back on the bed with a great sigh and lay comparatively still. Her eyes were closed and she had let go of my cock. She lay there, her breasts rising and falling with her heavy breathing which slowly subsided until she was more or less breathing normally. She opened her eyes and turned her head to look at me. 'Hey, that was good, Tony,' she said. 'Really good. You've sucked girls' pussies before. I can tell. Thank you. That was terrific.

Would you like to fuck me now? Please?'

'I can't think of anything nicer, sweetheart,' I said. 'I thought you'd never ask. Can I fuck you from the back? You know, doggie fashion?' Doggie fashion has always been a favourite fucking position for me. I'm not too sure why, except that it certainly guarantees deep penetration. The big disadvantage of this position for girls – and the reason why a lot of women aren't that fond of it – is that it almost always precludes any possibility of friction from the penis against the clitoris, thus making orgasm for the love of your life well nigh impossible. The answer, of course, is to frig the lady with your fingers whilst you fuck her from behind. Or if she knows you well enough, or if she's sexually confident, or both, she'll probably do that for herself. As with anal sex, the position ideally needs digital stimulation of the clitoris from someone.

Whatever Babs's feeling about being fucked doggie fashion, she agreed immediately. I suppose you could say that, having come three times whilst we were dancing earlier, and then having a very healthy orgasm, or series of orgasms, whilst I was performing cunnilingus on her, she wasn't feeling too badly done by. Remembering my *Water Babies*, she was playing Mrs Do-as-you-would-be-done-by. (You will remember that *The Water Babies* doesn't have a Mrs Be-done-by-as-you've-just-been-done). Whatever. She raised herself up on the bed and knelt down in front of me, looking like a sex maniac's dream as she waved her buttocks under my nose, still clothed, as she was, in her French knickers, suspender belt and black silk stockings. The view of her suspenders, strips of long, thin, black elastic, stretching up the back of her legs, along the naked, tanned flesh of the back of her thighs, almost made me come at the very thought of fucking her doggie fashion.

The little flap of the unfastened gusset of her knickers hung down like a tiny curtain, hiding her private parts from my anxious view. Anxious only in that I was raring to ram my rigid cock up her wet, waiting cunt, which I couldn't actually see. I pulled the piece of material out of the way, and thrust my stiff tool into her. She was so wet from my previous attentions that I didn't need to waste any time in foreplay. She wasn't so much warm and wet as *hot* and wet. Her muscles gripped me as I entered her, and they began to work all the way along the length of my member, stroking it, gripping and squeezing, until I felt as if it was her hand masturbating me – as it had done earlier on.

The difference this time being that my cock was totally encompassed, and her cunt was wetter and hotter than her hand had been. One of the great joys of fucking doggie fashion, for me, is watching my cock sink all the way into a cunt, dilating the outer lips as it delves, and then to see it as I withdraw, coming out all wet and glistening from where it has been. She was really working at me, using her muscles like no woman I could remember, sweating at giving me as much pleasure as she knew how – which was a great deal of pleasure. I took her silken-covered buttocks in my hands, squeezing and stroking and pinching and pulling them, at which point she looked over her shoulders at me, pulled her fingers from between her legs, offered them over her shoulders to me, and said 'Would you like some pussy-juice to suck?' Who could possibly say no? Not me, that's for sure. Pussy juice. My favourite tipple. I'd rather suck pussy juice than drink scotch. Truly. Think about it.

I leaned forward and took her fingers into my mouth, licking them, and enjoying the same slightly glutinous, strongly flavoured taste of pussy-juice as I had when sucking her pussy earlier on. There was something totally erotic about her offering me this nectar to lick from her own fingers. 'You like that, baby?' she asked me. 'I love it, darling,' I said. 'I know exactly what you mean,' she told me. 'I just love the taste of it myself.'

At which point my cock took its own decision. It decided that it had had enough. Enough physical, mental, oral, aural, nasal and visual erotic stimulation. More, in fact, than it could cope with. And it decided to explode, pulsing jets of hot, creamy semen into Babs's receptive pussy. 'Oh, yes, baby,' she said. 'That's nice. I can feel your spunk jetting up inside me. It's all hot. It's lovely. Ooooh, I love it. I'm coming again. Oh, yes. Oh, baby. Oh, wow. Oh, fuck. Fuck, fuck, fuck. Mmmmm. Oh, yes.' She put a hand behind her, grabbed hold of my cock around its base and squeezed it gently, holding it firmly in her cunt despite my member's dwindling stiffness, until all my semen was milked from it. She kept hold of it, but she pulled herself slowly and carefully off it. Then she turned around, knelt down, and kissed it. Long and hard. 'I love your cock, Tony,' she said. 'And I love the fact that you know what it's for. And the fact that you know what women are for. Sometimes we're for loving; sometimes we're for fucking. You do both, and you understand the difference. I think I might be falling in love with you. Would you like that?' 'Like it, baby?' I repeated. 'I'd love it. Well, for this week, anyway. Will that do?' I laughed as I said it, and she joined in with me. 'You're a bastard, do you know that?' she said. 'A real bastard.' 'Yes,' I said. 'I do. I wanted to make sure that *you* knew it, too.' How does it go? There's many a true word spoken in jest? Something like that?

We eventually fell asleep, and slept well and soundly, curled up together familiarly, a light blanket protecting us from the air-conditioning, our bodies generating mutual warmth. I awoke once during the night, and looked at Babs's face in the moonlight that was shining through the windows. I had opened the curtains just before we went to sleep. Her face was relaxed, unlined. Content, even. I wondered how seriously – if at all – she had meant her question about falling in love with me. Love was the last thing I wanted, right now. It is a complication that I don't seem able to cope with. It turns me from being a prince into a frog. Or perhaps it prevents me from being a prince in the first place. And it interferes with sex. Sex was fun. *Is* fun, I thought, looking again at Babs as she slept beside me, remembering the taste and feel of her. I inhaled, deeply, and I could still detect the sweet smell of female sex. It had the immediate effect of giving me a hard-on. I ignored it, and finally fell asleep, to dream erotic dreams of Annabel.

The next morning Fort Lauderdale was as Fort Lauderdale almost always is – the sky was a deep, cloudless blue, there was a light breeze off the sea, and the temperature, at ten in the morning, was pushing eighty. It would get hotter as the day progressed. The locals were already out and about, enjoying their tennis, golf, swimming, sailing, or whatever else took their fancy, before the full heat of the day began to really burn. The visitors – including Babs and me – were still enjoying their breakfasts on their various terraces and balconies, keeping in the shade wherever possible, and enjoying tall, tinkling glasses of what has to be the finest, most delicious freshly squeezed orange juice in the world.

We were in no hurry, Babs and I. Sex was out sport, and we took our exercise in bed. Work didn't start until noon, when we were attending our first wet T-shirt contest. We intended arriving at about eleven-thirty, in order to make ourselves known to the owner or manager of the bar, to ask his permission to take photographs, and to get the girls who were going to compete to sign model release forms for us, in order that we might reproduce their pictures, should we wish, in the magazine. It wasn't legally necessary, strictly speaking, in that we were simply taking photographs at a public function, but it could possibly save us a lot of hassle later on when any photographs appeared. Fred and I had agreed that we would pay a hundred dollars for any pictures printed in *Tiptop*, which meant getting the girls' names and addresses.

In fact, when we made ourselves known to Harry Mast, the manager of the bar restaurant, he was delighted. 'Hey, you mean you're one of the editors of *Tiptop*? Wow, just wait until I tell the girls this. You'll be our judge, Tony, won't you? I mean, I usually do it, but for God's sake, you're an expert. You just have to be our judge. If you aren't an expert on tits, who is? Oh, excuse me, Babs,' he said. 'Forgive me. I just get carried away sometimes.' He plied us with drink – on the house, he insisted – and introduced us both to anyone who came within a hundred yards of us.

We quickly discovered that it wasn't all that practical to try and get the girls' names and addresses before the contest started. We got some, of course, but there were a lot of last-minute entrants, egged on either by their boyfriends or by the other girls in the group that they were with. 'Oh, come on, Jenny,' they'd say. 'You've got better boobs than any of those girls. Go and flash them. Earn yourself a hundred bucks. It'll be a steal.' In the end, at the beginning of the contest, when I announced who I was, I asked that any girl who didn't want to be photographed for *Tiptop* only had to say so. Those who did should sign one of the release forms held by Harry, and give him their name and address.

When Jenny, or whoever, came up onto the temporary stage, it would be to resounding cheers from her friends and all the other youths and men in the bar, who were anxious to see as many tits revealed initially beneath wet T-shirts and, with luck, in the flesh, as possible. In fact, after glowing from the initial welcoming cheer that *I* got at the announcement of my connection with *Tiptop*, I soon discovered that being the judge in these contests was no piece of cake. All the contestants, without a single exception, were aged between about eighteen and twenty-two – and they all had perfect breasts. Secondly, as judge (expert or not) I quickly discovered that I was only there to confirm the decisions of the audience, who were extremely vociferous in their acclamations and dismissals. Any disagreement would probably have caused a riot. Not that this prevented the girls from attempting to fix the odds. Harry had insisted that I stand at the side of the stage and introduce each of the contestants as she first came up. I also had to give a sort of abbreviated running commentary as each girl appeared first dry and then with her T-shirt clinging to her lovely tits when made wet with the water from the bucket.

'Do you like them?' asked the first girl up on the stage, taking a deep breath and thrusting out her chest. 'Yes, sweetheart,' I said. 'I like them. They're very pretty.' 'They're yours to play with after,' she said. 'If I win.' 'I hope you do, sweetheart,' I said. 'I really hope you do.' I could just imagine, even if I *were* able to swing anything, trying to claim my prize afterwards. The second one said 'I've got great tits, Tony, but you should see my pussy. It's prime.'

'I'd love to, sweetheart,' I said. 'You'll find me right here after the contest.' I never saw her again, of course. But to be fair, she didn't win. I'm sure I wouldn't have seen her again if she had. The problem was, have you ever seen a young girl with bad tits? No tits worth speaking of, yes. *Bad* tits, no. If they had no tits to speak of, they didn't enter wet T-shirt contests. So, assuming the various pairs of pretty young tits were equally attractive, the audience actually voted for pretty faces, good legs, appealing personalities, anything which added to the initial essential qualification. In the end, the first prize went to a girl whom I got to know quite well during the two weeks that Babs and I spent down in Florida, in that she probably won something like half the contests that we attended. She had a pretty face, beautiful short blonde hair cut in a boyish style which really suited her, gorgeous legs, and tits which hovered just – but only just – on the right side of being over-large. They weren't sagging yet, but next week? Who could tell? This week's generosity was next week's excess. Perhaps.

She was called Corinne. She won her dry T-shirt heat largely and appropriately, I guessed, for her ample breasts, well supported by the tightest T-shirt this side of Miami Beach. Then she won her wet heat, I thought (again guessing, but the crowd was one hundred per cent with her, against two other really gorgeous young girls, both of whom would have got my personal vote, had anyone asked me) because of her gigantic nipples, which were really phenomenal both in size and shape. She had obviously made no promises, or payments, to the guy with the buckets of water. In fact, she possibly insisted on the cold water for the effect it had on her nipples. They immediately stood to attention, to the whole-hearted approval of the entire male section of the audience.

She won the final heat, out of four contestants, by taking off her T-shirt seconds before I called for the audiences' vote and, a split second after that, pulling down the front of her bikini bottom to expose tufts of tightly curled blonde pubic hair to a now wildly excited male audience. The other three girls, all of whom possessed far prettier, shapelier breasts, didn't get a look in. They were all amateurs, and they all kept their T-shirts on. It was a basic lesson in presentation. Corinne showed the boys what they wanted. That she didn't actually deliver didn't seem to matter. The amateurs retained their modesty. And their amateur status. Votes, by the way, were by a show of hands, but on every separate occasion they were overwhelmingly in favour of one girl against all the others.

Harry gave me the one hundred dollars in cash which I passed over to Corinne to the general approval of all present. A lot of the men crowded around her afterwards, but she ignored them, and made her way towards me. She was still naked from the waist up, carrying her wet T-shirt as she came. Her breasts looked eminently suckable close to. She grinned at me. 'I can see that you're a real tit man,' she said, as she arrived within speaking distance, 'by the way that you're looking at them. But are you really an editor from *Tiptop*?'

'I am, and I am,' I said, feeling witty. I probably shouldn't have bothered. I saw Babs coming over towards us, shooting as she came, taking pictures of a topless Corinne talking to me. 'Do you think I've got what it takes to model for *Tiptop*?' Corinne asked. 'I mean, you know, am I good enough to model for one of your nude photo features?' She looked at me directly through beautiful, dark blue eyes. I could see that she was serious. 'Do you want an honest answer?' I asked. 'Always,' she said. 'You might just,' I said. 'We'd have to take some test shots before I could tell you for sure.' 'You mean, I might not?' she asked. 'Why not?' I looked at her as directly as she had looked at me. 'Don't take this personally, sweetheart,' I said, 'But you asked me for an honest answer. This room is full of girls who have a better chance than you of modelling for *Tiptop*, simply because their breasts are smaller. The camera adds weight. Yours are very pretty – and extremely sexy,' I added, leering at her, 'but they're a tiny bit full for serious nude photography. There are things we can do, you know, with flimsy bits of gauzy material, and soft focus. That sort of thing. But the camera, at least in terms of nude photography, seldom lies. Take that little redhead over there,' I said, indicating a girl probably in her late teens. 'She'd be perfect for us. Can you see the difference? her breasts are firm and pointed. They lack the fullness of yours, but the camera will make them look a little heavier than they are, which means that they'll probably look perfect in the photographs. I could be wrong about yours, but I don't think so.'

I dug into my hip pocket, found my wallet and took out a card. 'If you're ever in New York, and you feel like it,' I said, 'give me a call, and I'll see if I can set up a test shoot. Here's my card. But I'll tell you one thing for nothing. If you're talking about personal preference, Corinne, I prefer your tits to that little redhead's any day.' It wasn't true, but it's always worth a try. Well, isn't it? She took my card. 'Sure,' she said. 'Thanks a lot, Tony.' Her look said, 'You've gotta be kidding, mister. If that's what you think, go fuck the bimbo.' She took herself off.

We did another show that evening and three more the following day. Suddenly two weeks seemed to disappear in a flurry of wet T-shirts, tantalizingly perfect young breasts, a great deal of alcohol and some elegant fucking at nights with Babs. Having her stay with me as we moved down along the coast of Florida was fun, and the sex was great, but it did totally preclude getting together with any of the pretty young girls who were trying their luck on the wet T-shirt circuit in Florida at the time of our trip. And there *were* opportunities. Not all the contestants were putting it about, of course.

A lot of them entered, as I mentioned earlier, on the spur of the moment, and for them the competition itself was the attraction, rather than the actual prize money. They were one-off competitors – and they seldom won. Not because they didn't have pretty boobs. Many of them did. But they didn't have the experience of the girls who were working their way around the circuit. They didn't know how to manipulate the audiences. Of the girls who were patently in it for the money – for whatever reason – about a third of them offered, one way or another, to drop their knickers for a little friendly help from the judge, a position for which I had, by now, achieved something of a reputation. I would have loved to have taken some of the girls up on their offers. Some of them. Bullshit. *All* of them. But apart from resorting to subterfuge, at which I drew the line, there was no way I could get away from Babs. Once I was finished at a contest, so, basically, was she. Whatever we did between that and the next one, be it eat, drink, sunbathe, swim, go to the movies or sleep, we did together. She was a delightful companion, and one whom I had no wish to offend.

But one thing that was a major pleasure on this Florida trip was to become something of an expert on young female breasts. Tits are actually an essential part of my business, and I had probably seen more than most long before I went down to Florida. But I suddenly found myself in a situation where I was surrounded for up to six hours a day, every day, by large quantities of gorgeous young tits. Tits near enough to reach out and touch. Tits, their nipples rigid, exposed through transparently wet T-shirts. Tits *totally* exposed, in the final stages of many of the contests, by the removal of the said T-shirts by the more enthusiastic – or the more exhibitionist – of the contestants. And many pairs of delectable tits flashed at me backstage just prior to the beginning of a contest, in the hope that the sight of these and the prospect of other little treats, often described in anticipatory detail, would help a particular contestant to win.

I was quickly reminded that there are as many different varieties of breasts and nipples as there are of pussies and pussy lips. I loved them all. The soft, slightly under-developed breasts, surmounted by largish but thinly-layered areolae from which peeped tiny, not-yet-fully-grown nipples. Even when doing their best to become rigid from the sudden shock of cold water, these nipples never really made it. Sweet. The breasts themselves were not developed enough to have become pointed, but they were still prettily formed. Then there were the young but firmly pointed, thrusting breasts, conical in shape, firm, but still small by comparison with what they would develop into eventually. They tended to have similar areolae to the first kind, but with bigger, slightly longer – comparatively speaking – nipples, which stood up proudly erect when wet.

Corinne's – of which I saw a great deal, on a regular basis – were about as full as a young girl's breasts can get and still stay firm, with very thin, almost non-existent areolae, surmounted by quite small-diameter but comparatively long nipples which swelled alarmingly when under water, as it were. These were positively the winning tits on the circuit. First of all, the fact is that most young men, given a choice, prefer big tits to small tits. (Sadly, quantity, not quality, is the criterion for breasts with most young males.) Added to which was the fact that Corinne's nipples were certainly, once made rigid by the water, the largest on display. And she could hardly wait to tear her T-shirt off altogether, thus exposing those beauteous tits in their full (and I do mean *full*) naked glory. Then, finally, as if all this was not enough, there was the glimpse of her pubic hair that she offered as she pulled down the top of her bikini bottom, to roars of delight and disconcertingly loud whistles from the entire assembled male population. The other girls didn't really have a chance.

One thing that struck me throughout this happy exposure of massed mammaries was something that I hadn't actually noticed before: all these lovely girls had nipples that were completely smooth. You know, no wrinkles, no puckering. No indication that there had ever been any wear and tear of any kind. Soft, smooth, unsullied skin. Beautiful. But anything becomes boring if you do it constantly and after the first week of these wet T-shirt contests I really did start to get bored. I began to fantasize, after a bit. I would stand there, doing my judge/compère bit, extolling and/or describing the charms of whichever example of jail-bait was exposing her jugs to the ecstatic audience, and I would be on autopilot whilst I was trying mentally to imagine to myself what kind of pussy matched the tits. Would the girl's pussy lips be pale pink? Dark pink? Pinky-brown? Brown? Black? Would they be long, short, butterfly-winged? Would her pubic hair be short and silky? Long and curly? The same colour as the hair on her head? Would her thighs be as smooth as silk?

Some of the girls wore abbreviated, cut-off shorts, rather than bikini or swimsuit bottoms. Would these girls be wearing anything beneath their shorts? Or nothing? Panties? If panties, what kind? G-string? Bikini? What colour? Black? White? Red? What material? Silk? Cotton? Would the girl be sufficiently sexually excited by now by what she was doing to have wet the cotton lining of her pantie-crotch with the moist evidence of her sexual arousal? When I had decided, to my own satisfaction, what lay beneath the tiny shorts or tight bikini bottom of the girl in question, I would then speculate about whether or not she was a virgin. Did she fuck? Was some lucky, long-haired, dullard, unappreciative student already shafting this delightful, sexually entrancing, enticing body? Or was she still at the stage where all she knew of sex was from the insertion of her own fingers into her young quim, the masturbatory fancies of a young girl as she lay back, played with herself, and fantasized about the real thing? Or perhaps she had progressed to lesbian sex with one or other – or more? – of her fellow female students?

Maybe she was familiar with the delights of being sucked off by one of her girlfriends as she returned the compliment, the two of them entwined in the classic *soixante-neuf* of lesbian love, bringing each other delicately and gently to orgasm. Or perhaps they fucked each other with dildoes? Maybe this gentle, pretty little blonde girl in front of me strapped on a huge black rubber prick, attaching it to her thighs and around her waist with leather straps, and fucked the living daylights out of her girlfriend? The combination of wet, hard-nippled breasts seen through translucent, tight T-shirts and my lust-laden imaginings caused Babs to join me one afternoon and whisper in my ear, 'I hope you don't mind my saying this, Tony, and I don't suppose, in fact, that too many people are looking at *you* right now, when they've got all these pretty young girls' boobies to look at. But anyone glancing in your direction could hardly avoid noticing your hard-on. Is there anything I can do to help? Fuck you? Suck you off? Masturbate you? Talk dirty? Anything?' I laughed. I had to, really.

I turned my back on the audience. 'Any and all of those lovely things, sweetheart, would be an improvement on what's happening here,' I told her. 'My problem is that I've seen it all before. Haven't we all? So I had to think of something to do to pass the time rather more amusingly.' I explained to her about my fantasies concerning each girl as she came on stage. 'What fun,' she said. 'No wonder you've got an erection. And what do you make of this girl who's up here now?' I looked again at the sleek, lithe brunette who had been the subject of my thoughts when Babs had interrupted me. I had come to certain conclusions about her, which I now related to Babs.

'Because her hair is quite dark, and she has something of a Latin appearance – a little mixed blood, I suspect, somewhere in her past – I decided that she has a very hairy cunt, and that unlike third or fourth generation American girls and pure-blooded English girls, she has no modesty which forces her to shave the hair around her bikini line. If pubic hair curls out around her bathing suit crotch, she isn't going to give a damn. She's only wearing shorts today because she believes that they show off her ass better than a swimsuit or bikini bottom. And that hair will be as thick around her asshole as it is around her pussy. If she didn't pluck them, she would probably be sprouting black, silken, curly hairs around her nipples. She does get rid of those, as you'll see in a moment, because all the American women's magazines tell her that only native women from the jungle have hairy tits. And it's simply not true. I speak from experience.

'As to her actual cunt, I think that her outer lips will be the same dark brown, almost black colour that her nipples and areolae are, that they will be fleshy and puffy when she is sexually aroused, and the lips themselves will be quite long, like butterfly wings. Whoever fucks her will probably have to use his fingers to hold them apart as he shoves his prick up inside them. And I bet she fucks like the proverbial nine ten from Paddington.' Babs looked at me blankly. And then I remembered that Americans say these things differently. 'I'm sorry, sweetheart. What I'm saying in English slang is that I bet she bangs like a little bunny. OK?'

'Oh, wow, yes,' said Babs. 'I have to agree with you there. Just look at that cock-sucking mouth.' She grinned at me. 'I wouldn't say no to that around my pussy, never mind your cock. Shall I ask her if she'd like to join us this evening?' 'You're kidding,' I said. 'No, I'm not,' she replied. 'But if you're not into that sort of thing, then say so. It's not a problem. I just thought it might be fun.' I looked at the slightly heavy-breasted, dark brown-haired girl, and at her pouting, full-blooded lips and mouth. It *was* a cock-sucking mouth, Babs was right. How old could this girl be? Eighteen? Nineteen at the very most. And I had already envisaged her thickly-haired pussy, with the dark brown, almost black, long fleshy pussy lips.

Not into that sort of thing? Babs had to be joking. It was, though, something of a surprise for Babs to tell me that she was into threesomes, and not only that, but that she fancied the Latin-looking girl's lips around her pussy. In the last couple of weeks, we'd done almost everything that two people can do together since we'd been sharing motel rooms down here in Florida, and I'd had not an inkling of any bisexual tendencies. Not that I'm bisexual either, I thought, but two girls together who like getting it on together are a tremendous turn-on, especially if they don't mind if I join in.

'Hey, Babs, that would be terrific,' I said. 'That really would be something. What do you think the chances are?' She gave me a long, clear-eyed, slightly amused look, and smiled at me. 'Chances?' she said. 'There's no question of chance about it. If that's what you'd like us to do, that's what I'll arrange. Leave it to me.' She began to walk away towards the girl we had been talking about, who had just won her heat. Babs stopped, turned back towards me and said: 'Put money on it, baby.' It looked as if was going to be a different kind of evening.

She turned out to be absolutely right about everything. The girl said that yes, she'd love to join us for dinner. And anything else that was on the cards. Her name was Jeannie, and she was a high school student on vacation. Over dinner at one of the many local sea-food restaurants that evening, we all got stuck into soft-shelled crabs sautéed in butter, with green salad and a bottle of Californian Chardonnay, whilst we began to get to know each other.

Jeannie was just eighteen, and from her conversation it was apparent that she was no virgin. I've no idea what Babs had said to her, but Jeannie's conversation was sprinkled with sexual innuendo that indicated that she was into relationships with both men and women, which I hoped augured well for later on. We all followed the crab with curried shrimp and more Chardonnay, and on the way back to the motel we stopped at a liquor store and bought a couple more bottles of chilled Chardonnay. It was one of those motels which furnishes its rooms in the American manner with two king-size beds. Whilst I found glasses and opened bottles, I watched Babs and Jeannie stripping off.

Jeannie was wearing tiny white cotton panties beneath her cut-off denim shorts. They were minuscule, and to my delight (it's always gratifying to be found to be right about something, isn't it?) I could see dark brown, curly pubic hair peeping around the edges of them. As she slipped her panties down her legs, she revealed that she was indeed exotically hirsute all around both her genitalia and her anal area, as I had also predicted. When she slipped out of her blouse, she exposed pert young breasts, with dark-skinned nipples and areolae, but there were no hairs around her nipples. I felt quite disappointed. I had seen her breasts at the contest earlier that day, of course, but it was pleasant to be able to go over to Jeannie, as I handed her a glass of wine, and look at them that close to, and be reasonably certain that I would have those succulent nipples between my lips before too long. Whilst I had been looking at Jeannie, I had also been watching Babs stripping off her skirt and blouse.

Like Jeannie, she too was bare-legged, scorning both stockings and pantihose in the heat of the Florida day. Babs was wearing a pair of white nylon panties that I had seen before. They were rather pretty ones. They were transparent all around, but they had a lacy panel at the front which covered but did not actually conceal her pussy. As I watched she pulled them down and stepped out of them. She looked at me, grinned, and walked over to Jeannie. She didn't say anything, but she took Jeannie in her arms and kissed her deeply on the mouth. Jeannie brought up her arms, put them around Babs and began to kiss her back. Babs then put a hand down between Jeannie's legs and began to feel and stroke Jeannie's pussy. Jeannie opened her legs to allow better access to the source of her pleasure and then, after a moment, Babs stopped kissing and said, 'Let's continue this on the bed,' She pulled Jeannie towards it as she spoke.

When they got there, Jeannie lay down on her back and spread her legs. I could see her snatch now and, as I watched, Babs began to stroke it with the palm of her hand. 'That's nice,' said Jeannie. 'I like that. Are you going to kiss me down there? I like being kissed down there.' Babs didn't say anything, but she used her fingers to spread Jeannie's labia and then she slid a finger deep inside her. I could see that Jeannie's labia were not the butterfly-winged shape that I had fantasized about at the wet T-shirt contest, but they *were* quite fleshy, and were of the same dark-skinned colour as her nipples (which I now noticed were firmly erect). As Babs's fingers massaged and stroked, I could see the paler pink inner flesh of Jeannie's vagina shining wetly under Babs's fingering ministrations. Then Babs withdrew her fingers and, leaning down between Jeannie's parted legs, she began to first kiss, then lick and suck at Jeannie's pussy. Jeannie wriggled her bottom in her enjoyment of this sexual gratification, and began to move her hips slowly beneath Babs's mouth. Her ass was quite beautiful and I watched it moving, her plump cheeks firm and full I could see the rich growth of her anal hair which didn't quite manage to hide her dark brown anus completely.

I fantasized reaching under Babs's neck as she sucked at Jeannie's pussy and thrusting a well-greased finger into that tight little orifice. I felt my cock swelling at the thought of it, which reminded me that I might as well get undressed. My turn at Jeannie had to be coming, surely? I stripped off and sat on the edge of the bed, much closer to the action than I had been previously. I was close enough to see Babs's tongue lapping at Jeannie's wet pussy, dipping into it as Babs's fingers held her labia apart. I guessed that, at its innermost depth, Babs's tongue was stroking Jeannie's clitoris to erect enjoyment, and sucking and licking it to eventual orgasm.

Jeannie was getting quite excited now, moving her hips strongly against Babs's mouth and tongue, and she began to speak again, her voice breathy and husky with mounting passion. 'Oh, Babs, darling,' she was saying, 'oh, that's so good. You're sucking my cunt. I love it when you suck my cunt. You suck so well. Oh, yes. That's sooooh gooood. Ohhhhhh, I love what you're doing to me. Oh, do it harder. Please do it harder. Oh, yes. I'm coming now. I'm coming, oh God, I'm coming. Oh yes. *Yeeeees.*'

And come she did, writhing up against Babs's mouth as she did so, shouting out her pleasure. Babs went on sucking until the final throes of Jeannie's multiple orgasm had completely subsided. Jeannie just lay there for a while, her eyes closed, her breath coming fast, her breasts rising and falling as she breathed, until she eventually opened her eyes and looked down at Babs, who was still gently sucking and licking. Jeannie said, 'Thank you, darling. That was so beautiful. Thank you. Thank you. Shall I do it for you now, my dearest?'

Shit, I thought. When am I ever going to get my end away? Babs stopped what she was doing, lifted her head up and looked at Jeannie. I could see that her lips and mouth were wet with Jeannie's juices. I wanted to fuck her mouth. I wanted to fuck anything. I just wanted to fuck. 'That would be nice, Jeannie,' said Babs. 'Yes, I'd like that. Thank you.' They changed places, Babs lying down on the bed, her legs spread wide, Jeannie now kneeling on the floor at the end of the bed, her head positioned over Babs's pussy. She began to stroke and play with it, pushing her fingers in and out of it, spreading the lips apart, opening it up for the action that was soon to come. I could see that it too was wet with love juice. Jeannie's fingers were soon covered in it. Fuck it, I thought, and I knelt down behind Jeannie and reached between her legs, feeling for her cunt lips. 'Oooh,' she said, as I found them. 'What a naughty boy. That's nice. Are you going to fuck me?' 'If you don't mind, sweetheart,' I said. '*Mind?*' she said. 'I thought you'd never ask.' So I got down to it while she got down to it, and a great time was soon being had by all.

She had a tight, welcoming, wet little box, whose depth I was able to penetrate fully from my position behind her, whilst the fact that she had her head down automatically raised her ass up in the air, making it a simple job to fuck her from behind. Bearing in mind that she had only recently achieved multiple orgasms from the cunnilingus so expertly applied by Babs, I didn't waste any time thinking about her feelings. It's a real pleasure to be able to be selfish occasionally, and especially without having to feel guilty about it afterwards. So I concentrated entirely on my own pleasures, to the exclusion of all else, gripping Jeannie around her firm thighs and shagging her deeply and quickly, concentrating on coming as quickly as I possibly could.

I put my heart and soul into it, as well as my cock, and was rewarded by an enormously satisfying climax in about one minute flat. I pumped my semen into Jeannie and she lifted her mouth away from Babs's pussy just long enough to say 'Ooooh,' and that was it. I pulled out of her and took myself off to the bathroom where I enjoyed a long, hot, relaxing shower, after which I went back into the other room, climbed into the vacant bed, and fell asleep watching Jeannie still giving lip service to Babs. I don't know how long they kept it up, but when I awoke the following day they were asleep in each other's arms in the other bed. I got myself up, showered, shaved, and was eating breakfast in the coffee shop in about twenty minutes flat. I decided that I'd had enough of Florida. When I got back to the room, I told Babs that, provided that she was satisfied that we had enough photographs of wet T-shirt competitions to run a four-page feature, I was ready to get back to New York. She didn't hesitate for a moment and said that she had more than enough to run four pages. So we agreed to give ourselves this day for a last day on the beach, and catch a plane back to the Big Apple the following morning.

Jeannie spent the day on and around the beach with us, and that night was pretty much a repeat of the previous one, other than that the order of play changed slightly. I fucked Babs first. Then I watched the girls playing lezzie games for a while, and then I fucked Jeannie, this time from the front. It beats taking sleeping pills. I was back in my New York apartment by the middle of the afternoon the following day, which was a Friday.

CHAPTER SEVEN:
A SURPRISE GOODBYE

Before I left Florida, I telephoned Eileen to tell her that I was on my way back. She told me that there were no problems waiting for me in the office, so I said that I wouldn't show up there until the Monday morning. That gave me the weekend to acclimatize myself and get the apartment organized. The first thing I did after breakfast on the Saturday morning was to telephone the lovely Katrina, my darling Russian ballet dancer. 'Darlink,' she cried when I said hello. 'How lovely. Where are you? Are you back in New York?'

'Yes, sweetheart,' I told her. 'Can you spend the day with me tomorrow? Please? I'm dying to see you.' (You will remember that Sunday was her one evening off.) 'Better than that,' she said. 'I'll come round now. OK?' 'Fantastic,' I said. 'How long can you stay?' 'Until Monday lunchtime,' she said. 'I've strained a muscle. It's nothing serious, but I've got to rest it until Monday afternoon, so I can't dance or rehearse or anything.' She lowered her voice. 'But I'm sure I can fuck,' she said. 'Shall I come now?' she asked, her voice back to normal. 'Yes, please, my darling,' I said. 'Fantastic. I'll be waiting for you.'

I checked the time. It was too early to telephone Fred. If he was at home, he would still be out to the world. I made a mental note to call him later, just to catch up with the gossip. I checked that there was champagne in the fridge. I'd stocked up with food and booze and bought some fresh flowers. The apartment was immaculate, thanks to the good services of my cleaning lady, and I had re-ordered the papers, bringing back a copy of the *New York Times*. It being Saturday, I thought I'd have a look at the sports pages. The baseball season was winding down, and American football training had commenced. I had become quite a fan of American football, having overcome my rugger bugger's initial contempt for a sport which superficially looked like rugger but where the participants dressed up in protective suits. If you take the trouble to understand it, it is actually an extremely intelligent game, and very exciting. And they really do need the protective clothing! I'd even been to Shea Stadium to watch a couple of baseball games and had thoroughly enjoyed those, too. At that moment, the doorman rang through to check that I was expecting Katrina, and I put the paper down and went to open the door.

The elevator doors opened and disgorged her, and she came flying down the corridor, strained muscle or no strained muscle. 'Darlink,' she cried, as I picked her up and held her close, twirling around in the corridor. I put her down, and she stood on tiptoe and kissed me, hard. I kissed her back. 'Sweetheart,' I said. 'Let's have a celebratory drink.' I took her by the hand, and led her back into the apartment. She was wearing a lightweight woollen suit, with a short skirt and a long jacket in a pale shade of plain grey, and she wore it with a bright red silk shirt and high-heeled, red leather, rather strappy sandals. Her long blonde hair was done up in a French plait.

I shut the apartment door behind us, took her in my arms and kissed her again. I put my hand up her skirt, and felt her pussy through her knickers. Her knickers between her legs were sopping wet. She felt for my burgeoning cock, found it, and squeezed it happily through the

A SURPRISE GOODBYE

material of my trousers. 'Fuck me now,' she whispered. 'Please fuck me now.' It was at that moment that the telephone rang. 'Let it ring,' she said. 'Take me to bed and fuck me.' 'Forgive me, sweetheart,' I said. 'It might be Fred. I haven't spoken to him yet, not since I've been back up here.' 'Oh,' she said. 'Then I suppose you had better answer it.' I looked at my watch. It was just after eleven. It was still early for Fred. I picked up the phone.

'Hi, Tone,' said Fred. 'It's me.' 'Hi, Fred,' I said. 'How are you?' 'I'm terrific,' he said. 'I'm at Kennedy.' 'Good Lord,' I said. 'Where are you off to?' 'I'm off to California to lie in the sun and forget about girlie magazines,' he said. 'I've had enough. You fucking look after it. I'm shagged out.' I couldn't believe what I was hearing. 'You can't do that, Fred,' I said. 'Watch me,' he said. 'I'm going to stay with Lulu for a while, but don't tell Wally where I am. Call me if you've got any problems, but promise me that you won't tell Wally where I am?' 'I promise,' I said. 'But what *shall* I tell him?' 'Just tell him that I've had enough,' he said. 'He'll know what I mean. Cheers now, Tone.' He put the phone down.

I sat down. Katrina came over and stood in front of me. 'Trouble?' she asked. 'You can say that again,' I told her. 'Can I help?' she asked. 'Thank you, sweetheart, but I don't think so,' I said. 'Except by being here. I took hold of her hand. 'Let me get you a drink,' she said. 'Scotch?' 'Please,' I said. He's gone mad, I thought. He's gone off his tiny head. I was in shock. Fred had always been there, if you know what I mean. Now I was seriously on my own. What should I do first? Think about it carefully, I thought. Don't panic. He'll probably be back by the end of the week. Thank God it's Saturday, I thought. At least I've got the weekend to think about it. Decision one, I thought. Don't tell Wally anything. Not yet. Katrina came back with a good stiff scotch and water, no ice. Good girl. She was learning.

'Thank you, sweetheart,' I said. 'Come and sit down.' She sat on the sofa beside me. I told her what Fred had said. She looked thoughtful. 'Who's Lulu?' she asked. Lulu was a very beautiful New York fashion model whom Fred had been fucking on and off ever since he'd been out in the States. She it was who originally introduced him to cocaine. Amongst other things. She was good at her job, but she was pretty flaky out of working hours. I tried to describe her to Katrina. 'I guess they'll have fun in California,' I said. 'For a while, anyway. Difficult not to, really. Especially if you're as rich as Fred is. And Lulu's not exactly short of money. Lulu's got an apartment down in L.A. But they'll get bored after a week or so. And Lulu must have work booked up months ahead.'

We were both silent for a while. Thinking our thoughts. I wondered how long I could get away with not telling anyone. I'd have to tell Eileen, that was for sure, but on pain of death that she kept it to herself. No one else. Certainly no one in the London office. It wasn't any sort of problem in work terms. I was more than capable. I was just uneasy. Fred was chancing his arm if Wally ever found out. Loyalty was Wally's big thing. Katrina turned to me. 'But this must be good for you, darlink,' she said. 'It must give you more responsibility, and more money. Both. Sooner or later.' I hadn't thought of that. I suppose she was right. But that wasn't important. Fred had always been my friend as well as my boss. We were mates, from way back. He was the first person ever to purchase my written work, and it was he who encouraged me to start writing full-time. It was he who had offered me my first job as an editor. If it wasn't for Fred I wouldn't be living in New York, leading the life of Reilly, and earning real money. I didn't want his job. Not even if he didn't want it. If loyalty was Wally's big thing, then loyalty to Fred was pretty big with me.

I suddenly remembered that Katrina was with me, and I

also remembered what it was that we had been going to do just before Fred's telephone call. I took her hand. 'Do you mind if we postpone the sex for a while, sweetheart?' I asked. 'What I'm going to have to do is see if I can contact Eileen, Fred's secretary, and ask her to come over here and talk this through with me. You're entirely welcome to stay with me – I hope that you will, please – but she and I are going to have to talk shop for a while. Is that OK with you?' She patted my hand. 'Is OK, darlink. We can catch up with the sex later. Maybe when Eileen comes, if you can get her, maybe I leave you and go into the bedroom and play with myself. You know, to help frustration. How you say it? Ah, yes. Masturbate. Is not a problem. Is OK.'

I managed not to laugh, but I did smile, and I leaned over and gave her a big kiss. 'I'll make it up to you, sweetheart,' I said. 'I promise.' Eileen *was* in. 'Hey, Tony. Hi. What's with you this bright Saturday morning?' she asked, when I announced myself over the phone. 'I've got a problem, Eileen, baby,' I said. 'A *big* problem. Is it at all possible that you could come over to my apartment and talk through it with me? Please? It really is quite serious.' 'Of course, darling,' she said. 'You know I'll drop everything and come running, any time you want me. And particularly my panties. What's the matter? Girlfriend let you down?' I laughed. 'No, it's something even more serious, sweetheart,' I said. 'I'll fill you in when you get here.' 'How lovely,' she said. 'I'm on my way.'

Twenty minutes later the doorman rang through to announce Eileen's arrival. When she arrived at the door I let her in and introduced her to Katrina, who was given a rather sour look. But when I told her about Fred, she settled down immediately. 'My God,' she said. 'You weren't joking, were you?' 'No, sadly,' I said. 'But I just can't think what to do for the best. I'm pretty sure I can track down Lulu's L.A. telephone number. Her agency will have it, if I can't get it from Directory. That's no problem. And obviously I'll talk to him later on today, when he's arrived out there. But what am I actually going to say to him? I mean, what *can* I say?' Eileen bit her lip, and gnawed away at it for a moment or two before she said anything. 'It's a sod, isn't it?' she said. She must have picked that up from Fred. It simply isn't an expression that Americans use.

'I had no idea,' she continued. 'He's been pretty good while you were down in Florida. You know, coming into the office, and all. He's been reasonably on time. He hasn't been *obviously* coked out of his brains, like he is sometimes. I've assumed that, ever since his stay in London, he's been a reformed character. And now this. Shit. Do you think he's serious?' 'God knows,' I told her. 'I've seen Fred angry. I've seen him bored. He's got quite a low attention span, actually. I've seen him pissed off. I've seen him drunk. I've seen him out of his mind on cocaine. But I've never seen him run away from anything before. I can't ever remember him taking anything seriously enough to run away from it. Least of all work.'

'How serious is he about Lulu?' Eileen asked. 'Does she have anything to do with this?' 'I honestly don't know, is the answer to both those questions,' I said. 'I don't think he's particularly serious about her, in that I don't think he's ever serious about anybody. Not for more than about twenty-four hours, anyway. But you never know. I guess she must have *something* to do with it or he wouldn't have gone away with her. I think she's a friend that he fucks rather than a lover, if you know what I mean.' 'Tell me about it,' said Eileen, raising her eyes to the ceiling. 'And she plays good backgammon, which he likes,' I added. 'Let's all have a drink,' I suggested. 'What will you girls have?' Katrina wanted a vodka on the rocks, and Eileen had a glass of white wine. I had my usual. I dispensed the drinks, and sat down again.

'I think I know what we *ought* to be doing,' I said. 'I'm

just not sure how to go about it. But let me try this on you both. Number one. We need to decide if this is temporary or permanent. Basically, whether it's going to go away, or not. That's vital to everything. If it's only temporary, we don't need to do anything. Right?' I looked at them in turn. 'Right,' said Eileen. A moment later, Katrina agreed too. 'Good,' I said. 'Number two. If it looks like it's permanent, i.e. genuine – that's quite a consideration, isn't it? – then we'll have to take some kind of action. Sooner or later, we'll have to tell Wally. That much is obvious. But it's a matter of when. The timing is vital. We don't want *him* stamping about, causing chaos out here, if we can possibly avoid it. So we'll shelve telling Wally until we absolutely have to. But I don't think we should deliberately lie. If Wally rings up you or me, Eileen, and says "Where's Fred?" I think at that stage we'll have to tell him. Do you agree, Eileen?' She nodded. 'Yes, I do,' she said. 'Not mentioning it until we have to is one thing. Deliberately telling Wally lies is something else.' 'Right,' I said.

'I think that's probably it,' I went on. 'Once we have decided whether or not it's serious, i.e. genuine, then everything else – like telling Wally – falls into place. So it all comes down to, how do we find out whether it's serious or not?' 'There are only two ways,' said Eileen. 'Either by talking to Fred. Or we simply wait and see. How long you reckon we should wait is probably your decision,' she said. I looked at her. 'Mmmm,' I said. 'It's not easy, is it? But let's take an arbitrary period. How about two weeks? If he's still over in L.A. after two weeks, and he's still saying that he's not coming back, then I think we'll probably have to accept that he *isn't* coming back. Do you agree?' I looked at the two of them again.

'I guess so,' said Eileen. 'Anything up to two weeks could be a vacation. After two weeks, if he's still saying he's not coming back, my vote is for telling Wally then.' I looked at Katrina. 'Is difficult for me,' she said. 'I not really know Fred. I meet him, yes. But I not really know him. But if what you say is so, then yes, after two weeks you must tell English boss.' 'What about the rest of the staff here in New York?' asked Eileen. 'We'll have to say *something*, won't we? They'll wonder where he is if they don't see anything of him at all.' I pondered on this question for a moment. What Eileen was saying was quite right, of course. 'I know,' I said. 'I've got it. When they ask where he is, we'll simply say he's on a trip to Los Angeles. Fred being Fred, we don't have to say why, or what for, or even for how long. If anyone asks those questions, we can simply say we don't know. We've no idea. All of which is absolutely true.'

'Terrific,' said Eileen. 'Perfect. And like you say, it's all true. Is there anything else we need to think about?' 'I don't think so,' I said. 'I can't think of anything. You can handle his office mail. If there are any problems, presumably you'll ask me?' She nodded. 'Sure. Fine.' 'Good,' I said. 'His apartment mail will pile up, but I don't see that as a problem. Presumably he's told the staff there that he's away for a while?' 'I guess so,' said Eileen. 'But I could call them and check. Shall I do that?' 'Please,' I said. 'That makes sense. What else? His salary goes into his bank account, the same as anyone else's. You know about his diary, Eileen.'

She chortled. 'As much as anyone does, I guess. Which isn't very much. But I'll check through it, and do anything that's necessary. When his coke dealer calls, I'll simply tell him that Fred's over in L.A. for a while. He doesn't need to know anything else.' 'What about girlfriends?' I asked. 'Will anyone be surprised that he's not around?' 'No, not really,' said Eileen. 'He's so often not around for most of his women that they're used to it. They'll simply think they're out of favour for a while. They won't cause any problems. Apart from driving me mad on the phone, of course.' 'Well, as far as I can see, that just about covers it, unless either of you can think of anything else?' I said. Neither of them said anything, so I went on. 'I'll call Fred at Lulu's this evening, and I'll tell you what he says.' I turned to Eileen. 'Bless you for coming over so promptly Eileen, sweetheart,' I said. 'I really do appreciate it. Two heads are always better than one for this kind of thing. To be honest, I just plain panicked. I couldn't think what to do first. Will you join Katrina and me for a spot of lunch now? That would be the very least I can do to say thank you.' She smiled at me. 'Thanks, Tony. I'd love to. Are you sure I'm not interfering? I don't want to play gooseberry. Katrina? Is that OK with you?' Katrina gave her a huge smile. 'Of course it's OK, darlink,' she said. 'We can talk about Tony.'

Oh, terrific, I thought. 'Let's go to Marty's,' I suggested. 'Up on Third Avenue at 73rd Street.' 'Oh, great,' said Eileen, 'I love Marty's.' 'Sounds good,' said Katrina. I called Marty's, made a reservation for the three of us, then rang down and asked for a cab. 'We're on our way down now,' I said. 'Don't bother to call me back.'

Marty's was packed. But then it always was. There wasn't anyone playing the piano this lunchtime. I guess they only do that in the evenings. The last time I had been in Marty's was with Annabel. Suddenly, I wondered what she was doing in London this Saturday. I looked at my watch. It was nearly one. Five hours ahead was six in the evening, London time. For all I knew, she might be in bed. I wondered with whom, or if she was up and alone. I plumped for up and alone, but that was probably because that was what I wanted her to be. I wondered why. She could have been here, sitting with me now, advising me with her wise head what best to do about Fred. The waitress arrived. She was really pretty, with a lovely smile. 'Hallo, folks,' she said, handing out menus. 'My name's Fran. Let me tell you about today's specials.' She ran through her list. I ordered a bottle of Italian white wine for starters, and Fran said that she'd be back for our orders 'momentarily.' I love the way Americans say 'momentarily'. Their use of the word in that context is totally ungrammatical, but it's fun.

The excitement of the morning had rather taken the edge off my appetite, but the two girls ate enough for the three of us. I couldn't believe it. The food literally just disappeared off their plates. 'Now, darlink,' said Katrina to Eileen, pushing her empty plate away. 'Tell me all about Tony. Is he a bastard in the office?' 'Oh, he's hell,' said Eileen. 'You just can't imagine.' 'But he's a great fuck, don't you think?' said Katrina. Eileen didn't turn a hair. 'I've had worse,' she said. 'Oh, sure,' said Katrina. 'Haven't we all? But this one gets top marks in my book. What marks would you give him out of ten?'

'Hey,' I said. 'Do you mind? This isn't the sort of conversation to have in front of me. When I've gone to the gents, maybe. Now, definitely not.' 'Spoilsport,' said Eileen. She turned back to Katrina and, in a theatrical whisper, intentionally loud enough for me to hear, she said 'Ten. But don't tell him. He's big-headed enough already.' 'Pack it in, girls, will you?' I said. 'Enough is enough. Now then, does anyone want anything else. More coffee? More brandy? No? I'll get the check, then.'

I waved to Fran, and made signs asking for the bill. When she brought it, she had folded it so that I could see that something was written on the back of it. I unfolded it, and read, 'I've enjoyed looking after you today. If you'd like to know just how much, call me,' followed by a telephone number, and her name, 'Fran O'Brien. I looked up at her and she gave me a lewd wink. 'Glad to be of service, sir,' she said, smiling. I over-tipped her, naturally, and made a mental note either to call her, or to drop by at Marty's when I was on my own one day. I slipped Eileen a ten. 'Take a cab on *Tiptop*, sweetheart,' I

A SURPRISE GOODBYE

said. 'And thank you again.' 'Don't mention it,' she said. 'Any time. And thank you.' She kissed Katrina on the cheek. 'I'll call you,' she said. 'We'll definitely have that lunch. Goodbye now.' I waved down a cab for her, and then one for Katrina and me. 'Sutton Place South,' I said to the driver. I opened the door for Katrina, and helped her in.

'Nice girl, that Eileen,' said Katrina. 'Do you know that she's in love with you?' 'Er, yes,' I said. 'And I'm very fond of her.' 'But you're not in love with her?' she asked. 'No,' I said. 'Not in the way that you mean.' 'Do you fuck her?' Katrina asked. I saw the driver looking at me in his rear-view mirror. He grimaced when he caught my eye. 'Er, yes,' I told her. 'Sometimes.' 'What do you mean, sometimes?' she asked. 'Well,' I said. 'Because I work with her, I see her most days. She's my secretary, as well as Fred's. And she keeps asking me to fuck her. So I do. Sometimes.' 'You don't always fuck *me* when I ask you,' Katrina said. 'How about this morning? "Please fuck me," I said, just like that, and you didn't.' 'But I was going to,' I said. 'Hmmm,' she said. 'We'll see about that.' The driver pulled up outside the entrance to the apartment block, and Katrina got out as one of the doormen opened her door for her. I handed the driver a note. 'I gotta take my hat off to you, bud,' he said. 'I don't know what it is, but whatever it is, you got it, that's for sure.' 'Thanks,' I said. 'Keep the change.'

Back in the apartment, Katrina seemed to have recovered from her minor sulk in the cab on the way home. 'Get 'em off, sweetheart,' I said, once we were in the apartment. 'Get them round your ankles.' She looked puzzled. 'Round ankles,' she said, looking down at her feet. 'I don't understand. What about my ankles? Are you saying that they are too fat? My ankles are quite slim. Dancers don't have fat ankles.' I had to laugh, and I went over and gave her a big hug and a kiss. 'Don't worry about it, darling,' I said. 'Your ankles are beautiful. I don't suppose they showed Budgie on Russian TV.' I explained Adam Faith's milkman's favourite greeting. I think she understood.

When we got to the bedroom, Katrina said, 'I take much trouble, dressing for you this morning. Since I have not seen you for so long, I make myself sexy for you. Now I undress slowly. You can watch.' She took off the pale grey suit, the jacket first, and then she unzipped her skirt, dropped it (round her ankles!) and stepped out of it. I took a deep breath. I could already see that she had indeed taken a great deal of trouble. Next she took off the red silk shirt, and stood there, slowly turning around, so that I might appreciate her exotic, indeed erotic, lingerie to the full. She was wearing matching nylon bra and panties in a deep blue that was darker than royal blue, lighter than navy.

The material was opaque, rather than transparent, in that it clearly showed shape but not visual detail. It was shiny, like silk, but it clung to her better than silk, the bra outlining the unmistakable shape of her erect nipples, and I could clearly see the shape of her sex lips through the tight nylon crotch of her panties. The blue was edged with white lace, the bra held in place by straps of it, and the knickers were similarly held up by a white lace waistband, while the rest of them were edged with it. Under the knickers she wore a matching white lace suspender belt, which was just lengths of elasticated white lace, the long suspenders clipped to the darker tops of the pale brown silk stockings that they supported. The whole was still set off by her strappy, red patent leather, high-heeled sandals. I felt my cock rising in appreciation of this delightful sight. 'You like?' Katrina asked.

'Like it, sweetheart? I love it,' I said. She came over and stood in front of where I was sitting. She put down her hand and pulled aside the crotch of her knickers,

A SURPRISE GOODBYE

displaying her full, puffy cunt lips, swollen with passion. I could smell the scent of wet pussy. I breathed in deeply, enjoying the anticipation. 'Look,' she said. 'My cunt is all wet for you.' Katrina put down both hands and pulled her outer labia apart, showing me the shining, wet, pale pink interior of her vagina. The cockteasing aroma increased tenfold. 'Come and fuck me now, Tony,' she said. 'No more excuses. You can see that my cunt needs your cock. Now. Please.' She turned away and walked over to the bed. She looked over her shoulders. 'I take off my panties now,' she said. 'The rest I leave on to make your cock hard while you fuck me.' She bent over and slipped the knickers down her long legs, stepping out of them and dropping them on the floor. As they reached her ankles, I could see that the cotton lining of the gusset was wet and sticky with her effluent. I was dragging my clothes off as quickly as I knew how. I had missed this lovely young lady while I'd been down in Florida. She had just reminded me of exactly what I had been missing. It was her inherent sexiness. She had the morals and habits of a tart, combined with the delight and innocence of a fresh young girl. It was a fantastic combination.

Katrina lay down on her back on the bed, waiting for me, her legs wide apart, her knees bent, one hand slowly fingering her pussy as she waited. 'Katrina do somethink she never do before, while you are in Florida,' she said, conversationally. I was at last shot of my clothes, and I went over to join her on the bed. 'Oh,' I said. 'What was that, sweetheart?' 'I stay faithful to you,' she said. 'I fuck only my fingers. No men. Not even women. No one.'

I took hold of her and kissed her, passionately, on the mouth. When I came up for air, I said, 'Thank you, darling. That was a great honour.' 'Yes,' she said. 'It was. Now fuck me.' I took my swollen length and fed it into her waiting wetness. She felt delightful. A whole erotic dream of my own, but living and breathing. Wet with desire. She wasn't just wet, she was positively hot, and her vaginal muscles closed around my cock as I began to shaft her with long, deep strokes. 'Oh, yes, baby,' she breathed, hoarsely. 'That's what I've been needing. Hard cock. *Your* hard cock. Fucking me. Oh, Jesus.'

Katrina went on in this manner as I fucked her as well as I knew how. I wanted it to last. I wanted her to be rewarded for her faithfulness. I didn't want it to be over until she'd come more than once. I leaned down and began to suck a nipple through the nylon of her brassiere. She moaned as I sucked, the additional sensation adding to her sexual pleasure. I bit the nipple. Not *too* hard. She moaned again. I could feel her orgasm building, from the signals and sensations that she was sending me with her vaginal muscles. I too was having fun. She felt terrific. She was doing beautiful things to my cock. But I'd been exercising it thoroughly all the time I'd been away. How long was it? Two weeks at least. A bit more. So I didn't feel the urgency that she was feeling. While I was thinking about all this, her first orgasm built up and broke, and she thrashed around on the bed quite wildly, shouting out her pleasure as she came. She started off with a series of small orgasms, which quickly built up into a more or less continual orgasm, for a while. This had her screaming while it lasted, until it finally, slowly, subsided. I kept fucking her all the way through these orgasms, and her enthusiastic enjoyment of what was happening to her helped to keep my cock hard as she came and came again.

It wasn't too long before I could feel Katrina building up to a repeat of this performance, and this time I decided that I would join in with her. After all, we had the whole weekend ahead of us. There was no need to try and break any records. I just wanted her to enjoy what she was doing. So I increased my rhythm, and I increased the pressure with which I thrust into her on my down-stroke,

A SURPRISE GOODBYE

so that the friction of my cock against her erect clitoris might become more urgent. She began to thrust back up against me again, and to moan in that throaty, husky way that she had when she was climbing up the long, slow incline to orgasm. And then she was there, and I was there, and we thrashed about together, and I felt my cock spurting into her in jets, and that in itself seemed to increase the intensity of her coming, so that she shouted out with a combination of excitement and pleasure. If she was a typical example, no one could accuse Russian girls of being repressed.

When we had recovered, Katrina turned to me and kissed me, seemingly lovingly. 'That was nice, darlink,' she said. 'Katrina enjoy herself. Is good for you, yes? We do it again soon, yes? Is so much better than fingers.' 'Yes, sweetheart,' I said. 'Is good for me, too. Very good. Thank you.' She was lying there in her blue lingerie, looking like a dream. Any red-blooded male's fantasy sex object. And she just loved to fuck. I just lay there for a while, thinking what a lucky guy I was.

We spent the rest of the afternoon in the bedroom, alternating between talking and fucking. During that time I took off Katrina's bra, then the little white suspender belt, and finally I peeled off the stockings, an enjoyably erotic act in itself, until she lay there totally naked, and then I fucked her again, after which I said, 'Enough, my darling, for now. Let's get bathed and dressed, and then I'll try and telephone Fred, after which we'll go and have dinner somewhere. OK with you?' We began to do exactly that. I looked up Lulu's L.A. number, which I discovered I did in fact have, and I pressed the phone buttons rather nervously. I had no idea what I was going to say to Fred, even supposing that he was there and agreed to speak to me. Lulu answered, immediately. I got the impression – I'm not sure why – that she had been getting a lot of telephone calls. Or maybe it was just that she had been making a lot of telephone calls. Who knows?

'Tony, darling,' she said. 'How are you?' 'I'm fine, Lulu, sweetheart,' I said. 'How are you?' It seemed slightly inane, in the circumstances, to be observing niceties of telephone good manners. 'I'm good,' she said. 'I expect you've called to talk to Fred. Is that right?' 'Please, Lulu,' I said. 'If he's available.' 'Hang on a second, darling,' she said. 'I'll put him on.' I heard her say 'It's Tony Andrews, darling,' and then Fred was on the line.

'Tone,' he said. 'How's it going?' 'Oh, fine, Fred,' I said. 'Everything's fine. But I've been thinking about our conversation this morning, and I just thought it would be a good thing if I checked in with you.' 'Great,' he said. 'Fire away.' Shit, I thought. He's being reasonable. That's always a bad sign with Fred. Whenever he sounded reasonable, it meant that he was doing something entirely *un*reasonable, but that he'd thought it through, he'd taken his decision, and he was going to see it through whatever the eventual outcome. 'Well,' I said, 'I wondered if you were serious about what you said. I mean, I can understand that you're tired. Bored, even. Fed up. You know? But you don't need to jack it all in. Why not just take a holiday? Lie in the sun out there for a while, and recharge your batteries. But what's all this about jacking it in? I mean, seriously. What's it all about?'

I heard him take a deep breath. 'I appreciate what you're saying, Tone, really I do,' he said. 'But I've thought this through carefully, over a long period of time. It's not a sudden decision. It's not the result of too much coke, or booze, or anything like that. It's just that, over quite a long period of time now, I've become fairly disenchanted with the way that I earn my living. It's a good living, you know that. I know it, too. But, to be honest, I've made enough money not to need to work any more. Ever. So I've just been thinking, why, in God's

A SURPRISE GOODBYE

name, am I busting my gut still working for Wally?

'He's not the easiest person in the world to work for, as you must know, and he's got strange ideas about things like office hours. That sort of thing. You know what I mean. I feel more like a fucking schoolboy being bollocked by the headmaster than the guy who's actually built up that business for Wally from nothing, and made him a fortune in the process. You'd think, by now, that he'd let me have my head. But no, Wally's still got to play "I'm the big boss" with me. Well, fuck him. He doesn't actually need me any longer. You know that. I know that. But *Wally* doesn't actually know that. So don't tell him. Let him think, now, that he needs you. But frankly, any wanker could run that magazine. It's all set up. Just keep giving the punters what they want, and bingo, the money rolls in.' Gee, thanks a lot, I thought. Any wanker, eh? I guess it takes one to know one. 'And anyway,' Fred continued, 'whatever I do, I don't need to work for Wally. If I get seriously bored, I can start my own magazine, for God's sake. I've got the money. I've got the know-how. And I've got some pretty good, pretty original ideas. But to come back to your original question, sure I'm sure. This isn't a holiday, this is it. I know I could have done it more tidily. I could perhaps have given my notice in, written Wally a letter. Perhaps even gone back to London and told him. I just thought, fuck it. That's it. So you tell him, OK? Or maybe you've told him already? What did he say?'

'No, I haven't spoken to Wally, Fred,' I said. 'The only person I've spoken to about this is Eileen, who sends her love.' She hadn't, but she would have done if she'd thought about it. 'But look, Fred, please don't think I'm trying to interfere, because I'm not. It's your life. Whatever you want to do with it is fine by me. But may I tell you what I think? I mean, you know, give you my opinion, for what it's worth?'

'Of course you can, Tone,' he said. 'We're mates, for God's sake. You know I always value your opinion.' 'Well,' I said. 'I see it like this; leave aside, for the moment, everything that you've just said, and look at the positive side. You're extremely well paid. Right?' 'Right,' he said. 'Next, despite what you say about Wally, you do actually come and go pretty much as you please. Now don't you?' 'Well, maybe,' said Fred. 'But not as much as I'd like to.' 'Well, leave *that* aside for the moment,' I said. 'I'll come back to that. But why don't you simply go to Wally and tell him that you want to alter your status within the company? Tell him that, so OK, you're the managing director, but that's only a title, really. You're still running around after him like a – what did you say, a schoolboy? Yes. That was it – so tell him that you want to be a full, main board director, with a proper shareholding, and all that, and that you want to alter and agree with him the parameters within which you are prepared to work. You could draft a piece of paper to give him. You know, perhaps only work four days a week, for example.

'You hold all the aces. Wally can't edit a magazine. Tell him that if he doesn't agree to your terms, you'll leave. Set up on your own. Go and work for the opposition. Paul Raymond. Bob Guccione. Hugh Heffner. Anyone. That doesn't mean that you're actually going to go and do it, does it? But he wouldn't know that, would he? As far as he's concerned, a move like that would make tremendous sense.'

'Oh, I don't know, Tone,' he said. 'Look, I appreciate what you're saying. It's all good, sound stuff. I know you're right, if you want me to say it. Of course I do. But I really *have* had enough. My get-up-and-go has got up and gone. I'm tired. I want to relax. I don't want to have to get up and go to an office. Mine, or anyone else's. I want to boogie all night, and sleep all day. You know me. That's what I *really* enjoy doing. I've been through all that working eighteen hours a day, worrying about the mortgage, wondering about whether the magazine will work or not, thank-God-it's-Friday bit. And I've made a success of it. I'm just a little lad from nowhere who had an idea and made it work. Made it work very well, to be fair to myself. And now I want to stop, and enjoy myself. What's so wrong with that? You tell me.'

'There's nothing wrong with that, Fred,' I told him. 'Absolutely nothing at all. Except that it isn't necessary. You can enjoy yourself, and *still* have the money happily rolling in. Think about it.'

'I *have* thought about it, Tony my old love,' he said. 'I've thought about little else, ever since I came back from London. While you were in Puerto Rico, remember? I was so bloody angry with Wally's attitude while I was in London, I could have strangled him. So OK, he wasn't poor when I went to him at the beginning. But he's a bloody sight richer now than he was then, that's for sure. And what does he say? Thank you? Not a bit of it. He tells me that I'm not keeping proper office hours, and that I'm setting a bad example to the staff. Who needs it? I've only been out here in L.A. a few hours, but I feel better already. Now you're telling me that you think I'm doing the wrong thing. Well, I'm sorry, old love, but I don't agree with you. I think I'm doing the first thing that I've done right for a very long time. Like I said, it's good of you to care enough to say what you're saying, and I appreciate it. I really do. But my mind's made up. If you need any help, at any time, you know that all you have to do is call me. Right? And of course, if you fancy a trip to the West Coast, come be our guest. Any time.'

Forget it, Andrews, I thought. Let it go. You're on a hiding to nothing. You've said your piece. You've tried to help. If he doesn't want to understand what you're trying to say, let it go. Any more, and you'll lose a friend as well as a colleague. 'Well, if that's how you feel, Fred,' I said. 'But I tell you what I'm going to do. I'm not going to say anything to Wally yet awhile. If he – or anybody else, for that matter – asks where you are, as far as I'm concerned you're on vacation. OK? What that means is that, as far as I'm concerned, you're not committed to any particular course of action for the time being. If you still feel the same way in a couple of weeks' time, well, then we can talk again. But until we do, you're on holiday. If I take you at your face value – no, that's wrong – if I accept what you're telling me (and I know that you believe what you're saying – very much so) then in theory I should telephone Wally, and say, look, Wally, old thing, I have to tell you that Fred's gone. Left you. Disappeared. And Wally's going to go potty. He's going to come out here with an army of lawyers and accountants and make everyone's life a misery. Certainly yours, and probably mine. And that is something to be avoided, as far as is possible. At least, that's my opinion. So I'll wind up now. Or shut up now. Whatever you want to call it. But do you hear what I'm saying?'

'Yes, of course I do,' he said. 'I hear, and I understand, and I would like to say "Thank you." I know that you're seriously trying to be helpful. And I appreciate that. As far as I'm concerned, I'll still be feeling the same way in a couple of weeks' time. But I'm happy to leave it like this. I shan't speak to Wally. At least, I shan't speak to Wally without telling you, one, that I'm going to, and two, what I've said to him. Or, if he should call me here, then I'll call you immediately afterwards, and tell you what we've said. In those circumstances, I'll tell him that you think I'm on vacation, and that you don't know anything about my thoughts, plans, feelings, or decisions. OK?' 'Well, yes,' I said. 'But say what you like. I'm not frightened of Wally. Tell him the truth. Just keep me in the picture. Look after yourself. God bless. Goodbye now, Fred.' 'Goodbye, Tone,' he said. 'Thank you. Seriously. Thank you.'

I put the phone down. 'How was it, darlink?' said Katrina. 'How did it go? What news?' 'Well, I *think* it was

OK,' I said. 'But no news. Nothing really to add. He's still saying the same things that he said this morning. In rather more detail. He seems to be set on doing what he's doing. But I'm not sure that I entirely trust him. Dear old Fred's always been a little bit devious.' 'In what way?' asked Katrina. 'Well,' I said. 'He says that this isn't a quick decision. He says he's been thinking about doing what he's doing for a long time now. Ever since he came back from London. Which was a little while before you and I met, with Fred in attendance, in the Russian Tea Room,' I said. 'What's that? Four, five weeks ago?'

'Somethink like that, darlink,' she said. 'It was a while ago.' 'And now,' I said, 'he says he's finished. He's had enough. He doesn't want to work for Wally any more. But I don't entirely trust him. I have a feeling that there might be a great deal more to this than meets the eye. I mean, if what he says is true – that he's been thinking about it ever since he came back from his trip to London – I'm surprised that he hasn't discussed it with me at some time since then. I mean, we *are* friends. Or, at least, we *used* to be friends. And then, the one thing that he didn't mention – or the one *person* that he didn't mention – in any kind of detail, was anything to do with Lulu. You'd think wouldn't you, that if a close friend decided to jack in his job in New York, and move off out to Los Angeles, that he might – just *might*, mention that he'd moved there with a girl. I mean, someone we all know. Lulu's been around for ever. She's one of Fred's few regulars. Why would he have so little to say about Lulu? As I remember it, he said that he was going to stay with her, as if she was out there anyway, and she was simply putting him up for a few nights. But I tend to think that there's more to it than that.

'You'd think he might have said, for example, that there wasn't anything significant about the fact that he'd flown out there with her. You know what I mean? I don't know. I think I'm beginning to imagine things. The whole thing is an enigma to me. It makes me think about things that I've never thought about before. I've never wanted Fred's job, for example. Ever. I don't particularly want it *now*. But I'm forced to ask myself, if he's serious about not coming back, whether or not I seriously want to make a pitch for it. I mean, at the end of the day, everyone's interested in money, and that job pays a great deal more than mine does. Not that Wally would pay me what he's paying Fred, obviously. But if I wanted the job – and if Wally would give it to me – he'd need to pay me more than I'm getting now, that's for sure. If only on a the-buck-stops-here basis.'

I looked at Katrina, and I suddenly realized that I had been ranting on about Fred for far too long. She was trying to look interested, because she knew that what I was saying was important to me, but her eyes were beginning to get that glazed look. You know, the one that tells you you've lost your audience. 'I'm sorry, sweetheart,' I said to her. 'Forgive me. That's quite enough, I know. I'll stop now. Just let me call Eileen and tell her about my telephone conversation, and then we'll go and find some supper. OK?' 'Is OK, darlink,' she said. 'Is no problem.'

I rang Eileen, and we went over Fred's telephone conversation. When I got to the end, I asked her what she thought. 'I don't really know, Tony,' she said. 'It's all very confusing, isn't it? It does rather sound as if he means it. But you know Fred. He might mean it today, but will he still mean it tomorrow? You tell me. I think you've probably done the best thing you can in telling him that, as far as you're concerned, he's on vacation for the next couple of weeks. Having said that, I honestly think that you've done *everything* you can, at least for now. It's wait and see time, I guess.' We chattered on for a bit, and then agreed to leave things until we met in the office on Monday morning. 'Just one thing, before you go, darling,'

A SURPRISE GOODBYE

she said. 'I think Fred's very lucky to have someone like you looking after things for him. Most people would be trying to take things over, rather than keep them open for Fred. I hope he appreciates it.'

I said something evasive like 'So do I,' and put the phone down. Katrina was, for Katrina, rather silent over supper. 'What's the matter, sweetheart?' I said. 'Why so quiet?' She smiled at me. 'Nothink is matter, darlink,' she said. 'I am just wondering whether to give you present. Is difficult to decide.' 'Then let me decide for you,' I suggested. 'Do it. Whatever it is that you want to give me, feel free. I love presents.' She gave me a bit of an old-fashioned look. 'This is problem,' she said. 'I don't want you to love this one. Just to enjoy.' Oh, shit, I thought. Women. There's no pleasing them. 'All right,' I said. 'I'll enjoy it, but I won't love it. How's that?' 'You promise?' she asked me. 'I promise,' I said. 'Cross my heart, and hope to die. What is it? Am I allowed to know in advance?' 'Oh, yes,' she said. 'You must know in advance, so that you can look forward to it. But is not an "it." Is a "who." I am going to give you my girlfriend, Valentina. Perhaps *lend* is better word.'

'Hey,' I said. 'That's some present. Do you think she will agree?' 'Oh, is all agreed,' said Katrina. 'While you were away.' 'Terrific,' I said. 'Tell me about her. What does she look like? Did you have to work hard at it to get her to agree?' She laughed. I noticed a man at the next table looking at her. I wondered if he could hear our conversation.

'One question at a time,' she said. 'She is blonde, like me. But her hair is short. She is also a dancer in chorus. And no, I didn't have to work hard. She suggest it. I tell her about your big cock, and she plead with me to let you fuck her. You will like her. She is called Valentina, after the famous woman astronaut. You know? Valentina Tereshkova? She has small breasts, like me, but she has big nipples. And she has very pretty cunt. No, how you say? Pussy. She has very pretty pussy. Small, tight lips. I know, because I kiss it, sometimes. We play naughty games. You know, lesbian games. Like me, she is fucked as young girl, and like me, she is taught to suck other girls, for old men to watch, Party members, to make their cocks stiff before they fuck her. And we learn to like it, sometimes, when there is no man to fuck properly. We will do it for you, if you like. Do you like to watch girls do naughty things to each other?' She looked at me with her blue eyes open questioningly. I wondered again if the man at the next table could hear her. From the expression on his face, I think he probably could. I felt as if my erection was about to tilt the table over. Did I like to watch girls doing naughty things to each other? Jesus. Yes. Yes. YES. Please God. 'Er, yes. Yes. I do.' I said, rather hesitatingly. I mean, girls in brothels doing naughty things for men to watch is one thing. Russian ballet dancers doing naughty things for me to watch is something else. And how. I suddenly saw no point in being shy about it. 'Actually, sweetheart, I love it,' I said. 'It makes me very excited. When can we get you together with Valentina?' She looked at me and smiled again. 'How about this evening?' she asked. 'If I telephone her now, she can be at the apartment by the time we get back. Would you like that?' 'Yes, please,' I said. 'I'd love it.'

When we got back to Sutton Place, Valentina was waiting in the lobby. I knew it was Valentina. She was youngish – about eighteen, I would guess – with her blonde hair cut short, and with a little fringe. Her legs were slim and muscular-looking, and she had that exotic look that I was beginning to recognize was a trademark of many young Russian girls. She wore a black dress, and had a multicoloured shawl around her shoulders. She was sitting down, looking idly at a magazine, and she jumped up when she

A SURPRISE GOODBYE

saw Katrina. 'Katrina, darlink,' she said. 'Valentina, darlink,' said Katrina. They kissed each other.

'And this is Tony,' said Katrina. 'Tony, this is Valentina.' she came over and gave me a kiss on the cheek. She smelt heavenly. I put my hand in my pocket to hide my rising erection. Valentina smiled. 'I've heard a lot about you,' she said. 'I hope it's all true.' I saw the doormen looking at me with a mutual sort of "How in God's name does he pull all these chicks?" expression on their faces. Fuck them, I thought. Tough shit. We got the elevator and went up to the apartment.

Once inside, Valentina went over to the windows. 'What a beautiful view,' she said. 'You are lucky to be looking out over the East River. And what's that little island there, just under the bridge?' 'That's Roosevelt Island,' I told her. 'I've never noticed it before,' she said. 'And people live there, I see. How do they get there? I can't see any road.' 'There isn't one,' I said. 'At least, not from Manhattan. There is one from the other bank. That's Queens. But from this side, there's a sort of aerial tramway. You can't see it from here. It's just the other side of the bridge. It's quite a fun trip. But there's actually nothing to do on the island. It's just apartments. But you can walk around it, and there are benches to sit on here and there.' 'Which bridge is that?' Katrina asked. 'It's the 59th Street Bridge,' I told her. 'It's my favourite New York bridge.' 'Why is that?' asked Valentina. 'No good reason, really,' I said. 'Except that it was the first bridge I came across from the airport on my first ever trip to New York. I never dreamed that I would live here then. And now I can see it out of my window. Mary Tudor had Calais written on her heart. I've got the 59th Street Bridge, and Roosevelt Island.' They both laughed.

Valentina came over and stood up against me. She put out a hand, and I felt her take hold of my cock through my trousers. I would never cease to be amazed by these

Russian girls. They were just so naturally, unembarrassedly sexy. 'I've heard a lot about your cock,' she breathed, smiling up at me. She unzipped my fly as she spoke. 'And I just can't wait to see it. And feel it, of course,' she murmured. 'Inside me, that is.' She pulled it out of my trousers and it grew in her hand as she looked down at it. 'Mmm,' she said. 'Beautiful.'

She turned around and looked at Katrina. 'Are you ready, darlink?' she asked. 'I'm ready when you are. I did what you asked me to do on the telephone.' She didn't let go of my cock whilst thus engaged in conversation. She just stood there, holding it. She began to move her hand in a slow masturbatory motion. I pulled carefully away from her. 'If you keep on doing that, sweetheart,' I said, 'you'll soon have a very sticky hand.' She laughed. 'What a naughty boy,' she said. 'I might have to spank you.' She looked at me, and I noticed that her eyes were a beautiful pale green. Quite unlike Katrina, I thought. 'Or would *you* rather spank *me*?' she asked. 'That sounds better than you spanking me,' I said. 'But how about a drink first, to take into the bedroom with us?' I offered them champagne. This was obviously a special occasion and needed something more exciting than just plain spirits. They both agreed with alacrity. Whilst I was opening the bottle, Katrina fetched three champagne glasses from the kitchen cupboard. She put them down on a table close beside me. 'Thank you, darling,' I said.

'Since Valentina is a present,' she announced, 'I thought she would be more acceptable if she came prettily wrapped. So when I telephoned her, I asked her to put on her naughtiest knickers. When we've had a sip of champagne, I'll open the package for you, if I may. Is that in order?' 'Perfectly, sweetheart,' I said. 'That will be lovely. Thank you.' I drew the cork, poured the three glasses, and handed one each to the girls. 'Cheers, darlings,' I said. 'Happy landings.' I waved the girls towards the bedroom

A SURPRISE GOODBYE

door. 'After you, ladies,' I said. Katrina led the way. I followed Valentina. She had a gorgeous ass, I thought. I could see the line of her knickers through the thin material of her dress. I sat on the bed.

'This is all for your enjoyment, darlink,' said Katrina. 'So as we go on, ask anythink you like. Stop us, start us, tell us to hold on. Join in. Anythink you like. OK?' Good God, I thought. How many men get offers like that? Not too many. 'Thank you, sweetheart,' I said. 'That's lovely. I will. I promise.' 'Good,' said Katrina. 'Now, then. First, I take off Valentina's dress.' She went behind Valentina, and unzipped a long zip which ran from Valentina's neck to her waist. Then, standing behind Valentina, she took the dress by its shoulders, and eased it down, slowly, over Valentina's breasts.

This revealed the fact that Valentina was wearing a rather minimal-looking, black, gossamer-thin bra. But the interesting thing about it was that it had holes where Valentina's nipples were, thus ensuring that they poked out through the holes. As Katrina had told me, they were big. They grew bigger as I looked at them, and Katrina reached around Valentina and took one between her fingers. She pulled it, slowly, and it became stiff and hard beneath her fingers. 'Lovely nipples,' she said. 'I have sucked them many times. They taste nice.' She let go of the extended nipple, and then drew the dress down over Valentina's slim hips, and down around her ankles. Valentina stepped out of it. I felt my cock growing harder as I saw what was next revealed. She was wearing French knickers in the same black, gossamer material as her bra, but the difference was that where the bra exposed Valentina's nipples, the French knickers lacked any pretence at a crotch, thus exposing to view her pale blonde pubic hair, through which I could see a glimpse of her snatch. It was pink-lipped, and glistened as if wet. She was also wearing black silk stockings, held up by black garters, which were decorated with little red bows. The white flesh revealed between the bottom of her French knickers and the top of her stockings was the sexiest sight I had seen for a while.

'Voilà,' said Katrina. 'Sexy, no? Turn around, my darlink,' she said to Valentina. 'Let Tony see your lovely little bottom.' Valentina obediently turned around, showing me her bottom, almost bare in the black, gossamer-thin knickers. It was indeed lovely. It was firm, round, tight, and muscled. I wondered if she liked to be fucked in the ass. And then I remembered Katrina's instruction to 'ask anything you like'.

'Does Valentina take it up her ass?' I asked. There was silence for a moment or two, and I wondered if I had perhaps gone too far. Katrina looked at Valentina. 'Do you take it up the ass, darlink?' she said. Still there was silence for a moment. And then Valentina burst out laughing. 'I take it anywhere, darlink,' she said, to my not inconsiderable relief. 'Up my cunt, up my ass, between my tits, in my mouth, in my hand. I don't mind. But I would like to start off with up my cunt. Once I have come, you can fuck me anywhere you like. In my left earhole.' She giggled. 'Except that it wouldn't fit.' She burst out laughing again. 'Russian girls take it anywhere, darlink,' she said. 'And as often as you like. Men like to fuck girls in the ass because an asshole is so tight, they tell me. Well, all I can say is, my cunt is tight, too. You will feel how tight it is. Very soon now. I do not think you will complain. But first, Katrina and me, we play lesbian games. No?'

She looked at Katrina. 'I think so,' Katrina replied. 'You want to watch us play dirty games?' she asked me. 'Make you stiff. Make you horny. Make you fuck us well?' 'Yes, please,' I said. 'I'd like that.' 'But first,' said Katrina, 'come and feel the quality of this present.' I didn't move, for a moment. 'No, I'm serious,' she said. She beckoned to me. 'Come on,' she said. 'Come here.

A SURPRISE GOODBYE

It's all right.' I got up off the bed, and went over to them. Katrina took my hand in hers, and placed it over one of Valentina's small but exquisitely formed tits. 'Feel that, darlink,' she said. 'Is good. No? Is firm. Lovely? Yes?' I felt it. It was firm. It was lovely.

I reached around behind Valentina and undid the hook of her bra, pulling it down her arms, taking it off. I felt her breast again, without the interference of the material, thin as it had been. It felt wonderful. I leaned down, and took one of the huge nipples in my mouth. It tasted gorgeous, just as Katrina had said it would. Musky. Sort of scented, if you'll accept scent as a taste. Put another way, it tasted like incense. It grew larger in my mouth. I put a hand between Valentina's legs, and found a moist, wet slit. I pushed a finger inside it, and she squirmed, and said 'Oh, yes. I like it. Do it some more.' I moved my finger about. It was certainly tight. I pushed another finger in. Valentina wriggled again. I reached the other hand behind her, and took a firm young buttock in my hand. It was sort of soft, but hard at the same time. Soft when it was pleasantly relaxed, as it was right now under my fingers. Hard, I could imagine, when she used the muscles that I could feel lay beneath the warm skin. I could feel Valentina's breath, warm on my face. 'Fuck me,' she whispered. 'Fuck me now. Please.' She moved her hips against my hand, my fingers sliding further into her hot, wet cunt. My cock was almost exploding.

'Right,' said Katrina. 'Now go and make yourself comfortable. I'm going to do things to Valentina that will make you feel really sexy.' She pulled my arm gently away from her girlfriend, and my fingers slid out of Valentina's cunt with a moist pop. I sniffed at them. They smelt, as you can imagine, of hot, wet, aroused pussy. I sucked them clean, revelling in the taste. Did I really want to watch these girls doing dirty things to each other? Yes, I thought. I really do. I'm going to fuck them anyway. And

I've got all Saturday night, and all day Sunday, and all Sunday night to do just that in. There's no hurry. Calm down, lad. I went and sat on the edge of the bed. 'I assume you're going to do it here, girls,' I said, patting the top of the bed beside me. 'So this seems like a good place to be. Let the action commence.'

Valentina came and lay down on the bed beside me. 'Take your clothes off, darlink,' she said. 'Let me see that beautiful cock of yours again. Please? I have been dreamink about it. Now I can actually hold it in my hand. Soon, it will be in my cunt.'

I stood up and dragged off my clothes. My cock, understandably I think, was fully erect. So would yours have been. Valentina reached out and took hold of it again. 'I love it,' she said. 'I just love cock. Good, stiff, hard, lovely cock.' She gave it a friendly squeeze, and then said 'Don't go away, darlink. I shall come looking for you very soon now.' At this point, Katrina came and lay down on the bed beside Valentina, but with her head down towards Valentina's thighs. She spread the thin, gossamer material of Valentina's split-crotched French knickers as widely as possible, and began to perform cunnilingus upon her, showing a skill which patently came from much practice.

Valentina reacted with alacrity to the attentions that she was getting, and very shortly was groaning out her pleasure as she achieved the first of a number of orgasms that she reached during the time that Katrina licked and sucked her to the ultimate feminine pleasure. After a while, Valentina rolled onto her side and buried her head between Katrina's thighs, which opened enthusiastically to receive her girlfriend's mouth, leaving me with the delightful sight of two pretty young things sucking each other's pussies with energy and verve.

When Katrina too had received her share of orgasms, Valentina got up off the bed and went over to her handbag where she had left it on a chair and, searching around inside it, she produced a large, double-ended, pink rubber dildo, complete with elasticated harness. She stood by the bed, spread her legs, stepped into the harness, and then inserted one end of the dildo into her by now well-lubricated pussy. She came and stood in front of me and, turning her back to me, she asked me to buckle and tighten the back of the harness together for her, which I did. I then watched delightedly as the two girls fucked each other. It was quite difficult to see who was fucking whom, since both girls were thrusting their hips into the other's crotch. I think the answer was that both were fucking, and both were being fucked. Interesting.

Eventually, both they and I became satiated with their lesbian games. Valentina suggested that, since she had been promised that this evening's main purpose was her getting fucked by me – and vice versa – then it was probably about time that she and I got down to business. This was a suggestion with which I completely agreed, and with which Katrina also sportingly concurred, so it was with both delight and fervour that I sank my cock through the slit in those exotic black knickers, deeply into Valentina's receptive love tunnel. It was hot, wet, tight, and alive. Vibrantly alive. All those things that a man sexually primed almost to the point of premature ejaculation has been dreaming about for what seemed like an eternity. But I was determined not to shoot my load too soon, and managed to get myself under control after a nervous couple of minutes. Valentina's vaginal muscles massaged both my cock and my ego, and when I did finally explode, my semen shot into her in long spurts until, seconds later, she too reached her orgasm and matched my ejaculatory spasms with her own orgasmic ones.

We didn't even uncouple, but simply lay there, entwined, until we both started moving again, and fucking again, this time both able to stay longer at what was patently extremely enjoyable for us both. Katrina had had the decency to leave us alone the moment we had originally started to fuck. However well intentioned she was – and obviously she was for, without her initiative and encouragement, it could never have happened – it needed an understanding, sympathetic woman to realize that we would want to be alone with our fantasies and our desires for this first coupling. It was, eventually, a long night, but I'm happy to be able to tell you that I managed to divide my favours between these two luscious Russian girls without fear or favour. Perhaps more importantly, neither of the girls seemed to suffer the slightest pang of jealousy, and a happy, if tiring, night was the enjoyable result for all three of us. I made a new friend as well as experiencing the delectable favours of a new lover, and I believe that I speak for all three of us when I say that we looked forward to continuing this tripartite erotic alliance.

I awoke on the Sunday morning at about eleven. It was rather later than my usual time, but I felt fit and relaxed, if suffering somewhat from insufficient sleep. I delighted in the sight to which I awoke: that of a beautiful blonde Russian girl on either side of me, one short-haired, one long, both still sound asleep. I lay there for a while, reliving in my mind the sensual pleasures of the night before. Then I arose and made my way to the bathroom, a healthy erection preceding me. I had shaved, showered and brushed my teeth, and was sitting in the kitchen in a bathrobe, drinking coffee and reading the news section of the Sunday edition of the *New York Times* when, to my surprise, there was a ring at the door of my apartment. I say surprise, because no one had telephoned me from the lobby to announce a visitor. Not that I was expecting any visitors anyway. I assumed that it must be a neighbour, perhaps in need of the temporary loan of some item of domestic trivia. I got up and went to have a look through

A SURPRISE GOODBYE

the spyhole in my door before opening it. To my amazement, who should I see but Wally, the London-based, British owner of Tiptop Publications, and two other men whom I didn't know. I opened the door. Wally brushed past me and into the apartment, before I could say a word. The other two men followed him. I turned around and looked at all three of them, just not believing their strange behaviour. 'Good morning, Tony,' said Wally. 'What's going on? Where the fuck is Fred?'

'Good morning, Wally,' I said. 'Do come in. And who might these gentlemen be?' 'Oh, shit,' said Wally. 'I'm in such a state, I don't know what I'm doing. Please forgive me. This is Ron Stapleford, one of my accountants, and that's Peter Woodson, my solicitor. Gentlemen, you will have gathered by now that this is Tony Andrews. Tony is Fred's assistant out here.' I nodded at them; they at me. I didn't feel moved to offer them coffee.

'Now look, Tony,' said Wally. 'I'm very concerned about Fred. I flew in on Concorde this morning, having been told that he's disappeared. What can you tell me?' I looked directly at him. 'I can tell you exactly what I would have told you if you had telephoned me, Wally,' I said. 'Fred's on holiday. He's out in L.A., staying with a girlfriend.' 'L.A.?' said Wally. 'When did he go to L.A.?' 'Yesterday,' I told him. 'When did you last speak to him, then?' Wally asked. 'Yesterday evening,' I said. 'About five o'clock.' 'Have you got a telephone number out there for him, Tony?' Wally asked. 'Yes, Wally, of course I have,' I answered. At that moment, Katrina walked through the door from the bedroom. She was naked. She looked sensational. Valentina followed on behind her. She was still wearing her black, thin-as-gossamer, transparent French knickers. Nothing else. She must have taken her stockings off when she eventually went to bed. She looked pretty good too. It's wonderful what a couple of hours' sleep can do. I tried not to smile. 'Girls,' I said,

'I'd like you to meet my boss. This is Wally, from London. And these gentlemen are two colleagues of his: Ron and Peter. Gentlemen, may I introduce Katrina, on the left there, and Valentina, on your right. Say hallo, girls.'

'Hallo,' they said, gracefully. 'Hallo,' said Wally, Ron, and Peter. They looked at each other. 'Oh, shit,' said Wally. 'I guess everything's as normal as it ever is out here. Let's go home. Let's go back to London, for fuck's sake. Sorry to bother you, Tony. Get Fred to phone me, will you, please?' 'Sure, Wally,' I said. 'No problem.' The three of them filed out, slamming the door behind them. I noticed that Ron and Peter couldn't keep their eyes off the two girls and were falling over the furniture as they departed, walking in one direction while looking back over their shoulders in quite another.

'Ready for breakfast, ladies?' I asked. 'Yes, please,' they said. I never did find out how Wally and his chums got up to the apartment without being announced. I think it's called buying your way in.